A TOUCH OF BITTERSWEET

Blessings!
Enjoy!
Nan

Nan L. Seefluth

A Touch of Bittersweet
by Nan L. Seefluth

Printed in the United States of America

ISBN 9781619969490

The story is based on Mark 5: 25-34, King James Version.

www.xulonpress.com

Dedicated to my loving husband,
Gus, always my champion
And my children, for their
never-ending encouragement

PROLOGUE

A burgeoning crowd jammed the Capernaum marketplace. Sarah's stomach clenched in a knot. She tried to steady her ragged breathing. Could she reach him? She had to! The heaving mass threatened to smother her. She'd surely be trampled, with no way out. Suddenly the mob shifted slightly, jostling Sarah closer to the rabbi.

He stood on the low stone wall surrounding the well. As she reached toward him, a large man stepped in front of her. Tears pricked the back of her eyes. She had been so close. Now she could see only the tassel on the corner of the rabbi's robe. Her gaze locked on the splash of blue.

If I can touch it—just the tip of his robe...Sarah squirmed forward, her arm reaching, stretching. *Only a finger's width...* Suddenly, a push from behind boosted her ahead and her fingertips tingled as they brushed against the coarse blue fringe. A surge of strength swept through her. Sarah knew she had touched absolute power.

A sweet sensation of euphoria enveloped her. The din of voices faded away. She touched her arm, her face. *Is it real?* She blinked. The crowd stood all around her, as before.

She heard his voice again. "Who touched me?" Though his question bore no hint of scolding, Sarah flinched.

One of the men with him laughed. "Master, with this crowd pressing around you, you ask who touched you?" Several others chuckled.

"I felt strength going to someone who touched my robe," Jesus insisted.

He turned toward Sarah, looking directly into her eyes. Her heart somersaulted and slammed against her chest. The crowd pushed back a little as she fell to her knees before him, barely breathing. Her pulse thundered in her ears in the dreadful penetrating silence. Slowly Sarah raised her face toward the rabbi.

She heard her own shaky whisper, "It—it was I, Rabbi." She bit her lips to keep them from quivering. "I have been ill for twelve years, and—and I thought—I hoped if I could only touch your robe, I could be healed. I—I'm so sorry." She hid her face in her trembling hands. *Is he angry? I didn't ask him first. Did I steal this healing?*

His hand felt warm, strong, gentle on her arm. Sarah lifted her eyes to his face and the kindness in those eyes drew her to her feet. "Daughter, your faith has made you well; go in peace, and be healed of your disease."

The tender pressure of his hand on her shoulder sent a wave of peace through her. She knew she was truly, completely well again.

"Thank you, Master," she whispered.

His warm smile, the slight nod of his head made her feel like a trusted friend, not a stranger.

She did not want to turn away from those clear, compassionate eyes. Her soul felt bare, clean—even beautiful. But when he moved to talk to another person, she let the crowd shove her back away from the master.

Deborah! She must tell Deborah!

CHAPTER 1

Capernaum, twelve years earlier

Sarah laid her wooden shuttle on the cross beam of the loom. She straightened her shoulders and pressed both hands against the small of her back.

"Where are you, Sarah?" Tamar yelled from the front door. Sarah winced. Her sister-in-law's screechy voice pricked at every nerve in her body.

"In the courtyard, Tamar."

Tamar's sandals slapped the straw mat as she flounced into the atrium. Her screech changed to a whine, "Have you finished my dress?"

Sarah clenched her teeth. *Not even a 'good morning,' much less a 'how are you?'* "It's over there, Tamar." She gestured toward the folded garment on a small table.

"At last!" Tamar unfolded the dress and examined it. "And I hope you don't have too many other customers right now, Sarah. I've brought the most beautiful piece of linen. Just look at this." She unrolled the package in her hand. "Won't it make a lovely dress? I'd like a plain tunic this time like—"

"No, Tamar." Sarah shook her head and waved a dismissive hand. "I'm not sewing any more dresses now." She picked up the shuttle and straightened the strand of wool. "I promised Nathan—"

"Oh, Sarah, don't worry about your over-protective husband," Tamar interrupted. "Why, you'll have this done before Nathan even knows you're working on it." She tittered. "I'll leave the linen here on the table with what I owe you."

Sarah put the shuttle down, heaving a sigh. "Tamar, didn't you hear a word I said? I will not be doing any more dress-making, fancy or plain. So please take your fabric with you." She winced as a pain shot through her back. "I'm having a difficult pregnancy, and the doctor insists I quit sewing. Only baby things now."

Tamar's lips puckered into a pout. "Well, I'd think by this time you'd have everything ready for that baby! How much can one little child need?" She sidled over to the loom.

"My goodness, Sarah, whatever are you making with that faded-looking stuff?" She reached to touch the soft wool.

Sarah glared at her, clamping her lips together to stop angry words. *If she doesn't get out of here...* She swallowed hard. "It's a coverlet, and it's not faded. I purposely dyed the wool this light shade of blue." After carding the wool many times, she'd spun it into fine yarn. Her fingers had ached, but she'd smiled at the color, a blue as soft to the eye as the wool was when she nestled her face in it.

Tamar tilted her chin up and peered down her nose at Sarah. "Oh, you poor dear! You do have strange tastes." She scoffed. "You must be copying those crude friends of yours."

Sarah's head shot up. "I've noticed you think my taste is fine when you want a dress made." She felt the flush rising to her face.

"Well, of course I do," Tamar agreed.

Sarah watched Tamar's arrogance show itself as she strutted back and forth in the small courtyard. She raked a finger across the smooth surface of a little table and straightened a cushion on the chair beside it. The woman always picked at everything around her, if not with her fingers, then with her words. Sarah struggled to stay calm.

"You're a very gifted seamstress," Tamar offered, her harsh tone negating what was supposed to be a soothing compliment. "It's amazing how you can design such lovely fashions for others, when you dress so plainly yourself."

Sarah flinched, biting back an angry retort.

Tamar finally perched on the edge of a nearby chair. "Nathan has come a long way since he first started his pottery business on the square. But, Sarah, the secret to real success is in mingling with the right people. And those two over there..." She tipped her head toward the house next door, her lips curled in a sneer. "What a giggly little nitwit Deborah is!" She snickered. "And that carpenter husband of hers—well, I think surely you could find better friends." She shook her head, clicking her tongue as if scolding a naughty child.

"But then I doubt if Nathan would ever be accepted among mine and Elon's friends. He'll always be a crude, ignorant country boy—so different from Elon. My friends find it hard to believe they're brothers."

Sarah slammed the shuttle down and whirled around. "Don't you dare talk about my husband like that!" She shook her finger at Tamar. "Maybe Nathan is a country boy, but he's neither crude nor ignorant. And neither are our friends!" Her chest heaved with ragged breaths. "Deborah has been like a sister to me since I first came to Capernaum when my father died. And David is a hard-working, honest businessman, like Nathan." She leveled her eyes at Tamar. "I wouldn't trade them for a hundred of you or your fancy friends!" She slipped off the stool. But one leg buckled under her, causing her to fall forward against the edge of the loom. Catching her breath at the sharp pain, she leaned over the frame to recover her balance before attempting to move her trembling legs.

"Sarah? Are you—"

"Just—go!" Sarah choked out. Bent in pain, she struggled across the courtyard toward her bedroom.

* * *

With her hand on the latch, Tamar hesitated. Slipping back across the room, she stooped and gently fingered the soft blue wool lying on the floor, still attached to the loom. Just as a tear dropped, she straightened, shook herself as if to throw off this uninvited emotion. With a deep breath, she stiffened her back, set her jaw firmly, and marched resolutely out the door.

* * *

The marketplace droned with the commotion of an incoming caravan. Tamar threaded her way through the crowded street, preoccupied with her own stupidity. Disgusted that she had allowed that baby cover to shatter her composure—to drag out old hurts she thought she had buried. And she couldn't help wondering about Sarah. Maybe she should have gone to her. But she had tried, and Sarah told her to leave. She'd never seen Sarah so angry!

Well, I can't worry about her. She's not my problem. Head down, her linen headpiece pulled closely around her face, she hurried on toward home.

"Umph!" Her right shoulder slammed into someone. As she pitched forward, the man grabbed her flailing arm and stopped her fall. Her gaze lit on his hand. The ring. A dolphin! Only a Nabataean would be wearing that! Her heart sank to her toes. An eternity passed before she could bring herself to look up into his swarthy face. Her breath caught in her throat.

CHAPTER 2

Tamar lay in the dark room, her pulse thrumming a staccato in her ears. The marketplace encounter with Reuel played over and over in her head. The horrible nightmare which had plagued her for years, and which she thought she had smothered permanently, had now materialized—in alarming reality.

Rueul! Why had he come to Capernaum? After so many years, why now? She had to find him. But where to start?

What was he doing in the marketplace today? She vaguely remembered being in front of Nathan's pottery shop when she—when they...*Yes! He must have been coming out of that shop.*

Of course! Her breath caught in her throat. *Why didn't I remember? Rueul used to be a potter! He's working for Nathan!* But she still didn't know where he would be in the middle of the night.

As soon as Tamar heard Elon's snoring, she scurried out of bed, slipped on her clothes and sneaked out of the house. After the disturbing events of the day, her head throbbed. But Reuel had to be dealt with. She must find out what his intentions were and where she stood with him.

An almost-full moon lit the streets with an eerie silence. Tamar darted from one shadowed area to another until she reached the pottery shop. At the bottom of the outside stairway she paused. Her heart pummeled her chest. *If he's up there, what will I say? I don't know him anymore*. Her resolve crumbled. As she turned to leave she heard a man clear his throat. *He knows I'm here!*

She willed her trembling legs up the stairs. At the top, she took a couple of hesitant steps and stopped. Her gaze flicked across the shadowy cluttered area, suddenly freezing on his dark form sitting cross-legged on the floor. Tamar sucked in her breath, jumping back against the parapet.

"You're losing your touch, Jeda. I could hear your feet before you got to the steps. But I expected you hours ago," he hissed as she willed her shaky legs to move in his direction. "You're afraid of me, aren't you, Jeda?" He beckoned her toward him.

"No! I'm not!" she retorted. When he scooted over, she eased down on the opposite edge of his mat. "But don't call me Jeda!" she snapped.

"Oh yes! What was it Nathan called you? Tamar, isn't it? Where did you get that name?" He smirked. "And by the way, you can call me Esli."

"Why change your name, if you're going to keep wearing that dolphin ring?"

"Oh, but it's no secret that I'm Nabataean. You know we have the reputation of being the best potters in the world. And that's my trade. Your brother-in-law needs me, and he doesn't care where I come from."

"Well, the sight of that dolphin took ten years off my life!" Tamar retorted in a coarse whisper.

He chuckled. "I'm hoping she will add many more years than that to mine."

"But the Dolphin Goddess only helps on the journey after death," she argued. "And, anyway, you surely can't believe in that nonsense. Nobody can know what happens in the hereafter." She waved a dismissive hand toward him.

"Well, the lady has been good to me." He flexed his shoulders and yawned. "But you didn't come here tonight to talk about the dolphin."

"No, I didn't. I want to know why you're here—in Capernaum."

"I didn't come looking for you, if that's what you think," he muttered through clenched teeth.

"Then how did you know that your employer is my brother-in-law?"

"He saw you run into me today and told me who you were. Simple as that."

"I don't believe you. Aretas sent you, didn't he? I knew it would happen some day! I—"

"Aretas? You're crazier than I thought!" His hateful laugh sent chills down her spine. "Remember, I stole just as much from the Nabataean king as you did. If I'd gone back there... Well, you know very well what would have happened to me!" He slashed a finger across his neck.

"There's no way you can make me believe you just happen to be in Capernaum working in a pottery shop. For my husband's brother!"

Esli narrowed his eyes at her. "You know something, Jeda? I don't intend to try to make you believe anything." He leaned his forearms on his folded legs. "You see, I don't care what you believe. The quicker you understand that, the better."

"You'll never forgive me, will you?" she whispered.

"Well, let's see. Am I to forgive you for running away with most of my half of the plunder? Or for making a fool of me? I've learned a long time ago that the money isn't worth worrying over. For pretending to love me?" He shrugged. "I got over that long ago. But destroying our unborn child... No, I'll never forgive you for that!" He slammed his bony fist into the mat. "You were using me, just as you use the fool you're with now."

"And how would you know that?"

In the pale light of the moon she could see his silent sneer.

A chill ran over her. *I've pushed him too far.* "You've got it all wrong, Reuel. If you could only believe how wrong! Yes, I'm using Elon. He's my way of getting where I have to go. What I'm reaching for is very important to me. Far more important than wealth, I can tell you." She leaned toward him. For a moment their eyes locked, and she glimpsed a softness—longing—and knew he was remembering, too. Then his eyes turned cold, stony. The moment was gone, but it had transported Tamar to another time, a time she would always hold dear.

She wiped a tear from the corner of her eye. "Rueul, I was not using you. I did love you. I still—"

"Don't say it!" He grabbed her arm, his fingertips biting into the flesh, and shook her. "Spare me your lies. Give me credit for learning a little over the years!"

"All right!" She jerked her arm out of his grasp, rubbing the bruises. "I don't expect you to accept anything I say. But I had to do what I did. And I have to do what I'm doing now."

"Well, good luck, Jeda!" he growled. "Just stay away from me. I don't want to know anything about your sinister plans. You leave me alone and I'll stay out of your way." He unfolded his long legs and stood. "Now go back to that other fool."

"I wish I could make you understand..."

"For your own sake, don't try. If you involve me again, I promise you—it will be your last time!" He swore under his breath.

The hate in his voice sent shivers all the way down to her toes. Tamar crept silently down the steps. Reuel's threat had come through very distinctly.

* * *

The Law decreed that a woman was unclean for forty days after giving birth to a son. Or in Sarah's case, miscarrying a son.

"And had you dared to have a girl, it would be eighty days of 'uncleanness'," Deborah complained one afternoon. "A veritable social outcast—almost completely cut off from everyone."

"Yes, it does seem unjust," Sarah agreed with her friend. "But sometimes, Deborah, it's actually a blessing." She fingered the hem of her sash. "I can't imagine ever wanting to go out again, only to be pitied."

Pity! How she hated that word. She had received more than enough of that to last a lifetime. Time. Another hateful word she was sick of hearing. *Time will heal.* That's all anybody could think to say to her.

Of course Tamar had thought of a few other things to say. She generously offered to pray for her deliverance from the sins that brought this tragedy upon her. Nathan had been furious. And Elon had whisked his wife away before real violence erupted, though it had been obvious that he was as angry as Nathan. Sarah shuddered to think how they would have reacted had either of them known that it was Tamar's visit that caused her to lose the baby. Sarah clenched her teeth. She would never forgive her. Never!

CHAPTER 3

Lucian turned a small scroll back and forth in his hands. "I wish I could offer a cure..."

Nathan grimaced. He leaned forward and whacked the table with the side of his fist. "Surely there's something you can do! It's been months since Sarah lost the baby, and she's still..."

Sarah laid her hand on his arm. "Nathan, it isn't Lucian's fault."

Nathan scooted back in his chair and took her hand. "I know, and I'm sorry, Doctor. It's just that Sarah's getting weaker every day. I don't know how long she can go on like this. Besides, she's isolated from everything. The Law..."

"Ah, yes. The Law." The doctor stood, tossing the scroll on the table. "And what a stupid one it is that would persecute an innocent woman because of an ailment over which she has no control." He paced back and forth, his dark eyes snapping with anger. "I can't believe God intended that. I've known other women with a similar problem who kept it a secret to avoid such discrimination." And waving an arm heavenward, he added, "And I don't believe God condemns them one bit!" He set his jaw defiantly, every bone prominent in the lean, bronze face.

Sarah drew back at the sudden outburst of temper from the physician she had thought to be so gentle.

Nathan laughed. "Oh, I agree, Lucian. I, too, think it's unfair, but neither of us has the power to change it. And if Sarah could get well, we wouldn't have to worry about it."

Lucian sat back down at the table with a sheepish grin. "Point taken, Nathan. Sarah's health is the most important issue here. I'd better stop my ranting about the Law and refer you to a doctor in Tiberias. Apollonius is a Greek physician with whom I studied. I know he uses the mineral baths in his treatments. In fact, his clinic is located near them."

"But Nathan can't leave his shop to roam around over the country with me from one doctor to another," Sarah protested, "especially with his new pottery contract. He's too busy."

"Oh, that's no problem," Nathan countered. "Esli's perfectly capable of supervising the shop. Besides, that new contract is with the garrison at Tiberias. I can take care of business while you're taking the baths." He slapped his palms together.

Lucian smiled. "Aah, Nathan, in my line of work I don't see many men who care that much about their wives' health." He shook his head. "If I ever do find the right woman, I'd like to think I'd treat her with that same kind of love and respect. And I hope I'm as lucky as you, my friend."

"I hope so, too." Nathan squeezed Sarah's hand. She blushed, dropping her eyes.

"But the matter at hand..." Lucian waved away the conversation that had become a little too personal. "Seriously, Sarah, you'll be feeling much better after a few times in the soothing water."

"It's sure worth a try, isn't it?" Nathan took her hand, smiling.

Sarah's chest tightened. "But—Tiberias? I—I just don't know..." She gripped the arms of the chair.

Nathan's smile faded. "Sarah, I know what you're thinking, but I'm sure most of what we've heard about the place was exaggerated. Lucian wouldn't recommend going there if it were that evil." He glanced toward the doctor.

Lucian shrugged. "Oh, I suppose there's plenty of evil there, but you'll be going to the Jewish sector of the city, and you'll find it very much like Capernaum." He pushed his chair away from the table and leaned back. "And I'm not sending you two down there on your own. My friend will take you in his carriage."

"A carriage?" Sarah put her hand on Nathan's sleeve. "Won't that be very costly?"

"No, Sarah," Lucian answered instead, "Santimar will take you for a very reasonable fee," he assured her. "You see, he has worked for me since I moved to Capernaum. But more than that, he's a good friend. And he knows Tiberias like a native. He'll take you to a very good inn and stay there to drive you where you need to go."

"Then it's settled. Right, Sarah?" Nathan put his arm around her.

She nodded, forcing a hesitant smile.

"I'll write a letter of introduction for you to take to Apollonius," Lucian offered. "I can't promise he'll work miracles, but I know he'll do his best."

"He won't be a better doctor than you, Lucian," Sarah insisted.

"Thank you, my friend, but I'm hoping Apollonius has learned more about your illness than I." Lucian pushed back his chair and stood. "Can you be ready to go tomorrow?"

"So soon?" Sarah looked at Lucian. "The driver will surely need more notice than that."

"Oh, Santimar will be ready." Lucian laughed. He laid his hands on their shoulders as they walked out. "Please forgive me, both of you, for the way I carried on about some of our ancient customs. I guess speaking out against Jewish

Law would be considered blasphemy in some circles, but I believe some of our laws are for the pleasure of men, not God, and it bothers me."

"I agree with you, Lucian, but then who are we to fight the whole system?" Nathan shrugged.

"Well, maybe someday there'll be someone who will have enough nerve and power to fight it and tell people how to treat each other. And I can tell you this—I'll surely be on his side, whoever he is!" Lucian promised, laughing.

"I will, too," Nathan agreed, "but I'm afraid his life won't be worth much if he tramples on too many toes."

Sarah's mind wasn't on Jewish law. A feeling of dread settled in her chest. *Tiberias. Herod's city! What are we getting into?*

CHAPTER 4

"You're worried about the cost, aren't you?" Nathan asked, after they left Lucian's clinic.

"Not the cost so much as..." Sarah let the rest of the sentence trail off.

"So much as what?" Nathan took her arm and slowed the pace.

"I still don't like the idea of going to that unclean place." Sarah admitted, turning to face her husband. "It's Herod's city, Nathan, and he's an evil man. You know the Nabataean King is said to be after him for the way he abandoned his daughter for Herodias."

"Yes, and I don't blame Aretas. But that's between the two rulers. And we're not likely ever to see either of them."

"Well, you never know." She shook her head. "I've heard the city is crowded with Romans and Greeks, some of them criminals. And they hate Jews."

He squeezed her arm, chuckling. "Don't worry. They'll be glad to get our business. Lucian is confident we'll be safe and the Greek doctor is his good friend. Let's just plan to enjoy the trip, with the hope that it will make you feel better again."

"All right. I'll try." *I owe Nathan that much,* she thought. *If only I could be well again for him!*

But her smile masked a deep, nagging fear. She could just hear her father talking about "Herod's evil city"—built over a graveyard. He couldn't believe that any decent Jew would go to live there. Most of those who did had been of the lower elements of society, enticed by Herod's offer to build houses for them.

But that was a long time ago. It was surely different now, with both Jews and Gentiles moving there because of business opportunities. Still, if her father were living... *Oh, Baba, you would be horrified if you knew I planned to go to Tiberias!*

* * *

The sturdy little four-wheeled carriage had certainly seen better days, but Santimar beamed with pride as he helped Sarah and Nathan onto the narrow platform between the driver's seat and passenger compartment. They entered through the front of the otherwise enclosed coach, and settled back in the comfortable, heavily-cushioned seat. Sarah wondered what sort of dignitaries had ridden here in the past. She looked at the two passive donkeys and pictured a magnificent steed pawing the ground. In the folds of a faded, heavy brocade curtain tied back on either side of the opening, she could see streaks of red, yellow, blue and purple in the once-bright fabric.

Sarah watched Santimar climb into the driver's seat above the large box where he had stored their luggage. The little man's sharp, crooked nose; dark, deep-set eyes; and swarthy, weathered complexion gave him a sinister appearance. But when he smiled and bowed to her, he made her feel very special.

Santimar turned the carriage down the hill toward Lake Galilee, where this morning a strong east wind ruffled the waters into a profusion of vigorous white caps.

As they turned south, paralleling the lake, Sarah shivered. The strong, cold Gadim wind blew spray completely across the road. She pulled the heavy woolen robes closer around them and snuggled against Nathan.

"I know this trip to Tiberias is terribly costly, but I have to admit it's exciting." She nestled closer to her husband.

He chuckled and squeezed her against him under the cover. "I'm glad you decided to enjoy yourself," he whispered in her ear.

"Nathan, do you think the baths will make me well?"

"I wish I could promise you that, my dear. I'd give anything in the world for you to feel well again."

"I know," she whispered.

* * *

In mid-morning, when they were well past Magdala, Santimar pulled the carriage over to a sunny, sheltered area near a well—the perfect spot to eat a late breakfast. Sarah found a smooth place in the warm sun and spread a clean cloth. She laid out the food she had prepared the night before—salted fish, freshly baked bread, dried figs and sweet cakes.

Santimar watered the donkeys before joining them. As he ate heartily, he lavished liberal compliments on Sarah's cooking. She soon learned that behind his deceiving exterior roughness was a unique character, warm and gentle, and surprisingly well-informed. His sense of humor emerged in his amusing little stories, and though his Aramaic was laced with a heavy Arabic accent, his command of the language was amazing. Sarah could easily understand why Lucian had become so fond of him. She genuinely liked the man and it was easy to see how well Nathan got on with him.

As she gathered up the left-overs and folded the cloth, Sarah recalled the last time they had traveled this way. Deborah and David had been with them in the caravan going to Jerusalem for Passover. Remembering the evenings of singing and laughing around the campfire made her long for those carefree times. It was hard to believe how drastically their lives had changed. They were much poorer back then, but she would gladly go back to that, if it were possible. Losing the baby had been devastating enough, but not recovering—never able to be a real wife for Nathan—was almost too much.

Maybe Tamar was right about my sins. But what did I do to deserve this punishment? I miss going to the synagogue, worshipping with my friends. So many things are forbidden to me now—an unclean woman!

Sarah's religion had always been a very important part of her life, but doubts were beginning to plague her. *Why?* The baffling question loomed continually in her thoughts. It was difficult to say her prayers lately. *God isn't listening anymore.*

CHAPTER 5

Nathan and Sarah saw the massive wall of Tiberias long before the carriage reached the West Gate. At that entrance they viewed Herod's paragon city for the first time. The tetrarch surely had spared nothing to make it a model metropolis. Luxurious white buildings gleamed majestically in the sunlight. The spectacular sight overwhelmed Sarah.

"Can you believe this?" she whispered, squeezing Nathan's arm. "It doesn't even look real!"

"I'm really glad Lucian insisted we hire this carriage." He shook his head. "I wouldn't have any idea which direction to take."

But Santimar threaded his way through the busy maze as if he knew exactly where he was going.

The curbed cobblestone streets were half again as wide as those of Capernaum—also noisier and busier. Displays of merchandise crowded the sidewalks in front of the shops, often making it necessary for pedestrians to walk into the street to pass.

As they came within sight of the palace, Sarah was so dazzled that she momentarily forgot her fears of the heathen city. "Oooh, Nathan, look at that beautiful castle! It must be Herod's. Do you think we could get a closer look?"

Nathan called to Santimar, asking him to go nearer to the palace. The old driver mumbled something vague and with obvious reluctance, turned down the street toward the tetrarch's headquarters.

Sarah stared open-mouthed at its magnificence, but as they came closer and saw the stone lions in front and pillars at the corners with figures of antelope and bear, she shuddered. Remembering the Hebrew teaching about the ungodliness of animal figures, she remarked to Nathan, "The paganism! You can just feel it."

"Yes, and I'm ready to get away from this part of the city." He hurriedly instructed Santimar to go back the other way. But just as the driver turned the carriage down another street, he met a large Roman wagon drawn by a couple of snorting, frisky steeds, speeding down the middle of the street. Forced to take to the sidewalk, Santimar was unable to avoid hitting a cart of vegetables. As produce flew everywhere, out stormed the dumpy little shopkeeper, blustering his gross disapproval. Nathan got out and offered to pay the man for the ruined merchandise. Santimar, hassled and threatened with jail by the Romans, kept quiet.

The bill for damages settled, Nathan got into the carriage and told Santimar to go on, leaving the shop owner fuming over the produce lying all over the place. Santimar pulled out without hesitation and surprisingly, the Romans went on their way, too.

Sarah clung to Nathan's arm and realized he was trembling, too. "I've never been so scared in my life! I wish I'd never asked to see that awful place." She clamped her teeth together to stop their chattering."

Whew!" Nathan swiped his hand across his brow. "At least Santimar was wise enough to keep his mouth shut. Now, if we're fortunate, he'll get us to the inn with no more trouble."

When the carriage pulled up to the front entrance of the Inn of the Seven Stones on the south side of the city, a young stable boy ran out to meet them, babbling to Santimar in Arabic as if they were old friends. The boy bowed to Nathan and Sarah, gesturing toward the door of the inn as he began unloading their luggage.

The innkeeper, a hefty, grizzly man, greeted them when they entered the large room which served as both the dining area and reception. "Welcome, sir, to our humble place. I'm John ben Abel and I hope you'll be comfortable here."

"I'm sure we will." Nathan shook the man's outstretched hand. "I'm Nathan ben Amon. Sarah, my wife."

John nodded. "I assume Santimar's staying to guide you about the city. Jews often find themselves in some very uncomfortable situations on their own."

Nathan chuckled. "Yes, I'm afraid we've already experienced one of those uncomfortable situations, even with Santimar, and I shudder to think about it without him!" He told John about the trouble near the palace.

"Old Santimar knows when to fight and when to play the dumb driver, eh?" John laughed loudly. "You're not the first to want a closer look at Herod's finery." He shook his head. "I take it you're from Capernaum, since that's where Santimar lives."

"Yes, and this is our first trip to your city, but then our ignorance has already revealed that." Nathan reddened.

"Well, you've come to the right place, since it's your first visit. You'll find this part of town very much like Capernaum. And there's not a better man anywhere to guide you than Santimar."

John pulled out chairs for them around one of the small tables, which seemed to be the cue for a girl to bring three cups of tea. "Maybe you'd like to sit with me for a cup of the best tea in Tiberias!" he offered. "I'm sure you're tired after the long, bumpy ride." He sat down across the table from them. His round belly shook when he laughed, suggesting that ale, not tea, was his usual fare. Sarah noticed his heavy, reddish-brown beard seemed to make up for a total lack of hair on top, and helped to lengthen his round face. She took comfort in her supposition that this man was quite capable of keeping his inn safe from intruders.

"Have you known Santimar long?" John asked Nathan.

"Not really. We met him when we arranged for this trip," replied Nathan. "But you seem to know him pretty well."

"Oh, I guess you could say that—as well as anyone ever knows the rascal!" He laughed. "He lived here for a short time. He comes from way down south, Arabia, originally. I believe he was a slave there, and then was sold to a Roman officer who transferred to the garrison here in Tiberias."

"That's interesting," Nathan mused. "I've wondered about his background. He was recommended to me by a good friend. Sounds as if he's had quite a colorful past."

"That he has!" John nodded. "The story goes that the officer that bought him took sick not long after he came to Tiberias. When he realized he was about to die, he gave Santimar his freedom, along with a nice pouch of gold pieces, and told him to get out of here." He took a drink of tea. "But wouldn't you know," he continued, "before he could get out of the city, he was robbed of all his gold and beaten nearly to death! I tell you, it was mighty lucky for Santimar that a doctor on his way to set up business in Capernaum found him, fixed up his cuts and bruises, and took him on with him, on his own donkey, yet. I guess those two hit it off pretty good, 'cause he stayed there and worked for the doctor. He just recently got his own rig to use for hire. He comes here often, bringing people on business."

Nathan and Sarah exchanged smiles. "Well, I knew Lucian ben Obed was a fine man, but now I've learned something more about him." Nathan nodded thoughtfully.

"Oh! You know the doctor, then!" John looked surprised.

"He's the one who sent us here to consult a physician named Apollonius, a friend of his. But Lucian is more than our doctor; he's one of our best friends." Nathan smiled proudly.

"Nathan, isn't that just like Lucian, never to mention how he got to know Santimar?" Sarah added.

A thin, gray-haired woman emerged from the kitchen area. "Folks, this is my wife, Anna, the real backbone of this establishment. Without this woman, there'd be no good food and clean rooms, that's for sure!" He laughed heartily and stroked her shoulder affectionately. "Anna, this is Nathan ben Abel and his wife, Sarah. You'd never guess who sent them here—Lucian, from Capernaum!"

The mention of the doctor's name brought a big smile, crinkling her entire face like tissue paper. "Well! It's good to have you here." She bowed politely to Nathan, who returned the courtesy. Taking Sarah's hand, she said, "You look a little tired, dear. Let me show you to your room, so you can rest. I'll have a girl prepare baths for both of you before supper."

Nathan stood, helping Sarah from her chair. "Thank you, Anna. She does need to rest after the trip. Sarah, you go on and have a nap and I'll wake you for your bath."

Exhaustion had slipped up on Sarah, and by the time she stretched out on the bed, she couldn't keep her eyes open. Several hours later, after the good nap and warm soothing bath, she, like Nathan, was able to do justice to the feast that Anna set before them.

When Sarah and Nathan finally retired to their room, sleep eluded Sarah. The strange city sounds drifting in through the open window alarmed her. Horses clomping over the cobblestones, a carriage jolting along, the driver cracking his whip. Did nobody sleep in this place?

Sarah dreaded the morning. She didn't know what to expect. Would it bring more fear and trembling? Or would she find new hope—hope of healing, of being whole again?

CHAPTER 6

The nervous fluttering in the pit of Sarah's stomach worsened by the second as Nathan helped her into the carriage. Her knees shook. She wished they didn't have to leave the inn. Actually, she wished they hadn't left Capernaum! But she was here now, and had better make the best of it. She wondered if she should have eaten breakfast.

She had hardly settled back in the carriage when it stopped outside a large stone gate, ornately carved with scrolls and leaves across the top, a caduceus on either side.

Sarah stifled a gasp of surprise as they entered the lovely courtyard, divided in half by a wide marble path leading to the colonnaded porch spanning the full width of the building. A fountain, topped by a statuette of a beautiful goddess and encircled with a wide bed of colorful flowers, dominated each half of the garden. Situated alternately around the walls were neatly trimmed shrubs and life-sized statues of various Greek deities.

The long covered porch paved with black and white marble seemed to be a waiting area, with cushioned white marble benches placed against the wall. A pleasant young man sitting at a table near the door took the scroll Lucian had sent, and offered them seats.

As the benches began to fill, Nathan muttered, "The man must have quite a following."

"I'm just wondering what kind of prices he charges for his services, to pay for all this finery." Sarah whispered uneasily. "What if it costs more than we can pay?"

"I'm sure Lucian would have warned me if it were that costly. Don't worry about it. Your health is worth whatever the price may be." He patted her hand.

Just as she opened her mouth to counter his remark, the young man called for them to follow him.

Apollonius rose from his desk and greeted them warmly. "I've read the letter you brought from my friend. My dear friend Lucian." He smiled, a faraway look in his eyes. "My, but I do have pleasant memories of our time spent together in Alexandria! We had the good fortune to further our medical training under the very best physicians in the world there." He shook his head, as if remembering made him a bit sad. "I wish I could have talked Lucian into coming in with me here. He would do well in Tiberias. But no, he wouldn't be happy here—not Lucian."

"And how fortunate for us in Capernaum." Nathan affirmed. "It would be a sad day in our city if Lucian should leave us for the more lucrative practice in Tiberias."

"Well, I doubt very seriously that you need worry about that. Not for a moment."

After the examination, Sarah dressed and sat down with Nathan to wait for Apollonius to return to them. Ambling back into the room, he rubbed his fingers across his forehead as if trying to sort out his thoughts. He explained to them that he had no miracle cure for Sarah's ailment.

"But the mineral springs will be very beneficial, Sarah—perhaps even help your body heal itself. They'll make you feel stronger, more relaxed. When you feel better, your body can deal with the problem more easily."

He pushed back his chair. "The large spa is just next door, and my assistant will take you there and arrange for your scheduling.

"But, sir," Sarah countered, leaning toward the desk. "I don't quite understand how I can use these public baths—in my condition."

"Oh, that's not a problem for the staff there. In spite of what you may have thought, your ailment isn't at all rare, and the woman who will be attending you is familiar with the condition, I assure you. In fact, you won't even have to discuss it with her, for I'll be sending the information for your file there."

Sarah looked down, feeling heat rising to her face. "I—I meant that..."

"Ah!" He nodded. "You're worrying about being unclean!" He hesitated, as if groping for words. "Well, Sarah, that is a Jewish notion, and between you and your God. But these springs are international. We Greeks enjoy the spa and of course the Romans frequent the bath houses in large numbers. In fact, you're likely to see many different nationalities represented there." He laughed and spread his hands. "You'll wonder who is contaminating whom!"

His reference to the contempt that most Jews had for the Greeks and Romans embarrassed Sarah.

He turned to Nathan. "Seriously, your wife will find everyone at the bath house extremely courteous and competent. They like to please, and they'll give you your money's worth. Sarah will be guided in everything and will be perfectly at ease in the bath. Just don't expect the springs to be an instant cure. That may take some time.

He turned back to Sarah. "If, for any reason, you don't find things comfortable and pleasant there, feel free to come to me. I'll wager, though, that you'll not want to leave, once you've tried the warm bath."

Nathan laughed, taking Sarah's arm. "Thank you, doctor. I'm sure everything will be fine."

"Then I'll have you scheduled for two spa treatments a day for five days, two hours per treatment. The morning after your last visit to the spa, I'd like to see you again." Apollonius escorted them back to the porch where the secretary waited to take them to the bath house.

* * *

The outside of the building was similar to the one they had just left. The entry courtyard, the flowers, columns, fountains, marble statues and benches seemed to be standard. But this building was two or three times the size of the clinic.

A plump, matronly Greek woman named Iona was assigned to attend Sarah. She spoke Aramaic barely well enough to be understood, though probably better than any of the other therapists there. Sarah understood very little Greek and spoke none.

Iona, smiling broadly, invited them both for a tour of the facilities, first to a very large atrium. The simple but elegant peristyle framing the courtyard suggested a mixture of Greek and Roman culture.

Behind the white columns a covered, marble-paved walkway led to numerous rooms. In the large, open area fifteen or twenty people, wrapped in loose robes, lounged on soft couches in the sun. Attendants were rubbing what appeared to be oil on several of them. Though this atrium was open to the sky, warm air flowing from vents in the walls kept it quite comfortable.

"This is where you rest after bath," Iona explained.

Sarah nodded, noticing many large, beautifully decorated stone planters, some containing a profusion of flowers, others holding tropical plants and miniature trees.

"All baths in these rooms." Iona pointed to the doors that opened onto the walkway around the atrium. "Some for many people." She opened one of the doors, revealing a large room with a rectangular pool taking up most of the floor.

Sarah gasped involuntarily and quickly turned away, feeling the blood rushing to her face. About a dozen women lounged in the waist-deep water, completely nude. Several male attendants wandered in and out of the room, as if oblivious to the nudity.

When Iona saw the dismay in Sarah's face, she burst out laughing. But when Sarah obviously wasn't amused, the smile quickly faded. She put her arm gently around Sarah's shoulders. "Not to worry, lady—I have a room for only you."

"By myself?"

"Oh, yes!" The woman laughed again.

Sarah decided at that moment that she and Iona would get along fine.

Iona started to take them around to the opposite side of the atrium, explaining that the other large bath over there was reserved for the men. "You want to see?" Her eyes twinkled with mischief.

"Iona!" Sarah stopped dead still, feigning dismay.

The therapist giggled with delight. Sarah's modesty obviously amused her. She shrugged, opening the door of the suite Sarah would be using each day at the same time.

The ten by twelve main room had a bath in the center about six feet square. Steps led down into one end of the pool. A lovely sculpted maiden stood at the opposite end, pouring water from a small blue and green pitcher. The walls and floor, including the bath, were covered in geometrically designed mosaic tiles, the blue and green colors prevailing. Everything was sparkling clean, much to Sarah's appreciation.

Adjacent to this main room were two small preparation rooms. The attendant called the first one the apodyterium, in which Sarah would change. From there, Iona told her, she would go to the tepidarium. In this room of gentle heat the body would be prepared for the warm bath.

Nathan explained, "From what I've heard, the air is heated by a hypocaust located underground. Then it flows through ducts in the floor along the wall."

At this point, Iona excused Nathan, informing him that he could return to the atrium in two hours to wait for Sarah.

In the changing room Sarah learned how to wrap herself in a small garment resembling a loin cloth. After a few minutes in the tepidarium, Iona led her down the steps into the warm water. When she sat down on a ledge, the water almost covered her shoulders. She could feel it circulating around her, caressing her entire body with its warmth. Sitting back against the side, she allowed herself to drift into a state of utter tranquility.

Iona taught her some exercises and instructed her to alternate between these and resting quietly. Then the therapist left her alone for awhile, looking in on her from time to time and checking the water temperature. Sarah followed the directions precisely and when Iona came to tell her the two hours were over, she couldn't believe it.

After a few minutes more in the tepidarium, she was given a soft, loose robe and taken to a couch to lie in the sun for a few minutes. Iona massaged her arms and legs with lightly perfumed oil and she was so completely relaxed when Nathan came, that he sat down across the courtyard, reluctant to interrupt her rest. When the allotted time was up, Iona took her back to the dressing room.

Nathan met her when she came out ready to go. "I've never seen you look more peaceful as when you were lying on that couch."

"You wouldn't believe what a wonderful experience this has been." She squeezed his arm. "Apollonius was right when he said I wouldn't want to leave. Why, if you had been in there with me I could have stayed in that water forever!"

"That good, eh?"

"I just don't see how I can help getting well, with this kind of treatment. I can hardly wait until the next session."

After a couple of days of this routine, Sarah had convinced herself that she would surely leave there cured. But on the fifth day, she had to face the truth. Remembering what the doctor said about not expecting an immediate cure, she tried not to become too discouraged. But perhaps this had been simply a nice respite—a very expensive one, at that.

Then the old bitter feelings returned. Tamar caused this! She thought of the baby she and Nathan should have had. He would be getting big now, smiling and playing—a joy to her and Nathan. But they had been robbed of that. And she had been left ill—permanently ill! All because of Tamar's hatefulness. She could never forgive the woman!

"Sarah, after our lunch, I'll go to the garrison for awhile," Nathan suggested. "You can just relax here this afternoon and visit with Anna. We'll stay one more night and go back to Capernaum in the morning."

* * *

Situated on a hill just outside Tiberias to the northeast, the camp overlooked both the city and the lake. The installation covered a sizeable rectangular-shaped area, enclosed with a high, heavily-guarded wall. Nathan was surprised to find the camp so much larger than the one at Capernaum. It was a complete city within its walls—a collection of large, stone buildings, at least one well, a marketplace, a temple, and much more.

He found Atticus, the Roman Centurion, surprisingly friendly. The man was eager to show him around the camp, where he was able to see for himself what was needed in the pottery line. He felt fortunate to be the potter chosen from all of those in the area to do this job, which he could see would be continuous, if his shop was made the sole source.

* * *

When Nathan arrived back at the Inn of the Seven Stones, he found Sarah in the bedroom, packing their clothes. When he saw the sadness in her face, his heart ached. He put on a playful smile, and popped into the room.

"Nathan, what are you up to?" She reached around him and tugged on his arms. "I know you're hiding something!" After a bit of teasing, he let her take the gift from his hands.

Her eyes lit up with excitement when she saw the beautifully carved box. "Nathan! A lovely box for my dressing table. Oh, I love it!"

"But you haven't looked inside."

Lifting the cover, she gasped with delight. "Perfume! Oh, my! I haven't seen this much nard in my whole life!" Her eyes filled with tears. "You must have spent a fortune."

"But you, my dear wife, are worth many fortunes. And don't you forget it!" He took her in his arms. "I wanted to buy something special for you." He had shopped for the gift one day while she was at the bath house and he recalled telling Santimar that Sarah would be furious if she knew he had spent thirty denarii for it! Santimar had laughed and promised that it would be their secret.

"Nathan, you really know how to lift me up when I'm feeling sorry for myself. I'll treasure this forever and ever."

"I'm glad I can make you feel better. We must keep positive thoughts about your getting well. Let's remember what the doctor said—it takes time."

"Yes, I know, and I promise." She hugged him tightly.

* * *

Arriving back in Capernaum in mid-afternoon the next day, they went directly to Lucian to report on Sarah's treatment in Tiberias and to give him the scroll from Apollonius.

"I must say—the baths must have been just what you needed." Lucian exclaimed to Sarah when they walked in. "You look like a new person." He read the letter while they sat down in front of his table. "I know you're disappointed, both of you. But I believe you'll gradually get better now, Sarah."

"I hope so, Lucian. I do feel good right now, and I'd like to stay at home for awhile and give Nathan a chance to tend to his shop. He has so much new business."

"We'll just be patient for awhile. Plenty of rest. And I mean rest! And you must eat well, too. If you take good care of yourself, your body will have a better chance of getting well."

He turned to Nathan, who was very quiet. "Congratulations, my friend, on such a growing and prosperous business!" He patted his back. "You've done wonders with that little pottery shop you started with. Turned it into a successful business in a very short time. You're surely doing something right."

"Thank you, Lucian." Nathan smiled shyly. "God has blessed my business—so much, in fact, that I've outgrown the shop." A frown crossed his face. "But all the money in the world is worthless if it can't buy what I want most—a cure for my wife. That's all I really want."

"It will come, Nathan," Lucian assured him.

But Nathan wasn't convinced of that at the moment. Other people seemed to be able to buy anything they wanted with their money, but now that he'd finally accumulated enough, the only thing in the world that would make him happy wasn't for sale. These doctors were very good at saying "be patient", "her body will heal itself", "it will come"! He wasn't interested in their promises. He wanted results! Now!

CHAPTER 7

Nathan's mind whirled with indecision. Yes, he had found the ideal place to move his pottery shop. So many advantages. It couldn't be more convenient. The Seven Wells area of Tabga was about a mile south of his house. Perhaps the most important benefit was that the springs here provided all the water he would need. Except for a few broken tiles, the trough bringing that water into the building seemed to be in reasonable shape. Those very springs had made Seven Wells a prosperous industrial community. And it would certainly be a bonus to be located near other successful businesses. Besides that, the price was right.

But its violent history weighed heavily on his mind.

Since it was still early in the day, Nathan went on into Capernaum to the shop. As he walked, he considered all the facts he had gathered. When he reached the shop, he called his men together. He described the equipment, the water system, and the size of the building.

"Sounds perfect to me," Esli spoke up.

"Except for one thing." Nathan raked his fingers through his hair. "The potter who owned the place killed his wife, his father-in-law, and then himself. Since the murder and suicide, nobody has been willing to use that building. It's considered cursed. The pottery equipment has sat rusting for five years. So, do I dare break the spell? How do you men feel about it?"

The lead potter was the first to speak. "Nathan, it was a terrible thing that happened, but it was a long time ago, and I can't see what the tragedy has to do with us, or this business."

"I'm glad you feel that way, Esli." Nathan looked at the others.

One of the new men from Tiberias shuffled his feet nervously. Nathan watched him for a moment. "Japeth, you have a problem with this, don't you?"

"Well," he started hesitantly, "I—I just don't know about workin' where the curse of death has—"

"Man, what are you talkin' about?" One of the younger men pushed his arm playfully. "You lived in Tiberias, the town Herod built right on top of the dead!" They all laughed.

Japeth reddened. "I guess I never thought about that."

Esli rested his hands on his hips. "I think everybody here is ready to start working on the place, getting it ready to move into. We've got deadlines to meet."

"I probably ought to sleep on it, Esli." Nathan laid his hand on the lead potter's shoulder. "It could be fatal to jump too fast. I'm not superstitious, myself, but I have to think about how my trade might be affected."

"Well, just remember that the Roman soldiers don't care who died in your place of business, as long as they get their wares on time," Esli reminded him.

Nathan nodded. "I'll have a decision in the morning. Let's call it a day." He lifted his hand to them and began putting things away for the night.

* * *

At supper, Sarah noticed how Nathan picked at his food, obviously preoccupied. "Nathan, you haven't said a word about whether you went to Tabga to see about that big building. Did you decide against it?"

"Not really." He told her the story about the murder and suicide there. "I don't know whether to take it or not."

"My poor husband!" She reached to stroke his forehead. "I wish I could help you decide."

"Just by listening, you help more than you know." He smiled and squeezed her hand. "I think if I could get those old wheels oiled up and running, we'd be able to get our contracts filled on time. The place has all sorts of possibilities, Sarah. There's plenty of room for all the crew to work. And by the way, I think the three men that Santimar found in Tiberias are going to work out well. They're quite skilled."

"Nathan, do you have any fear of working in that place?" Sarah raised an eyebrow.

He shook his head, laughing. "Of course not. That superstitious stuff is nonsense."

"Well, don't you suppose most other people would feel the same?"

"Probably. At least the intelligent ones, and they're the people I do business with." He nodded his head, grinning. "Who said you didn't help me make decisions?" He picked her up and whirled her around.

They were laughing when Tabitha came to the door. "My, my! I'm glad to see folks so happy!" She smiled with admiration at the two. "Sarah, I just came to bring the things you wanted me to get for you at the market. And I can do some of your chores for you, while I'm here." She looked at Nathan. "I think she still needs me with her in the daytime. I'm afraid she does too much when she's here by herself." She dropped her head shyly. "And I wouldn't want any pay for it. You gave me too much when I was coming everyday."

"Why, Tabitha!" Sarah shook her head. "As hard as you worked, you certainly were not overpaid!"

"Sarah's right." Nathan nodded agreement. "But, Tabitha, I was wondering..." He gestured to her to sit. "Would it be possible for you to come here to live, as our housekeeper?"

Tabitha's mouth dropped open. "You mean—me—live here in this house—all the time?" She put her hand to her chest and breathed in deeply.

"Yes, but if you can't—"

"Oh, I can!" She smiled broadly. "Nothin' would make me happier!" She jumped up. "When do you want me to come?"

"As soon as possible—"

"Wait a minute!" Sarah put a hand on her husband's arm. "Don't let Nathan rush you, Tabitha. Take whatever time you need to tie up loose ends where you're living now."

"Oh, I make it a rule never to have any loose ends to tie up! How about if I just go and get my things? I can move in today."

Smiling, Nathan shrugged. "Well—sure, if you want to."

Without another word, she rushed out the door and down the street.

"Can you believe that?" Nathan laughed, watching her go. "I didn't expect such immediate response. I wasn't even sure she was free to take the job."

"Nathan, that old woman just loves to come here. I don't think she's treated too well at her brother-in-law's house. Your offer was a dream-come-true for her." She hugged him. "My husband is truly a kind man."

"I'm not hiring her out of kindness. I want you to have someone here to do the work. And, Sarah, I want you to let her do it. She's strong."

* * *

Tabitha obviously took her job very seriously. Keeping the house clean seemed to be pure joy for her. She allowed Sarah to do nothing more than supervise the cooking.

Tabitha told Sarah she had learned housekeeping skills from her grandmother, who had also taught her to be an expert midwife. She bragged about being able to work circles around the younger women. Nobody seemed to know just how old she was. It was doubtful she knew, herself. But her weathered face and stooped shoulders gave evidence of many hard times. A few extra pounds had collected mostly around her middle. Her drab tunics and the way she wore her gray hair pulled back and fastened at the nape of her neck with two very plain combs, would lead one to assume that she considered homeliness a virtue.

Sarah knew the old woman believed in the ancient cures that had been passed down through the generations. There were cures for every ailment imaginable, Sarah's illness notwithstanding.

When Tabitha insisted that she carry the ashes of an ostrich egg in a rag, as a sure cure, Sarah went along with it, not wanting to hurt Tabitha's feelings. But she drew the line at being saddled with a barley corn wrapped in the dung of a she-ass.

* * *

With all of the "sure" cures, the baths, rest, and everything else that had been tried, Sarah's problem still persisted. The winter had been unusually long and she had stayed inside a great deal of the time.

Nathan's business prospered. He had so many contracts that he had to work long hours, even with Esli and the other extra men he had hired. But now spring was near. Passover was only another month away.

"I think it's time to make plans to go to Jerusalem together—like we used to do," Deborah proposed as the two couples sipped tea in Deborah's and David's courtyard.

"Now you know I can't..."

"Sarah, hear me out," Deborah raised her hand in protest. "We can travel by carriage, and we'll find an inn in Bethany, or somewhere else nearby. You can relax while the rest of us go to the temple."

"Well..."

Nathan reached for her hand. "It would be nice to get away. I've been so busy we haven't had much time together.

And by Passover time I should be able to leave things with Esli that long."

Sarah reluctantly agreed. She didn't want to spoil things by admitting she really didn't feel like a trip. But maybe she'd be better by then. Did she dare to hope?

CHAPTER 8

The black-shrouded figure slipped inside the front door of the pottery plant at Seven Wells and stood in the small vestibule formed by an anteroom on either side. The room on the left contained very little except a row of pegs on each wall on which outer cloaks were hung. The one opposite, however, appeared more important. Through the doorway, whose heavy curtain was pulled to one side, she could see that the room was furnished as an office, plain and practical. A heavy wooden table took up the center of the room. Three chairs were placed casually around the front of the table. Nathan sat in the other one behind the table, his head bent over a scroll.

She stepped back out of Nathan's line of vision and stood silently observing the men at various tasks in the huge workroom. Six potter's wheels stood in a row down one side, facing the same number of large tables against the opposite wall, where different stages of finishing work was in progress. One of the two doors in the back of the workroom was open, revealing a couple of young boys treading together the clay and water in shallow vats. When a thick-set, muscular man opened the other door briefly, Tamar noted his heavy mitt and apron and the perspiration standing on his forehead, suggesting to her that the ovens for firing the finished product were going full blast in that room.

Esli sang a playful ditty while he painted a polished urn. The other men hummed along as they worked, laughing occasionally at the slightly crude lyrics.

Young Joseph whistled as he set the heavy water jar on the small table in Nathan's office and skipped out of the room in time to the tune. Suddenly spying the dark figure out of the corner of his eye, he let out a startled shriek and jumped back.

Work stopped dead still as Esli jumped to his feet and dashed to the vestibule. Nathan came out of his office, the small scroll in his hand. "Esli, would you please see to our visitor? I have to check on our stock in the back room."

"Certainly, Nathan." Esli nodded and turned to the stranger. "What can I do for you? Are you looking for someone?"

"It's you I want to talk to!" the woman snapped.

"Well, well! I can at least assume now that our guest is female!" He chuckled, pretending not to recognize the harsh voice.

Throwing back her mantle, the woman glared. "My good man, you may also assume that I don't take kindly to rudeness!"

"A thousand pardons, Madam. But disguised intruders cannot expect to be greeted with open arms. So what may I do for Elon's lovely wife today?" Esli bowed. "A gracious creature like you truly brightens an otherwise dull workshop, Lady Tamar! Please let me offer you a chair in Nathan's office." The potter led the way into the room where Joseph had left the fresh water.

"And just what are you doing here?" Esli spoke quietly between clenched teeth. "I thought I told you..."

"I came only to try to persuade you and your crew to get out of this place—and soon!" She sat down across the table from him.

"Look, I don't know what you're up to, but I'm doing my job here and that's what I intend to keep on doing."

"Are you crazy?" She sprang from her chair, moving near the doorway. "Don't you know that everything here is cursed by death? And has been since the murders and suicide took place here years ago!"

Esli walked over and closed the curtain. "Please keep your voice down!" he whispered coarsely, grabbing Tamar's arm roughly to pull her away from the doorway. He hustled back to Nathan's chair. "and don't try to tell me that you've started believing in curses."

She sneered, rubbing her arm where he had gripped her. "I think you're taking chances." She sat up on the edge of her chair. "Nathan is part of my family, and I don't want—"

He laughed, shaking his head. "I don't know what your game is, Jeda, but you're not worried about Nathan—I know that much. If he died, Elon would get part of the profit—a large part, if my guess is right!" Esli rose. "And I'm not worried in the least about this so-called death curse."

"Well, maybe you'd better worry about it!" she snapped. "I can tell you right now that Sarah is aware of the danger. You haven't seen her here, have you?"

"Of course not! She doesn't bother her husband at work." He pointed a finger at her. "And I don't think Nathan will appreciate your interrupting work here, either."

"I know, and I'm taking a risk by coming to warn you. Nathan didn't recognize me. And if Elon knew I was here..." She gave a little gasp and feigned a swoon.

Esli started out of his chair to go to her, but hesitated, settled back, sighing disgustedly. "Jeda, your devious little mind is up to no good and I'll not falling for your tricks!" He shook his head. "In the first place, you've never been superstitious in your life. And in the second place, you don't care about Elon—even how many other women he has!"

She frowned. "It's Sarah he really wants. He has said as much! I can't afford that! After all the years of planning, I'm getting so close to—"

"So you're trying to stir up trouble. A morale problem among my crew could ruin the business. Nathan and Sarah would have to move away. That's what you want, isn't it?" Esli frowned. "I'm warning you—you ruin this business and you ruin me. And I promise—you'll be sorry!"

"Oh? Does that mean you'll tell about my past?" She twisted her fingers together nervously. "You really hate me, don't you? And how do I know you haven't already told someone? Like Nathan! Did you tell him? He would have told Sarah! Remember, dear Reuel, you have a past, too!"

"Oh, but I have far less to lose than you." He laughed. "You're really scared, aren't you? Scared Elon's going to leave you." He chuckled again. "It would serve you right, since by your own admission you're just using him."

"I hate you!" she hissed. "I thought you were a decent man. I've actually loved you all these years. And now I find you despised me all along! You're cruel. As cruel as Herod!" A tear rolled down her cheek. "I'll get even with you if it's the last thing I do!"

"I want you out of here." He was no longer laughing. "Now!"

She laid her head back, closing her eyes. "I—I don't feel well. I'd like some water, please."

"I don't believe this!" he mumbled, pouring a mug of water for her. "I don't have time for these stunts of yours! He shoved the mug across the table, spilling part of its contents in the process. "Drink your water and get out, so I can get back to work!"

"Go on back to your pottery." She reached for the cup of water. "You've upset me so much that I have to rest before I leave."

"Suit yourself, but I'd advise you to get out before Nathan finishes in the back room." He looked at her with contempt. "And I don't ever want to see you here again! Understand?"

"Believe me, Reuel, you won't!" she retorted through clenched teeth.

He returned to the workroom, shaking his head. "I can do without hysterical women around here," he remarked in a low voice to the men who now worked halfheartedly.

* * *

Tamar smiled to herself, feeling smug. Now she knew where she stood with Reuel. She'd never have a minute's rest with him on the scene. He couldn't have told her secret yet, or she'd have known. Nathan would have told Elon. And if she moved very quickly, Reuel would never have the chance again! He would be out of the picture, as would the whole business! And when precious little Sarah was penniless...

* * *

"Esli, we heard that woman talking about the curse of death on this place," Japeth began. "If she's worried about it..."

"Japeth, you sound like another superstitious woman!" Esli spread his hands. "Now I intend to keep working here as long as I can make money for Nathan. I'm sure that's how long he'll keep me on! Now you can stay, or you can go. That's your decision. But if you choose to stay, it had better be wholeheartedly, for I can't afford this moping around!" Esli walked toward the rear for more clay. The mumbling and nodding among the others indicated agreement with him.

Tamar came out of the room wiping her face with a lacy handkerchief. With a quick glance toward the working men, she covered her head with the veil and slipped quietly through the door.

Esli breathed a sigh of relief. "We can't keep our schedule and entertain guests, too!" he grumbled.

Nathan entered through the back door. “By the way, who was the guest? And what did he want?”

Esli laughed. “Oh, your sister-in-law was here—trying to tell us how dangerous it is to work in this cursed place,” he raised both hands.

Japeth laid down his polishing tool. “I can’t believe I’m the only one here with doubts!”

“Man, can’t you see that woman is a bit strange?” one of the other men asked, shaking his head. “Sorry, Nathan, I shouldn’t say that about your brother’s wife.”

“Don’t worry about it.” Nathan grinned. “Look, since your work has already been rudely interrupted,” he suggested, “suppose we wet down our dry throats with a fresh drink of water.” He went to the office and got the jug, calling to the workers in the back. “We can use a break anyway, and what better time to discuss and clear up the doubts?”

Each got his mug and filled it to the brim.

CHAPTER 9

Sarah choked out a cry. She sat stunned, horror frozen on her face.

"Sarah, are you all right?" Elon leaned toward her from the edge of his chair. "Sarah?"

She slowly shook her head. It couldn't be true. Nathan's dead. And all of his crew. "Please tell me this is a bad dream—a nightmare." Her voice was barely more than a whisper.

"I wish it were, Sarah."

"Who—who found them?"

"A young fellow happened along. Probably a friend of one of the men. Said he first thought everybody was asleep on the job. But he soon realized..." Elon visibly shuddered. "They said the boy was hysterical when he ran to the tannery. Then someone had presence of mind enough to send for Lucian. He must have sent word to me as soon as he found out, because we got there about the same time." He sighed. "It didn't take him long to conclude that they were poisoned."

"Poisoned?" Sarah clenched her hands together under her chin. "How? Was it their food, or—"

"The water, so Lucian thinks." He sat back in the chair, sighing. "The half empty jug of water was still cool from the spring, like it had just been drawn. Evidently somebody put poison in it. We figure they all took a rest and had a drink." He spread his hands. "Beats anything I ever heard of."

Sarah shivered. "Elon, why would anybody want to kill Nathan and his men?" Her hands knotted in her lap. "Did they rob the place?"

"No, I don't think so. Everything looked perfectly normal to me—no ransacking or anything." He leaned forward, resting his forearms on his thighs. "The boy who found them saw a woman dressed in black leaving the place earlier, when he was talking to a fellow in front of the tannery." He shrugged. "He said he didn't think much about it then, and, of course, she had long since disappeared when he finally went down there."

He shook his head. "I've been racking my brain for some idea of who the woman could be, or what reason anyone would have for such a crime."

"A woman!" She frowned. "You know, Elon, a woman was the cause of the other tragedy that happened there years ago." She shivered, rubbing her folded arms. "I still can't believe it! All that Nathan worked so hard for, all his life—gone!" The tears finally came. She fumbled in her sash pocket for a handkerchief.

"Yes, it seems so. There's probably not much hope of rebuilding the business now, with all that's happened in that place. But you don't need to worry about money."

He told her about a conversation he'd had with Nathan right after Nathan had moved the pottery shop. He had Elon promise that if anything happened to him, he wanted Sarah to have the house and whatever money there was. Nathan didn't intend for Sarah to be a penniless widow—ever. Elon assured Sarah that she would be taken care of exactly as Nathan had requested.

"Sarah, the doctor's here," Tabitha said as Lucian walked into the room. "I'm sorry I couldn't get here sooner, Sarah."

He bent and took her hands. "I can't tell you how sorry I am. You know Nathan was a good friend to me."

"It's a terrible shock to her, Lucian," Elon offered. "Nathan never should have moved to Seven Wells."

"I doubt the move to Seven Wells had anything to do with it," Lucian countered, "but I'm afraid that's the way many people will look at it."

"I feel so bad for all the families," Sarah said, wiping her eyes. "And I don't know how I can live without Nathan."

Lucian pulled a chair near Sarah. "We'll all be here for you. And you don't need to worry about money. Nathan had money in the bank, and he told me Elon had promised him you would have it, in case..." He looked at Elon.

"I've already told Sarah about my promise to Nathan." Elon glared at the doctor.

* * *

Nathan's burial left Sarah consumed with overwhelming grief and loneliness. How could she ever go on without him?

The dreadful, agonizing days dragged. It wasn't that she was really alone. Tabitha was her constant companion and caretaker. Never a day passed without a visit from Deborah. And Lucian was faithful to check on her daily. But the emptiness she felt inside could not be filled by a crowd. She felt as if half of her had been brutally severed.

Elon couldn't have been kinder to Sarah, helping with all the arrangements and giving her as much comfort as he could. He seemed genuinely concerned for her welfare and her feelings, as well, for he made a point of keeping Tamar away from her except for the traditional courtesies of the funeral.

A few days after the burial Elon came by to bring her the money from Nathan's bank account. Since there was a substantial sum, he tactfully suggested that she find a safe place for it. She agreed and thanked him for his concern, knowing that he wanted her to ask him to take care of it for her. But she also knew that would be an unwise move. Finance was a man's world, and few women used the bank. So she decided to ask Lucian to look into the matter for her.

"I really appreciate your honoring Nathan's request, Elon. I know you are under no other obligation to do that."

"It's the least I could do, Sarah, and I promised my brother." He shifted in his chair. "I care about you, and want to take care of you." He got up to leave. "A woman as beautiful as you could run into real problems." As Sarah stood, too, he stroked her shoulder in a brotherly, comforting caress. Then he hugged her, his hand slipping away from her shoulders and down her back, pushing her body against his own. As his lips hungrily sought hers, she wrenched herself free and backed away from him, her face burning in embarrassment and anger.

"What do you think you're doing?" she half-whispered, hoping Tabitha hadn't heard.

"Oh now, Sarah, don't be such a prude! As Nathan's brother, I'm supposed to take care of you—like being a substitute husband."

"I don't need a substitute husband, thank you! The very idea! Nathan's been gone less than a week! Besides, you have a wife, and you'd better not forget it!"

"Don't remind me!" he snapped hatefully, hustling toward the door.

She glared at him as she sank into a chair, trembling. He smiled patronizingly and left.

* * *

Elon decided against telling Tamar about his promise to Nathan, or about any of Sarah's business. She didn't need to know how much money he gave Sarah. Or how much he kept. He knew she'd like nothing better than getting all of the inheritance and doling out necessary little bits to Sarah.

But somehow Tamar heard that Elon was letting Sarah have all of Nathan's estate. Though he knew she would find out sooner or later, he underestimated her anger when she heard about it.

He arrived home one afternoon to find her pacing the floor, as furious as he'd ever seen her.

"You are the most spineless, stupid idiot that has ever been born!" she screamed the moment he walked into the room. "I can't imagine what I ever saw in you! I know there's something going on between you and that shrewd little vixen, and I intend to know all about it!"

"I don't know what you're ranting about, Tamar." He sighed. "Must you always talk in riddles?"

"Riddles? I'm referring to your blundering attempt to handle Nathan's money!"

"Oh, I might have known." He spread his hands. "And what makes you think Nathan's money is any of your business? But if you must know, I'm merely honoring a request Nathan made some time back. We don't need his money and Sarah does. I owe him that much, and I'm keeping my word."

"Your word!" She paced the room. "Don't you know Sarah is totally ignorant about money? She has never handled any before. Without help, she'll be broke in a month!"

"I'm sure you could help her go broke much quicker than that." He threw back his head and laughed loudly.

She drew back her fist to hit him, her black eyes flashing with a fury that Beelzebub himself would have trouble matching. But the Elon she claimed was so spineless and stupid took her by the shoulders and shook her hard. Clearly stunned, she wilted.

He released her by shoving her into a chair—not gently. "I have no intention of arguing with you. You've become a veritable witch. The matter of Nathan's estate is my decision, not yours, and my decision is final."

Like a spoiled child, when the tantrum failed, she began to cry. He looked at her with a mixture of contempt and pity. "Spare me the theatrics, Tamar. You don't need Nathan's money. I buy everything you could possibly desire. You're simply jealous of Sarah, and let me tell you—it's not very becoming!" He walked to the window, his back to her.

"Sarah's just after you for the money, and you're too dumb to see it!"

Elon sighed disgustedly. "You obviously don't know Sarah at all." He shook his head. Turning to face her, he looked her in the eye. "Actually, I wish she were interested in me." He narrowed his eyes, shaking his finger in her face. "I wouldn't give a second thought to divorcing you." He turned away from her again.

As she left the room, her teeth clenched like a vicious animal, she hissed, "I promise you, my husband, you will regret this with all your heart, and so will your precious little Sarah! Don't think for one minute that I'll let her take my place!"

When she was gone, he wondered if he had done a grave injustice to Sarah, completely innocent. She would never be interested in him. He knew that, but Tamar would never believe it. He knew she was capable of keeping her promise to make him regret his generosity to Sarah. Her mind was filled with many little dark corners, packed full of devious plans that could be activated at any moment she saw fit.

* * *

Totally unaware of her part in the fight between Elon and Tamar, Sarah continued the struggle to get her life back in order. As thankful as she was that Tabitha wanted to stay on as her maid and companion, she knew she must not give in to the grief and loneliness. Plans had to be made for her future.

Since she loved creating fashions, and was confident in her ability to do that well, she decided that weaving and dressmaking would be her best option. This would keep her busy with something enjoyable, as well as profitable.

Lucian's daily visits meant a great deal to her. She considered him a close friend, hers and Nathan's alike. Since society considered her unclean, her doctor was the only man who could have anything to do with her, other than Elon. She needed someone strong like Lucian whom she could trust completely. He had taken care of opening an account for her at the bank, so that her money would be safe. He sent Santimar over when something about the house needed repairs. She depended on her doctor for so many things.

On one of Lucian's late-afternoon visits, after Tabitha had cooked an especially nice meal, Sarah invited him to eat with the two of them. After supper, while Tabitha was cleaning up, she and Lucian relaxed with another cup of tea.

"I'd like to suggest that you go to Tiberias for another round of baths." He leaned his forearms on his thighs, holding the cup in both hands. "The traumatic experience you've just come through would naturally aggravate your illness. You'll come back from the baths feeling more like making a fresh start."

"I hate the thought of going to Tiberias without Nathan, but I suppose you're right."

"You don't need to go by yourself. Take Tabitha with you. Santimar will drive you in the carriage and stay there to bring you back, just as he did before."

"Tabitha could use a nice rest, too. I'm sure she'd enjoy the trip." She brightened at the idea. "Lucian, I'll do that. Next week."

* * *

The Inn of the Seven Stones simply wasn't the same without Nathan. John and Anna did everything to make her stay as pleasant as possible, but it was plain to see that in her thoughts she was reliving every happy moment that she and Nathan had there together such a short time ago.

She took with her the alabaster vial of perfume that he had given her on the last trip. Before she went to bed the first night in Tiberias, she took out the box and lifted the alabaster to her lips, tears rolling down her cheeks. "I'll always treasure this, Nathan," she whispered. "It will remind me of you forever, my darling."

In spite of the painful longing for her husband, the baths were even more helpful than she had expected, and returning to Capernaum, things seemed a little less bleak. Her future looked far from rosy to her, but at least she didn't have to worry about money. Nathan had left her in excellent shape financially. Yet uneasiness crept over her when she thought about Elon's trying to seduce her. What would Tamar do if she knew? By law, Nathan's brother actually inherited everything he had. His giving it to her was out of a desire to please his brother. Or was it? After awhile, Elon might change his mind and take it all back, especially when she didn't respond to his advances. The thought sickened her. Just what was he going to expect of her in the future? She shivered.

CHAPTER 10

"I dropped by to see if you needed anything." Elon flashed a wide smile as Sarah invited him in. His grin vanished when he caught sight of Lucian. "Oh, I didn't know you had company." He glowered at the doctor.

"Take a seat, Elon. Tabitha's bringing tea and cakes for us. I'll tell her to add another cup," Sarah offered.

Lucian stood, nodding toward a nearby chair.

"Don't let me interrupt your visit," Elon said, hesitating.

Lucian waved a dismissive hand. "You're not interrupting anything."

Sarah came back into the room. "Lucian, you started to say something about seeing Ezra at the bank."

"Oh, yes, he asked me to bring him the record that Nathan had on his account. He needs it to close the books on it. Do you know where it is? It would be a small scroll."

"Oh, that would be in his office." Elon popped out of his chair as if it were hot. "I'll—uh—I'll take care of that for you." He sputtered, turning to leave.

Sarah put up her hand. "No, Elon, he had that here. It's probably in the box where he kept important things. I haven't looked through that yet. I'll go right now and find it, while you two talk."

Elon shifted, color rising to his face. "I'm afraid I must go, Sarah." He moved nervously toward the door.

"Before you leave," Lucian motioned for Elon to sit down. "I want to talk with you about a piece of property just outside of town."

"Well—uh—are you interested in buying property?" Elon appeared quite disconcerted.

"This must be what Ezra wanted." Sarah returned to the room unrolling a scroll. "But..." She stopped, looking closely at the record. "Surely that can't be." She looked puzzled.

"What is it, Sarah?" Lucian frowned.

"Elon, I thought you said you had drawn out all the money in the account."

He reddened. "Y-yes, I thought I did," he stammered.

"But this shows..."

"Sarah, may I see that?" Lucian reached for the scroll and looked at the figures.

"See, Lucian?" She pointed to the bottom line. "That shows that there was almost twice as much as Elon brought me. Why, I'm better off than I thought I was!" She laughed.

Lucian shook his head. "No, Sarah, there isn't any left in Nathan's account. Ezra told me Elon had emptied it. That's why Ezra wanted this record." He looked inquiringly at Elon.

Elon squirmed in his chair. "I'm sure Nathan must have drawn out the difference—he had plenty of expenses at the plant."

"According to this, Nathan put money in the same morning he died." Lucian and Sarah exchanged glances and both gazed knowingly at Elon.

Sarah dropped her head for a moment. "I don't understand why you would lie to me, Elon."

"I didn't lie, Sarah. I brought you all of it except for some—well, some expenses." He fidgeted.

"And what expenses would take almost half of the entire account?" Lucian lifted his brows.

"Well, I can't remember everything. I'd have to look that up." He jumped up angrily. "And who are you to be questioning me? You have no right to interfere, doctor! No right at all!" He clenched his fists. "My brother's money is none of your business!"

"But Sarah's welfare is, and it seems that she has trusted the wrong man with her affairs." Lucian retorted, his eyes narrowed. "You know very well there were no expenses that you had to pay out of that money. Nathan had taken care of everything."

"I resent your insinuations!" Elon snarled. "You're not qualified to tell me how to run my business—or Nathan's! I'm perfectly capable—"

"I don't doubt your capability—only your honesty. Why weren't you man enough to tell Sarah the truth? You told her you were giving her all of it, an out and out lie!" Lucian glared at Elon. "It made you look good, letting her think you were so generous, didn't it? And Nathan trusted you to keep your promise."

"You may think what you like! Remember, I didn't have to give her a single shekel." Elon stormed out, banging the door behind him.

Lucian stamped his foot. "I'd like to..."

Sarah put a hand on his arm. "Don't worry about it. He's right, you know, about my not having claim to anything." Sarah dropped her head sadly. "Legally, it all belongs to Elon, no matter what Nathan wanted."

"That doesn't excuse his lies. That two-faced—"

"Lucian, what good does your raging do?" Sarah slumped into a chair. "I hate the fighting. As disappointed as I am over the way Elon has treated me, I'd rather just let it go. I'll get by. I have my sewing to fall back on."

Lucian looked at her face, pale and thin. Her forced smile. "You don't have to do that, Sarah. I know it's very soon to bring it up, but if you were my wife—"

"Yes it is soon! Lucian, Nathan has been gone only two weeks. How could you...?"

"I'm sorry, Sarah. I had no right." He turned to go, avoiding her eyes. "I'll be back soon." He patted her shoulder. "Please don't start working too hard."

* * *

Lucian's proposal was the first of many. Sarah kept reminding him she couldn't marry him in her condition. No rabbi would allow it. She was unclean by law. But he insisted his being her doctor would be taken into consideration.

Days, months, seasons—all evolved into uneventful monotony for Sarah. Eleven years of the debilitating illness took its toll. The effort it took to keep up the dressmaking was often too much, leaving Sarah even more jaded and depressed. At those times, Lucian urged her to spend a few days in Tiberias, taking the refreshing baths. She returned each time rested and ready to tackle the tedium again for awhile, only to have the cycle repeated.

Lucian sent her to other doctors, none of which were able to do her any good. Her savings disappeared rapidly, more with each trip to another doctor and with each visit to the spa.

Lucian worried constantly about her. Her eyes, once sparkling and clear, became dark-circled and lackluster; the rosy cheeks and smooth, radiant complexion were now pinched and dull; and the lovely body that Nathan had compared to that of a goddess was almost emaciated.

Lucian never gave up trying to persuade her to marry him. Though he knew that marriage to him would hardly solve her physical problems, it would alleviate the financial strain, freeing her from the drudgery of sewing for other people. Besides, he loved her dearly, and though he felt he had failed her as a doctor, he knew he could be a good husband for her.

His daily visits became routine, and several times a week he had supper with her and Tabitha. On one such evening, while Tabitha was in the kitchen taking care of the cleaning up, he reached for her hand. "You're having a lot of pain this evening, aren't you?"

"Oh, a little. I'm pretty tired and my sides hurt worse when I've sewed too long. I guess I just get carried away sometimes and forget when to quit." She laughed.

"My dear, why won't you let me take care of you, so you won't have to do all this dressmaking? I hate to see you so exhausted!"

"But you know I need to keep busy, and sewing is what I like to do best."

That she didn't jump down his throat for suggesting marriage, as she usually did, encouraged him. "You're probably right, but I know you'd be better off just to sew for yourself, and maybe Tabitha. You don't make that much on the dresses, and you have to put up with those arrogant women. I could take away all of your financial problems."

Sarah sighed wearily. "Oh, Lucian, I wish you'd be content to keep our relationship the way it is. You would have nothing to gain by marrying me, you know." She felt her face flush.

"And that's why you won't marry me, isn't it? You think I wouldn't be satisfied without—"

"Please, Lucian, don't start nagging me again. When I can be a real wife, in every way, then I'll—"

"Do you know what a real wife is, Sarah?" he interrupted. "I know you love me, and just to be able to stay with you, hold you close to me every night before I go to sleep and wake up each morning with you beside me—that's all I need in a wife!" He took both her hands. "Yes, I'd want more of you, of course, if you were physically able. But since you aren't..." He looked pleadingly into her eyes. "Can't you understand that, my love?"

Sarah looked down, tears in her eyes.

"Did Nathan consider you any less a real wife when you became ill?"

She looked up, surprised. "No! I-I'm sure he didn't. But we were already married—and that's different. Lucian, the rabbi wouldn't marry you to an unclean woman, you know."

"Our case is different, Sarah, as I've told you before. I'm your doctor."

Sarah's shoulders sagged, as she sighed wearily.

He dropped her hands, raising both of his. "I know when to concede. I won't keep nagging, as you say, but remember I love you and I'm here for you if you ever change your mind."

She smiled. "You're so wonderful to me, Lucian. I really would like to see you find a woman you could marry, who could give you children, keep house properly for you and everything that goes with a happy home. I'd certainly understand, and be very happy for you. Honestly! You know that wouldn't keep us from being friends."

"Friends?" He shook his head. "Is that all I am to you—a friend? I can't believe that. We're in love! And it's you, or nobody!" The muscles in his jaw tensed. "Sarah, don't start match-making for me. I won't even discuss another woman."

"I'm sorry, Lucian." She saw that he was angry with her. "I didn't mean to offend you, and I won't mention it again."

Realizing that he would have to make the best of what he had with Sarah, he decided not to push her anymore. He was, however, concerned about her welfare. Her money was about gone and she certainly didn't make enough with her sewing to pay for the badly needed trips to Tiberias. She would do well just to feed herself and Tabitha on what she earned.

"I guess if I hadn't sent you to all those worthless doctors, including myself, you'd still have plenty of money. I thought someone would surely have a cure for you."

"You've done everything possible to find help for me, Lucian." Sarah reached and put her hand on his arm. "But I've accepted the fact that there is no cure. And I don't want to go to any more doctors. I've got the best one of all, right here."

He moved closer to her, taking her hands in his. "I'm glad you still have confidence in me, my dear."

"I'll go to the spa as long as my money holds out, because it helps me a great deal."

"Sarah, I'm going to see that you continue those visits to Tiberias." When she opened her mouth, he held up his hand. "Please don't deprive me of that pleasure. And I promise—it'll be our secret." He ran the back of his finger down her cheek. "And someday you'll realize how much I love you. Then you'll consent to be by wife. I'll always be here for you."

CHAPTER 11

"Sarah, I want the nicest dress you can make, sparing no expense!" Tamar informed Sarah. "This is such an important occasion!"

Tamar had wangled an invitation to Herod's birthday party at Fort Machaerus in Peraea. This important event would take her further than the monotonous little dinners and balls at the palace in Tiberias. Tamar's apparent greed for social standing was misleading. How little people really knew about her. And Elon...He was the biggest fool of all! Her motives for getting in with Herodias and Herod were totally unknown to him. And that's the way it had to remain.

Sarah examined the fabric Tamar handed her. "I guess I can do it for you, but I'm setting the price in advance." She named a higher figure than Tamar was accustomed to paying.

"Well, I must say, Sarah, this is something new! And it's much more expensive than usual."

"Actually, Tamar, it isn't. You usually pick up your finished dress and pay whatever you want to at the moment. I'm just telling you ahead of time what the price will be. I do know what my work is worth, and I need the money."

"Then perhaps I should find someone else to sew for me. I'm sure I could get a seamstress for less that that." Tamar tilted her chin in the air.

"That would be wonderful, Tamar. I really have too many to sew for already." Sarah handed the fabric back to Tamar.

Tamar backed away. "Well, I—I really don't have time to find someone else. I suppose just this once, I'll pay your price," Tamar replied, knowing she was definitely at Sarah's mercy.

* * *

Sarah worked every day until late at night for a week. She wished she had refused Tamar. This was by far the fanciest garment she had ever tackled. Working the intricate embroidery on the yoke was extremely time-consuming and tedious, and she thought her eyes would fall out, looking at those small stitches. The yoke topped dozens of tiny pleats, and dipped into a deep "V" at the bust. Sarah thought it would have been much prettier in a round neckline, but Tamar liked the daring Hellenistic style. Lucian and Tabitha scolded Sarah every day for what she was doing to her health, working such long hours.

The day Tamar came to try on the finished garment, Sarah was exhausted, having completed the last few stitches as dawn broke. She was hardly in her most tolerant mood.

Tamar put on the dress and paraded around the room, obviously delighted with the gown and with herself.

She changed back into her other clothes, got out her money bag and said to Sarah, "Please fold it so it won't be wrinkled, Sarah dear. I'm afraid I can't pay you quite as much as you asked. I talked to Elon about it, and he agreed that you were over-charging. He said you probably just didn't know too much about business. Here's your payment, though. Quite generous, really, and I hope you won't be too unhappy with it." She handed Sarah the money.

Speechless for a moment, Sarah gazed at the pitiful coins in her hand. Then surprise turned to anger. Trembling, she clutched the dress to her chest. Fighting back the threatening tears, she reached to hand the money back to Tamar. When Tamar drew back her hand, refusing the money, Sarah let the coins fall to the floor. Open-mouthed, Tamar stared at the scattered money.

Struggling to keep her voice under control, Sarah announced firmly, "I set the price for the dress well in advance. You had a choice to accept it or not." She looked Tamar straight in the eyes. "Until I receive that amount, the dress will remain with me."

"You can't be serious!" Tamar laughed. "You wouldn't dare!"

"Oh, wouldn't I? I worked harder on this dress than I ever have on any garment! Just look at the embroidery!" She spread the top of the dress in front of Tamar. "How many hours of tedious work do you suppose that took? Well, I can tell you—it took a week, night and day. And my time is worth just as much as anyone else's! I put too much of myself, literally, into that dress not to know its worth." She quivered all over with rage.

As she began to put the sewing material away, along with the fancy dress, she remarked more to herself than to Tamar. "This will bring plenty from someone who knows the true value of nice things."

Tamar appeared to be in total shock. Sarah had never stood up to her like this, and she had to admit—it felt good. Seeing Tamar's face as she stooped to retrieve her coins, Sarah turned her back to keep the woman from seeing her smug smile.

Tamar straightened up, tossed her head contemptuously and flounced toward the door. Sarah wondered how long it would be before Tamar realized she was without a dress for the important party.

Before Tamar opened the door she stopped and slowly turned to face Sarah, who was still busy straightening things in the room. She said, sheepishly, "Sarah, I'm afraid I was too hasty in refusing to pay your price. I guess I'll take the dress, after all."

"I think not, Tamar," Sarah responded sternly. "It's best that you leave now, like you started to. We really have nothing else to say to each other."

Tamar threw back her shoulders. "Sarah—I tell you I—"

"Goodbye, Tamar!" Sarah raised her voice, looking into Tamar's eyes with contempt. The deal was off. The high and mighty Tamar defeated. She stormed out.

Sarah turned to Tabitha, still standing in astonishment where she had listened to the confrontation.

"I probably just cut my own throat, Tabitha, but I absolutely could not control my anger. Now I'm ashamed of myself." Sarah dropped into a chair, burying her face in her hands.

"Well, my lady, you just stop being ashamed, right this minute, because I don't know when I've ever been so proud of anybody!" exclaimed Tabitha. "A human can only take so much of that witch and I was beginning to think you'd let her run over you the rest of your life! I'm glad to see you're as human as the rest of us."

"But of course you know that I'll end up letting her buy the dress. Elon will come over and talk me into it!"

"So, make him pay twice the price."

They were still talking about it when Lucian came. Tabitha began telling him all about Sarah's angry speech to Tamar.

"Sarah, is Tabitha exaggerating?" he asked, winking at the old woman.

"Oh, Lucian, I'm afraid not. I was such a shrew. I'm not very proud of acting like that, but it did feel good to have the upper hand, for a change."

While Lucian was laughing over it, Elon came, just as Sarah had expected. While Tabitha let him in, Sarah whispered to Lucian, "Now I'll handle this myself." He shrugged and smiled.

She turned to her brother-in-law before he could open his mouth. "Yes, Elon, she told you the truth, if she said I got very angry and refused to sell her the dress I had made for her," Sarah said before the man could utter a word.

"Sarah, I don't understand how you could do that to Tamar. I—"

"Well, maybe you'll understand when I tell you that I cannot take any more of her abuse, Elon. I worked night and day for a solid week on that dress. Here, I'll show it to you." She reached for the dress which was still lying across a chair. "Do you see all that embroidery work? Have you any idea how long and hard I worked on that?" She groaned a sigh. "No, of course you haven't, but I know, and I know how much it's worth!" She threw the dress back over the chair in disgust. "Elon, I told her the price in advance, a price way below what she would pay anywhere else. She had the gall to offer me half of that."

"I—I didn't know—"

"Oh? She said she had consulted with you about it. You supposedly said I didn't know anything about business and was over-charging."

"Oh, now, wait a minute! She didn't say a word to me about the price." He looked down. "I'm sorry, Sarah. I should have known. It seems I never learn to discount ninety-nine percent of what my wife tells me."

"You do learn slowly, Elon," Sarah agreed.

"I'll tell you what—if you'll reconsider, I'll pay you just double the figure you set. You see, Sarah, I do want her to have that dress. She has her heart set on it for the big party, and truthfully, I don't want to have to live with her if she doesn't get it. Now I know I sound like a spineless man, but—"

"Yes you do, Elon, and I feel sorry for you, for being so weak. I think you're wrong to do that."

He reddened. "Sarah, I'll see that she comes with me and apologizes to you for the way she treated you and—"

"No, thanks, Elon. In spite of the joy it would give me to see her have to humble herself just a little, I want nothing to do with your wife. You may buy the dress from me for twice the original price, but you tell Tamar to find another dressmaker. I will never sew for her again. That's final."

Elon agreed, paid her, mumbling apologies and thanks all the while, and then left.

Lucian and Tabitha, having stayed completely quiet during the whole scene, were ready to burst when Elon left. They laughed hard now, and Lucian, catching his breath said, "My dear, you're really something when you get riled, aren't you?"

"Well, I'm glad you two find my bad side so funny!" she replied, but then the whole episode suddenly struck her as hilarious and she began to laugh, too. She had been so tense with anger that the laughter spilled out until she was breathless. "I'll probably pay for it later, but I really don't care. I think it was worth whatever it will cost. Of course, Tamar is getting her way in the long run, but it's Elon that is babying her—not me!"

* * *

By the time Elon reached home, his anger at Tamar had built to the point of explosion. Tamar was waiting for him, and when she saw that he had brought the dress, she smiled victoriously.

"Tamar, you needn't look so pleased! Thanks to your infantile behavior, I had to pay double the original price for this dress! And it's the last one you're going to buy for a long time. I'm so disgusted with you, I could gladly choke you!" he stormed, throwing the dress at her.

Tamar held up both palms as if to ward off an attack. "But it wasn't my fault! Sarah—"

"Sarah made a dress for you. And I don't want to hear any more of your lies! You told her I advised you on the matter, which I don't appreciate at all, and then you offered her half price for that fancy dress. Why, she should have spit in your face! You're an idiot, Tamar! You didn't have sense enough to pay the perfectly fair price she asked and take the dress. No, you had to be a dunce and make her mad enough to quit sewing for you!"

"Oh, Elon, you know she'll sew for me again."

"No she won't, for I won't allow you ever to go near her again. She said she didn't want anything to do with you. And I'll tell you something else, she's no more fed up with you than I. If I have any more of this sort of thing, I will divorce you, and you can see how the other half lives. And believe me, Tamar, you'd better take me seriously!" he shouted at her. "I've already cheated Sarah by withholding nearly half of the bank account Nathan left. I'm certainly not proud of myself for doing that, after Nathan asked me to give her all of it."

"Oh! Elon, I didn't know." She smiled. "Why didn't you tell me?"

"Because it was none of your business!" Elon snapped. "Just get out of my sight," he snarled through clenched teeth.

* * *

Tamar slipped meekly out of the room. No use to rile her husband further.

She awoke early, eager for the trip to Macchaerus for Herod's birthday party.

* * *

Joanna, however, did not share Tamar's feeling about this day. She didn't feel well to start with, and even at her best, never looked forward to Herod's banquets. She knew that there would be a disgusting orgy before the whole thing was over, and although she would not be subjected to it, her husband would. Chuza hated it, and attended only because as Herod's steward in Capernaum, he had no choice. Joanna knew Herodias would have a gathering planned for the women, since the banquet would be for men only, and it would almost certainly be another meaningless, boring boasting marathon. She wondered how she could go through another one, with each pompous, egotistical woman trying to outdress, outshine and upstage the other. Sometimes she thought that Herod would do them a favor if he should fire Chuza, but then she remembered what usually happened to people who got "fired". No, she and her husband were in with that crowd and there was no getting out alive—at least for now.

Joanna knew how thrilled Tamar was to be included in this birthday celebration. She felt sorry for the pompous woman who had no idea what trouble she could find herself in, mixing with Herod's crowd.

CHAPTER 12

PETRA - Capital of the Nabataean Kingdom...

Aretas IV paced the stone floor, first to the narrow window overlooking the garden where Rafi sat with her young cousin, and then to the table where the scrolls lay waiting for his seal of approval on the dull, but necessary, logistic decisions.

Syllaeus was a good steward who carried out his duties well. These carefully itemized lists proved that. But the king was hardly in the mood for such tedium. He walked back to the window and stood watching his daughter, her delicate face pinched and unsmiling. The dispirited, faraway look in Rafi's eyes cut him to the quick.

His eleven-year-old niece darted across the grass, squealing with delight over the family of ducks on the pond, and suddenly Aretas was back in another time. It was the young Rafi playing in the garden, the sound of her carefree, childish laughter echoing through the palace.

Could it have been almost two decades since she was that happy, light-hearted little girl? Remembering was painful. His own selfish political games had cut short that sweet, innocent childhood. But how could he have known Herod would treat her so badly? The fox had convinced him that as his wife, Rafi would have the perfect life. For some reason, though, blaming Herod didn't alleviate his own guilt. He had played with a life that was so precious—two lives, in truth. His dear Tesla would probably still be with him had not Rafi's unhappiness broken her mother's heart and spirit.

His little girl had not laughed or sung since she came back to Petra to live again. The scoundrel had robbed her of every shred of dignity and crushed her liveliness. If he could get his hands on that monster, he'd... As Aretas was about to pound his clenched fist on the table, the steward appeared.

"Well, it's about time, Syllaeus! I'm running out of patience."

"I'm sorry, Sire," the steward apologized, bowing graciously. "I was kept busy with the servants. Did you check the lists I left for you, Sire? They need your seal."

"It's not those parchments I'm thinking about right now. I'll do that later." The king paced faster. "I'm anxious to know what you've found out about Herod Antipas and that John fellow, in Peraea. Did the preacher agree to spy for us at Macchaerus?"

"Your Majesty, I'm afraid things didn't work out as we had hoped." Syllaeus answered hesitantly.

"Didn't work out?" Aretas slammed a chair against the table. "And why not?"

"Well, Sire, Saikas came back from Macchaerus to report to us, while Nimri stayed on at the fortress to be at the tetrarch's birthday party. Clever man, that Nimri!" Syllaeus chortled. "Believe it or not, he's got himself hired on in the palace. Those dummies would take on anyone, so long as he'd work for practically nothing." He cleared his throat nervously. "But as to the baptist, I'm afraid we had him pegged all wrong."

"How's that?" The king frowned. "He's got a big following hasn't he?"

"He has, but it turns out that building an empire for himself is not his goal, after all. Apparently he's very sincere about what he's preaching. He's got a message for the people, and the way he lives... well, from what I hear, he wants nothing for himself, not even clothes or food! But, anyway, my lord, he couldn't help us now that he's been thrown in the dungeon."

"Herod put him there?"

"Yes, my lord. Seems that the man had quite a conversation with Herod. Actually had the tetrarch listening to him. More than once. But he made the mistake of accusing Herod of adultery—even incest—since, as you know, Herodias is not only his sister-in-law, but his niece, as well.

"Well, I'll say one thing for the preacher—he's got plenty of guts. Though I'm not so sure about brains." Aretas threw back his head and laughed loudly. "But surely he didn't tell the old snake anything he didn't already know. Herod's mean, but he's not stupid. When he brought that witch back from Rome, planning to get rid of my little Rafi, he knew exactly what he was doing." He looked out toward the courtyard again. "Why, if my daughter hadn't been smart enough to get herself down to the Macchaerus residence before Antipas got back to Tiberias, she wouldn't have had a chance of getting out of the province alive. Herodias would have seen to that." He sighed heavily. "It was fortunate for Rafi that he took his new queen to the Galilean palace first, instead of Livias. And now the vulture has the gall to bring the harlot right down to the fortress-palace with him to celebrate his birthday! That's a slap in Rafi's face. He couldn't get much closer to my border with her than that!" The old king was fuming now and pacing even faster.

"Yes sir. A pompous viper, he is!" Syllaeus agreed. "By the way, Your Grace, Nimri and his men have orders not to go ahead and kill Herod outright. I trust I instructed them correctly. I assumed that at this point, you are only after sources of information in Tiberias and Livias, and other places in Galilee and Perea."

"You assumed right, Syllaeus. That's why I depend on you so much." Aretas stopped pacing. "And what do you hear from Shamri? Is he still keeping up with Jeda's whereabouts? Is she still in Capernaum, trying to get in with Herod's crowd?"

"Affirmative, Your Grace, on all counts! Her greed is setting her up to be of great value to us." The steward laughed. "If we're lucky, she'll have wangled an invitation to the Fox's big celebration! It'll make Nimri's job a lot easier!"

"She always was a greedy little vixen!" Aretas meandered to the window. "But she made my daughter happy. If she had been content to stay here, she'd have far more than Herod could ever give her." The king shook his head sadly. "He's the one who mistreated her. Why would she want anything to do with him?"

"Maybe it's all pretense, my lord. Have you ever considered that she could be after revenge?"

"No, but..." Aretas folded his arms, stroking his beard thoughtfully. "Syllaeus, you may have something. Jeda could be just the one to help us make that murderer squirm." His face lit up. "He thinks he's so powerful, with his new Galilean palace at Tiberias and the Peraean place at Livias. And when he tires of all that he comes to that monstrous castle at Macchaerus. But I suspect he's down there now because of the soldiers I've put on the border below the fortress. Oh, I like keeping him nervous!" He rubbed his hands together and smiled with satisfaction. "Yes, our little Jeda may be motivated by something other than greed!"

* * *

Fortress-Palace Macchaerus...

"Elon, aren't you ready?" Tamar asked, fingering her tight, titian curls.

"As ready as I'll ever be, I guess." Elon sighed wearily.

"Then you'd better go on to the banquet hall. Herod won't like it if his male guests aren't all there when he arrives. I'm almost ready, but I don't want to be too early. It would be crude for me to appear eager, like a vulgar peasant." She began carefully darkening her eyebrows.

"You're really enjoying this foolishness, aren't you?" Elon shook his head disapprovingly. "To me it's all so very childish."

"But that's because you're a fool, my husband. I just happen to know how to get somewhere in this world, and you'd do well to take notice." she retorted. "If you think I'm actually enjoying all of it, then you're very naive. It's merely the means to an end. I think you'd actually be content to be nothing the rest of your life." She lifted her chin haughtily. "Well, not I!"

"And you think that cheap-looking paint on your face and your bosom showing is going to make you something?" Elon shrugged and opened the door just as a servant was about to rap.

"Tea for you and your lady, Sire," he said, bowing politely to Elon.

"Well, it's a bit late for me. I'm on my way to the banquet hall. Tamar, would you like tea while you're finishing?" he called. "I'm sure she would. Take it on in."

"I have a tray prepared, my lady," the servant said, bringing the tray into the inner room. "May I set it right here beside you?" He moved a small stand next to the dressing table. "We wouldn't want to interrupt such important artistry." He stepped back to observe unabashedly.

"How dare you come into my chamber!" Tamar exclaimed. "Where is my husband? Elon?" she called nervously. "Why did you allow this man to come in?"

"Sorry, Madam, your husband was going out. He told me to bring the tray to you." He smiled. "I must say, Lady Tamar, you must be the most beautiful lady in the palace tonight."

She blushed. “And surely you are the most flattering man.” she purred. “Not that I’m averse to compliments, but do you tarry in every lady’s dressing room so presumptuously?”

“Hardly, my dear lady. Few dressing rooms are so interesting, you see.” He smiled. “And flattery is insincere, empty talk. But as a connoisseur of beautiful women, I speak only the truth about you, Lady Tamar. And I can honestly say your loveliness puts the queen herself to shame tonight.” He tapped his chin pensively. tilting his head slightly. “In fact, perhaps you shall be a queen someday.”

“Oh, my! You do have a way with words, don’t you?” She tittered. “I really doubt that I’ll ever be a queen, but it’s a nice thought.” She sighed deeply, frowning. “I’m afraid, dear boy, that it’s too late for me. I made the mistake of marrying the dullest man in the world, who has few ambitions. And being king would not be among them, even if it were possible.”

“Oh, but I’m not so sure it’s as late as you believe, Madam. You see, I know more about you than you think. My connections in high places...”

Tamar whirled around, facing him. She felt the blood drain from her face.

“And those connections are not with a mere tetrarch, such as Herod.” He raised his hand as she opened her mouth. “I have a message for you from a real king.” Nimri winked.

“Whatever are you talking about?” She was shocked that he would be so bold as to speak of another monarch right here in Herod’s palace. “I have loyalty to no other ruler than Herod Antipas!”

“Oh?” He winked again. “I don’t suppose you owe just a tiny bit of allegiance to Aretas—and Rafi? Even a little?”

Tamar gripped the edge of the dressing table. Her heart slammed against her chest. “I don’t know what you’re talking about!” She looked away, her mouth trembling. “I’m from Galilee.”

"Right!" He nodded his head. "Capernaum, I believe. But, my dear, don't feign ignorance about King Aretas. I know all about you and where you used to live." He was no longer smiling. "And Aretas needs you. Remember the time when you needed him?" Nimri sat down in a chair nearby.

"No! You have me mixed up with someone else!"

"Please spare me the games. They're too time-consuming, Jeda!" He grinned as Tamar gasped. "Did you really think you could rob Aretas and get away free?"

"But—but that was..." Her shoulders sagged and she dropped her head in despair.

"Many years ago?" Nimri rose slowly and walked around the room. "He's never lost track of you, Jeda. Never."

A tear started down her cheek. "Is he going to have me killed? I can explain..."

"Had he wanted you killed, you wouldn't have made it to Jerusalem!" He shook his head. "The king still thinks of you with affection, because Rafi loved you so much." He waited a moment while Tamar absorbed the words. "Now allow me to tell you exactly what part you are to play for him."

Nimri pulled the chair closer to her and perched on its edge. "And remember, Jeda, if you have any notion that you can inform on me, you'd better think carefully. Your background would hardly endear you to Herod. Or his wife!"

"Oh, stop it!" She clenched her fists in her lap. "And don't call me by that name. I'm Tamar." She took a deep breath, relaxing her hands. "All right, what do you have in mind?"

CHAPTER 13

In another part of the palace...

Receiving no reply to her gentle knock, Herodias gingerly opened the door and hesitated before walking into the room. "Whatever is wrong, my husband? I rapped several times and you didn't seem to hear me. Now I find you tramping around the room, almost in a frenzy. What is it, love?"

"Aahh, nothing really important, I guess." Herod folded his arms as he walked. "I guess I'm having second thoughts about jailing the eccentric preacher. John, the baptizer." He shook his head. "I don't think he's such a bad sort. He was doing no real harm. In fact, I rather enjoyed my little talks with him." He smiled, nodding his head thoughtfully. "I may send for him again tomorrow. I have more questions for him."

"No real harm? You're out of your mind!" she exclaimed. "My lord, he insulted both of us. Are you going to give him another chance to do more of the same? Or maybe you don't care that your wife was offended," she pouted.

He laughed. "Since when do you worry about anybody's opinions about our private life?"

"I'll tell you when!" Herodias wagged her finger at her husband. "Since I've realized that old Aretas might have sent him. You know his little Rafi would like to see you destroyed, and John may just be their way of doing it. He was deliberately inciting the people against you, with his accusations."

"I suppose Aretas could have sent him. I wouldn't be too surprised. But when you say Rafi would like to see me destroyed, you're wrong. That gentle little thing never had a vicious thought in her life." Herod turned his back to her and looked out the window, as if reminiscing about his little Arabian princess. "And as for John's accusations...Well, they weren't exactly unfounded, you know."

"I suppose you're sorry you gave up your precious little Rafi?" Herodias tilted her chin in the air. "You certainly gave her no thought when you were seducing me!"

"When who was seducing whom?"

"Oh! My master's insults give him pleasure, no doubt!" She puckered her lips in a pout. "It may be your birthday, but don't go too far. Rafi was a dolt. She was afraid of you. That's the only reason she gave in to your every whim. It was not love, I promise you! I, on the other hand, am not afraid of you, and I know how to keep you happy. In fact, I find it quite challenging. You, love, enjoy being seduced." She moved her hips suggestively, smiling at him impishly.

Herod grinned. "You keep that up, and we'll have a party of our own right here," he threatened.

"And have you miss all I've planned for you?" She slipped her arms about his bulky waist, squeezing him playfully. "I just want you to stop worrying about that John fellow, and have a good time tonight, my dear!"

"I'll do that. And perhaps you're right about John. Anyway, he's been put away for awhile. I'll let him go when his followers all give up on him. He'll certainly be in no hurry to spend another week or two in the dungeon."

"Oh, how foolishly soft you are, my husband. But I suppose that's the reason I love you so much," she cooed, patting his cheek and kissing him lightly on the nose. "But right now, there's only one thing you should be thinking about. The guests are here for your birthday feast, and it's going to be simply glorious!" She stepped back, clasping her hands together under her chin. "If I do say so myself, there was never a more splendid party even in Rome, than is taking place here in Macchaerus tonight. I've seen to it that everything's perfect for you. The men are all in the ballroom, so I'll have your valet bring your fanciest robes and get you ready." Opening the door, she turned. "And, my king, the ladies will be breathlessly awaiting your arrival. I do hope you'll take a bit of time with them on your way to the hall. We wouldn't want to disappoint them, now would we?" Blowing a kiss in his general direction, she swept out of the room, brocade skirts swishing.

Watching her go, Herod thought how well she arranged things, so much better than Rafi could ever do. What a pity she lacked Rafi's gentleness and compassion.

* * *

The great hall buzzed with conversations among many important people. Prominent landowners, traders and various other distinguished businessmen represented the major cities—Capernaum, Tiberias, Livias, and Magdala. Wine flowed freely, served by girls obviously selected for their physical attributes.

The magnificent banquet room opened out upon a large atrium, decorated profusely with marble furniture, flowers, hanging lanterns and tapestries. Herodias had obtained her husband's permission to have the women's celebration in this beautiful courtyard, cleverly convincing Antipas that if he made the wives happy, he would find greater loyalty from their husbands. And what could please the women more than to be noticed by each distinguished guest as he entered the ballroom?

Lamps of imported Eqyptian glass, each one a different color, enveloped the entire atrium in an enchanting rainbow of soft pastel light. The effect was pleasing to Herodias, especially when Antipas entered the courtyard, obviously enthralled by the sight of the beautiful women in such a romantic setting.

As the tetrarch walked through to the ballroom, he dutifully flirted shamefully with the women, kissing the hands of a few, each of whom gushed over him obligingly. As he came to the ballroom door, Herodias curtsied to him. "Happy birthday, my lord," she murmured softly.

"Thank you, my queen," he replied, kissing both of her outstretched hands. "You were right. This is the finest party I've ever seen."

"It has only begun, love." she assured him as he left the atrium.

Tamar was thankful that Herod had not passed close to her in the garden. The thought of his touch made her shudder. Even his presence had brought the usual sickening chill to her. Every time she saw the tetrarch she remembered with disgust the first time she actually met the savage beast. At least that's what he had been that night. Of course, he didn't remember her at all. He had been too drunk to get a good look at her in the dimly lit bedchamber. And though she was hardly the only servant girl he had ravished, she doubted that any other had vowed to take revenge. And tonight Nimri had brought that possibility closer.

Deep in thought about her conversation with the Arabian, Tamar was startled when Herodias suddenly spoke to her, "My, you're really lost in your thoughts, Tamar! I trust the party isn't boring to you!"

"Oh, no! Quite to the contrary, Your Grace!" she stammered, shaking the earlier thoughts. "Why, you've certainly outdone yourself on this party. Everything is lovely! I'm sure the king is pleased, as well," she gushed.

"That's nice of you to say. You obviously have good taste, my dear." Herodias laughed, staring shamelessly at Tamar's gown. "And I see it goes double for your clothes. I'll have to speak with you about your dressmaker, before you leave Macchaerus." She turned away to greet another guest.

* * *

As the diaphonic tones of the flutes, zither and lute drifted from the banquet hall, a bevy of dancing girls gathered in the courtyard. At the sound of the timbrel, each girl draped in a filmy, scanty costume went into her erotic dance as she passed through the doorway, swaying and twisting to the beat, ready to drive the drunken men insane. Tamar, at this point not too sober herself, envied them, wishing she could don one of the colorful scarves and dance into the roomful of excited men. The thought of changing places with one of the dancers was delicious, especially as she recalled the dark, handsome Livian palace steward who had arrived just as she was entering the atrium. What fun it would be—a fling with an exciting man such as he! But she wouldn't dare. Here, of all places. Any fun she could manage would have to be in secret. Discretion was important if she was to carry out her long-term plans. As it was, she knew she was playing a very dangerous game, one which to lose would be fatal. She would have to be content with the idle chatter of these empty-headed women tonight.

Tamar walked over and engaged in conversation with Joanna, the one woman in the entire atrium with an iota of intelligence.

* * *

When after a few glasses of wine and a dozen or so dancers Herod began to show signs of boredom, Chuza seized the opportunity to speak with the Tetrarch. "Highness, your birthday celebration is certainly a tremendous success. I trust you're enjoying it?"

"Yes, Chuza, my wife knows how to please me in many ways. The parties she arranges are no exception," Herod answered thickly.

"Your Majesty, might I take my leave now without insulting my lord? I ask only because my wife has been ill, and I think she should be escorted to her bedchamber. I'm a little concerned that she will stay up too late enjoying the queen's entertainment and become ill again."

"Why, yes, by all means! Always take care of your wife, Chuza. I always say...Well, I...Yes, good night, Chuza..." The man was too far gone to know or care who left or stayed, so the steward quietly exited the room.

In the garden, he thanked Herodias and asked that she excuse him for taking Joanna away from the festivities so early, explaining that she had been ill and needed her rest.

"Why, Joanna, I didn't know you weren't feeling well. Please go and take care of yourself." They both bowed to her as they left. "Sleep well," she called to them.

* * *

As Joanna and Chuza said good night to Tamar, she had to envy them a little for having a good excuse to leave. How she wanted to do the same! Oh, in a way she loved the social whirl, the challenge to learn all of the sophisticated ins and outs. But at times the pretense was tedious. Most of all she hated bowing and scraping to Herodias, whom she considered a dreadful boor. But to get where she wanted to go, she must play the part, a tittering idiot, elated over every little attention paid to her by the royal family. Some day...

* * *

The garden now began to buzz with excitement. Another dancer had entered the courtyard, one whose identity in this particular role sparked a flurry of whispering from the women. Even more beautiful than the other dancers, her hair fell in soft, silky wisps over her bare shoulders. Her pale blue costume brought together at the bust in sheer folds with a jeweled pin, exposed more of her voluptuous bosom than it covered. The filmy material of the dress left very little of her young, shapely body to one's imagination. Herodias escorted her to the door of the banquet hall, for this, her own daughter Salome, was her special surprise for the birthday celebration. As the girl disappeared into the hall, the women fell silent, trying to hear what came next. Though the music muffled the voices, except for whistles, it was hardly difficult to imagine what was being said in that room full of men.

Soon the music changed to another beat, as Salome came through the door toward her mother. While the curious women listened, she said breathlessly, "Mother, my stepfather was so pleased with my dancing that he told me to ask for anything in the world and he would give it to me! But, Mother, what should I ask of him?"

The thought of Herod's unlimited offer sent the guests in the atrium into a flurry of excited babbling, but Herodias took her daughter to one side, whispering something in her ear. Since she was obviously not going to divulge the secret, the women returned to their mingling again, with something new on which to speculate.

The minglers in the garden kept their bleary eyes on the ballroom door as they still chatted, though clearly less enthusiastically than earlier, as if hoping to hold out until Herod's stepdaughter returned. After all, it would be a shame to give up and go to bed without knowing what the girl had requested from Herod.

* * *

Still rushing to and from the banquet hall, the exhausted servants kept the wine glasses filled, and removed dirty dishes and scraps, as some of the men continued to eat and drink, even at this late hour. Then suddenly the servants all stopped dead still, staring numbly toward the entrance to the garden. When the women facing that direction began to stare, too, conversation halted. As Tamar turned to see what everyone was gaping at, she almost collided with a manservant carrying a very large tray. The colored lights played on the tray and its contents, as he moved slowly across the atrium. As the edge of the platter bumped Tamar's arm, she found herself staring into another pair of eyes. Just before she collapsed, she saw that the eyes belonged to a head, the head of a man—in a pool of blood. The eyes staring at her...

* * *

Tamar was only one of many who fainted at the sight, but Herodias was definitely not. Instead, she smiled smugly, feeling triumphant as the head of John the baptizer was taken into the banquet hall to be presented to Salome. Herod had granted her daughter's request!

There was a commotion in the hall. Salome came running through the doorway. Even in the dim, colored light, Herodias could see that her daughter was as pale as a corpse. She ran from the courtyard, disappearing into the bedroom wing. Behind her emerged most of the remaining men, visibly sickened by what they had witnessed.

Then Herod appeared. Herodias paled when he stopped for a moment, searching the room with his eyes. When he found his wife, he stared unblinkingly. It seemed to her an eternity. He walked past her, staring straight ahead. When she went after him, seizing his arm, he jerked away, shoving her roughly.

His face ashen and voice trembling, he turned and faced her. "Don't ever give me a party again. I don't like your finale!"

"But wait, love..." She reached for him.

"Get away from me!" He pushed her fiercely. "Don't talk to me now!" Between clenched teeth he continued, "You used your own daughter. How could you do that to her? And you used me! I shall never forget it, woman. Never!"

Watching her shaken husband leave, Herodias stood for a moment, embarrassed that he had put her down in front of the others. But the few women still standing were so stunned by what they had seen earlier that they were oblivious to Herod's departure. Herodias dismissed the women and their husbands and asked the servants to revive the others and send them to their quarters. She was now faced with the task of regaining favor with her husband, and to do that she must make up for this blunder. No little challenge!

CHAPTER 14

Tamar slept fitfully, plagued by nightmares of crowded rooms where men carried trays toward her. Each time one approached, she expected to see those staring eyes, only to find the tray empty. But when she ran into another room, she collided with a different tray. It carried a head. Not John's, but Esli's! Another tray followed, with the head of a second potter. Then another, and another. The whole crew! "No! You can't come back! You're dead! All of you!" she screamed. Then there was John's head again. The eyes! If she could only tear her gaze from their hypnotic grip! "No! No! Go away!"

Elon leapt out of bed and ran to Tamar. As he entered the room, she sat up in bed. "Get away! I had to do it, Rueul! I had to do it! Can't you see? Stop it! Stop it! You can't come back, I tell you!"

"Tamar! Wake up!" Elon took hold of her shoulders. She collapsed in his arms, sobbing uncontrollably. "Now, now, dear. Just a horrible nightmare. It's all right now." Elon forced her to take another dose of the sedative,

* * *

Elon watched Tamar as she tossed in her sleep, and the garbled, disjointed phrases were unintelligible. But the things she had screamed earlier bothered him. *I had to do it, Rueul! You can't come back!* Who on earth was Rueul?

"No! Get out of here!" Tamar screamed, sitting bolt upright in bed. "I don't want that on me!" She rubbed frantically on her hands and arms, as if trying to remove something.

"Tamar, are you awake? What in the world is the matter?" Elon sat beside her.

"The blood! I can't get it off. Rueul—get it off!" Her wild piercing eyes unnerved Elon.

He shook her awake. "Tamar, you're just having a bad dream." He smoothed her damp hair away from her face. "But you keep calling a man's name. Rueul."

Tamar choked out a cry, and clamped her hand over her mouth. "Ru—rueul?"

"Yes, but who is he? Do you know anybody named Rueul?"

"N—no," she whispered hoarsely.

* * *

Tabitha brought home a variety of tales about John's murder at Macchaerus, all very colorful. Sarah let her talk, sometimes hardly hearing what she said. But one evening Tabitha was particularly wound up over the stories she had heard that day in the marketplace.

"Some folks think that John could've been sent by old King Aretas, to spy on Herod. But most think he was a real godly man, preachin' good things. He sure must've been a spunky one, though, to tell old Herod what a sinful man he was to get rid of his wife." She threw back her head and laughed. "Oh, and I hear the baptizer was a cousin of this rabbi that's been goin' around Galilee, preachin' and healin'."

"Deborah mentioned hearing about the man. What is his name?" Sarah asked.

"They call him Jesus. Why, he grew up right over at Nazareth. They say he just touches people, even blind folks, and lepers. And they get well, right there on the spot." Tabitha gestured with both hands.

"That sounds pretty far-fetched," replied Sarah, smiling. "I suppose a magician can look believable, if he is skilled. But, Tabitha, you know he couldn't actually heal those people."

"Maybe not, but I bet you'd have a heap of trouble convincin' a lot of people around Galilee that they didn't get healed by him. He's drawin' more and more followers every day. I don't mind tellin' you, I'd really like to hear him talk the next time he comes to Capernaum," Tabitha declared.

"Well, dear, whom you listen to is your own business, of course, but I do hope you won't get all involved with some fanatic. He might cast some sort of spell over you."

"Over me?" Tabitha chuckled. "Sarah, you know it's not easy to cast a spell on a stubborn old mule like me. He'd have his job cut out for him, to change me!"

"I can believe that." Sarah laughed with her. "And I'm thankful you are strong. Otherwise, you wouldn't be such a rock for me to lean on."

* * *

Shopping in the marketplace a few days later, Tabitha noticed a crowd gathering in front of a small house nearby. As a woman rushed by in that direction, Tabitha asked what was happening.

"The rabbi, Jesus, is there!" answered the woman without slowing.

Tabitha joined in the push to see and hear the man, but the crowd had assembled so quickly she was unable to get close. She supposed that the preacher had gone into the house. Determined not to be outdone, she sat down on a large stone in the shade of one of the shops, to wait until he came out. Maybe she could at least get a glimpse of him.

As she watched the house intently, four men carrying someone on a mat climbed the stairs to the roof. Setting him down, they proceeded to dismantle the roof. Then to Tabitha's amazement, they let the man, mat and all, down through the hole they had made.

Her full attention on the baffling activity, she startled when she felt a gentle tug on her sleeve. She turned around to find Mary, her second cousin from Magdala, smiling at her.

"Why, Mary Hiram! What in the world brings you here?" She hugged her cousin joyfully.

"I've been looking for you, of course." Mary laughed. "And I had about decided you had left the country. Where have you been hiding?"

"Oh, child, I've moved since I saw you last and I've been pretty busy. You see, I keep house for Sarah, a widowed friend of mine. You must visit us, Mary, and meet her."

Tabitha stepped back, looking her cousin over from head to toe. "But, my goodness, girl, I haven't seen you in a crowd like this for years! You must be feeling better."

"Yes, Tabitha. Believe it or not, I've been cured of the seizures I used to have. Jesus took away my problem. Some say it was demons." Mary smiled. "Maybe so, but whatever it was, it's gone and I'm a completely new person. But, Tabitha," She laid her hand on her cousin's shoulder and looked into her eyes. "he did more than heal my body—he healed my soul. You see, he changed my entire life." Her face was radiant.

Tabitha stood open-mouthed, listening to her cousin's testimony. She started to ask a question but Mary looked toward the house where the crowd was gathered. "Jesus must be leaving now. I see people coming away from the house. I must hurry to Peter's to help Rebecca with the dinner. But I'll come to see you before I leave Capernaum. In fact, I'll try to get there tomorrow." And with a quick hug, she was off, before Tabitha could find out anything more.

"But how will she know where I live?" she asked aloud. Shrugging, she turned toward where Mary went. That's when she saw the man walking away from the house, hands raised high, tears streaming as he pushed through the crowd. With him were the four men she had seen on the housetop, and one of them carried the folded mat. Trembling, Tabitha turned and started toward home. No one had ever accused Tabitha of being gullible. She was not easily deceived, but there was something going on here, and it was more than a magician's show. Tabitha was determined that she would learn more about it.

Tabitha could hardly wait to talk with Mary again, to hear the whole story. She smiled as she thought about the change in her cousin.

She remembered how vibrant Mary had been as a young girl, and how beautiful. Her long, thick auburn hair fell over her shoulders with just enough natural curl to be the envy of any woman. She had married John, very successful in the fishing industry in Magdala, and was about as happy as a young woman could be. He had built a beautiful home, set back into the hill, overlooking the lake.

Then the convulsions had begun, becoming worse and worse, until she could seldom leave her home. She was afraid to be in public, not knowing when a terrible fit would strike her. People pointed at her and whispered about her demon possession. The stigma was bad enough in itself, but the illness was very weakening.

John was a good man who loved Mary dearly and took good care of her. Then he had died quite suddenly, leaving her with one son, barely grown but already part of his father's business.

Tears came to Tabitha's eyes as she remembered the real tragedy in Mary's life. With John gone, she had somehow taken up with an undesirable crowd in Magdala. Tabitha had no idea how it happened, but she was told that Mary was living a very shameful life. Of course, Mary became estranged from the family and Tabitha hadn't even known where she was.

But today Mary had said the old trouble was gone. And Tabitha had to admit that she certainly looked like the Mary of years ago. If this man Jesus had really changed her cousin's life that much, she surely wanted to know him. Maybe he could touch Sarah, as well!

* * *

As soon after the midday meal as she could get away, Tabitha made her way to the palace of the steward, a long walk to the northeast of the city.

Arriving at the servants' entrance, she found her friend Delmia sweeping the steps, singing happily.

"Well, look who's here! My, my, Tabitha! Whatever are you doing way over here? Your legs must be about to fall off after that walk! Come on into the kitchen and let me get you a cool drink of water."

"That does sound good, Delmia. These old bones don't hold up like they used to." Tabitha laughed, taking the water and dropping herself wearily onto a bench. "But I just had to come over here to see you, since you didn't go to the market this mornin'. I need to find out about that preacher, Jesus, and I thought maybe you could give me some answers."

Delmia pulled up a stool. "I don't know all that much about him, Tabitha, but I'll be glad to tell you what I can." She smiled. "What is it you want to know? Have you heard him talk yet?"

"No, but I was in the marketplace yesterday and I saw somethin' mighty curious." She related the story about the men and the invalid. "And then, on top of that, I ran into my cousin from Magdala, who has had convulsions for years, and she told me that the man took the spells away and left her as well as she ever was. I tell you, Delmia, I hardly knew her. Why, she just glowed!" She sighed wearily. "I don't understand any of this." She raised her palms. "What kind of power does the man have? I'm scared of witches and that kind of thing, and I don't know what else it could be. Still, I just can't believe Mary is under that kind of spell." She looked at her friend, her eyes filling.

Delmia smiled warmly, patting Tabitha's hand. "You don't have to be afraid of Jesus, Tabitha. There's no witchcraft to what he does. He's the most gentle person I've ever seen. And I know about your cousin. He did touch Mary and she's really well again, just as she told you. You probably haven't heard, though, that my mistress Joanna, was also touched by him. She's been sick, off and on, for quite a time. She just kept going, but was hardly able to hold her head up. Jesus healed her, and this household is just bubbling over with joy today! But, Tabitha," she continued, "there's only one way you can learn about him. You'll have to go and listen to him. When you do, your heart will be warmed." She smoothed the pocket on her sash. "You see, Tabitha, he touches people in many ways, not just by healing their bodies. He changes the inside, too, believe me!"

"Mary said something about that, too, and I didn't understand."

"But when you hear him, you will." Delmia took Tabitha's cup to refill it. "We're just praying he won't get himself into too much trouble with the Pharisees. They keep coming and trying to find something to go and tattle to Herod about!"

She handed Tabitha the fresh water and sat back down. "Last Sabbath Jesus and his helpers were walking through a field, and they ate a little of the grain, being hungry, of course. Well, the Pharisees said he was wrong to do that—said he was harvesting on the Sabbath." She leaned toward Tabitha, whispering. "I'm afraid Joanna and Chuza may get into trouble with Herod, too, if he hears that she's following Jesus. But Chuza is so happy over his wife's healing, I believe he'd take Jesus' side against Herod, if it came to that!"

"Well, I sure don't understand any of this, but I'll go hear the man, like you say." Tabitha clasped her hands together. "I'd give about anything if he could touch Sarah and make her well, too."

"He can do that," answered Delmia, "but only if she will believe. And I hope she can, my dear."

On the walk home Tabitha tried to sort out the things she had heard. Both Delmia and Mary talked about how he touched people on the inside. "What were they talking about? Do I need to be touched like that?" she wondered aloud.

CHAPTER 15

"I thought you'd gone back to Magdala!" Tabitha hugged her cousin and drew her into the front room.

"Now, Tabitha, you know I wouldn't think of leaving without visiting you." Mary looked all around the room. "What a lovely place."

"Yes, Sarah has good taste," Tabitha agreed. "God really blessed me when he brought me and Sarah together. When she lost her baby, the doctor asked me to come here and help her, and—well, we just got to be real good friends. She never did really get well and finally her husband hired me to be their housekeeper." She gestured toward a couple of chairs and the two sat down.

"I'm so glad for you, Tabitha. You deserve a good home."

Tabitha told Mary about Nathan's pottery shop and about the tragedy in which he died. "Sarah seems like my own daughter. Poor little thing." She shook her head sadly. "And, Mary, the poor child is gettin' weaker an' weaker every day." She lowered her voice to a whisper. "She goes ever-so-often to Tiberias and takes the baths and then she'll be better for a little while, but it don't last long." She looked toward the bedroom area. "She's havin' her rest now. I was hopin' you'd get here while she was awake. I wanted her to meet you."

"Well, I won't be leaving the city for a day or two, so maybe I'll get to meet her."

"Mary, I've sure been thinkin' a lot about you since I saw you in town. I couldn't get over the way you'd changed. And you're still lookin' just as good today."

Mary moved her chair closer and took her cousin's hands. "I knew when I left you yesterday that you were confused about everything. I'm sorry I didn't have time then to explain." She squeezed Tabitha's hands before she released them.

Tabitha leaned back in her chair. "Well, it's plain to me that you're well again. You look as good as you did when you were a young girl!"

"Tabitha, it was Jesus. He touched me and I was whole again."

"I'm so happy for you." Tabitha pulled a handkerchief from her sash and wiped her eyes. "I sure wish it could happen for Sarah. I worry so much about her. I've tried all the cures I know, and of course, she's gone to doctors and takes the baths. Nothing has done any good. I guess there's just no cure for her. But, Mary, the little dear never complains."

"Tabitha, don't be too sure there's not a cure for her," Mary challenged. "Jesus might heal her, too. I don't know if he heals everyone who asks, but I do know he can, if it's his will, and if she believes in him."

"But, Mary, you know the law—she's not even allowed to go to the synagogue. She'd have to tell Jesus her problem and then everybody'd know she was unclean. There she'd be, where she wasn't supposed to be, and..."

Mary put up her hand and leaned forward. "When you get to know Jesus, Tabitha, you'll find that he doesn't put as much importance on the law as he does on individuals. Besides, I wasn't healed in the synagogue." Mary rose and walked to the window where the view of the hills sloping toward the lake was especially pretty on this sunny afternoon. "You see, Tabitha, he speaks other places, too." She turned to face her cousin. "I know you're wondering how he could change a... well, someone like me."

Tabitha reddened, lowering her gaze.

"It's all right, dear one. I was mixed up with people I thought could help me, and I allowed myself to be drawn farther and farther from a decent life." She sighed, wiping a tear from her cheek with the back of her hand. "I was trying desperately to turn myself around, when I heard Jesus speak—down by the lake. That's all it took." She clasped her hands to her breast. "He changed my life. I was free, not only from my disease, but from my sinful, mixed-up life."

"Oh, Mary..." Tears blurred Tabitha's vision. "Did Joel..."

"Yes, my son and his family forgave me and took me back. I live with them and help him with the business, which is what I should have been doing all along."

Tabitha stood and hugged her cousin tightly. "If the rabbi can change a person that much..."

"But you must hear him for yourself." She took Tabitha's hands. "How about tomorrow? Jesus will be speaking at the synagogue and we'll go together. You'll see other women there that you know, too."

"I'll go with you," Tabitha promised.

"I know you must still have a great deal to do before sundown." Mary got up to leave. "I'd best leave you to your chores. I'll meet you at the synagogue in the morning, Tabitha."

* * *

Tabitha busied herself preparing food for all three Sabbath meals. Since the holy day began at sundown, the housecleaning, cooking, and everything else was done before twilight.

Just as Tabitha finished everything, she heard hazzan blow two notes on the trumpet to warn the workers in the fields to leave their work. A little later, he sounded two more notes to tell the shopkeepers to close, and the third blowing meant that it was time to light the lamp, which had been carefully filled so that it wouldn't run out. The Sabbath had truly begun.

When the lamp was lit, Sarah and Tabitha sat down to the first meal of the Sabbath, with the traditional wine and herbs a part of the dinner. When this meal was over, no more was to be eaten until after the service at the synagogue the next morning.

* * *

Tabitha caught her breath at the beautiful sight before her. The early morning sun coming into full view over Lake Galilee had transformed the white synagogue into a gilded basilica. The marble columns of the porch spanning the east side took on varied shades of rose and gold. Tabitha arrived about the same time as most of the crowd and joined Mary and the other women near the side entrance. As they slipped quietly into the women's gallery, which ran around the north and east sides, Tabitha saw one of the Scribes preparing to read from the Holy Scriptures. The men sat either on floor mats, or on the two rows of stone benches, one above the other, that ran around three sides of the rectangular building. This morning both places filled rapidly with an unusually large crowd.

Everyone listened closely as the scribe read the Word of God, and when he sat down, Jesus stood and faced the people. Tabitha's eyes never left his face. He was a fairly tall man, slim, but not scrawny. In fact, she thought him to be moderately muscular. As he looked around over the group of people there, he turned toward the women, and unlike any speaker before him, nodded and smiled. Tabitha sensed that as he looked over the crowd he saw each person individually.

As he spoke, one of the men in the front row interrupted him with a question. The rabbi stopped and answered him, even though the man obviously tried to trap him into saying something injurious to his reputation. Tabitha couldn't help noticing that the man's tassels on his prayer robe were almost twice as long and showy as those on Jesus' garment.

As another of the same group of men put up his hand and leaned forward to interrupt the speaker again, Jesus said, "Don't criticize, and then you won't be criticized. For others will treat you as you treat them."

Then, changing the subject, he continued, "Ask, and you will be given what you ask for. Seek, and you will find. Knock, and the door will be opened. For everyone who asks, receives. Anyone who seeks, finds. If only you will knock, the door will open. If a child asks his father for a loaf of bread, will he be given a stone instead? If he asks for fish, will he be given a poisonous snake? Of course not! And if you hardhearted, sinful men know how to give good gifts to your children, won't your Father in heaven even more certainly give good gifts to those who ask him for them?"

Tabitha noticed how some of the most pious men squirmed when he called them hardhearted and sinful, and they scowled at him. She was glad someone had nerve enough to say a few things that many people were quite often thinking about these men.

Jesus continued, "Do for others what you want them to do for you. This is the teaching of the laws of Moses in a nutshell."

As Tabitha listened she thought the man surely must be from God. He didn't even speak like the other Jewish leaders. He had a kind of authority, as if he were God himself!

He went on, "Not all who sound religious are really godly people. They may refer to me as 'Lord', but still won't get to heaven. For the decisive question is whether they obey my Father in heaven."

Then Jesus looked at a man farther back in the crowd, and said to him, "Friend, I see you have a crippled hand."

The man answered, “Yes, Sir, it has always been deformed.”

Everyone was very quiet. The hecklers in the front watched him closely, casting smug looks at each other.

Jesus asked the man to come and stand in front of the congregation. Then, turning to the cynics, he asked, “If you had just one sheep, and it fell into a well on the Sabbath, would you work to rescue it that day? Of course you would. And how much more valuable is a person than a sheep! Yes, it is right to do good on the Sabbath.”

The men did not reply.

Flashing a withering glance at his accusers Jesus said to the man, “Stretch out your arm.”

He did, and instantly his hand was normal.

The dissenters rose and pranced out of the synagogue.

With sadness in his eyes, Jesus moved toward the door. He raised his hand toward the people. “Bless you all,” he said and departed. His disciples got up and went with him, leaving the dispersing crowd mumbling among themselves.

Tabitha sat stunned for a few minutes before she joined the other women already leaving. Squeezing Mary’s hand, she whispered, “Thank you for tellin’ me about Jesus, Mary. I know now what you meant about him touching a person on the inside.” Tears slipped down the wrinkled old cheeks.

Mary put her arm about Tabitha’s shoulders, her own eyes brimming. “Tabitha, I knew it would be like that when you heard him. You’re wise enough to recognize his greatness.”

Walking back home that Sabbath day, Tabitha felt as light as a quill. Now she could tell Sarah about Jesus. Surely she’d have no trouble convincing her that he could heal her, after what she had seen this morning.

* * *

“Well, Tabitha, how was the service today?” Lucian asked as she walked in the door. “I decided to keep Sarah company this morning, instead of going to the synagogue. So you’ll have to tell us all about it. And spice it up a bit, if you don't mind. The service is usually quite boring." He laughed.

"Well, Doctor, you wouldn't have been bored this mornin', I can tell you! Jesus was there speakin' and you'da liked him, both of you. I never heard anybody put them uppity Pharisees in their places like he did. I might get struck down for sayin' it, but I'm thinkin' it, and that's just as bad!"

They all laughed as she sat down to tell about the meeting. She told them everything she could remember about his talk, and Lucian said, "Sounds like the kind of preaching I'd like. Maybe I'll go hear the man next time."

"Oh, but I've saved the best 'til last!" Tabitha leaned toward them. "There was this man there with the crippled hand. You know—that shopkeeper at the marketplace who runs the little vegetable and fruit stand on the end of the row?" They both nodded. "Would you believe his hand is as good as yours right now?" She slapped her knee emphatically.

"Now, Tabitha, I said I wanted it spiced up, but let's not overdo it." Lucian raised both hands.

"But I'm tellin' you the truth! You just go down there tomorrow and take a look at that hand, yourself!" She frowned. "But I'm afraid Jesus will be in big trouble now. The Pharisees who came to the service left in a huff after the healin'. Everybody says they'll go right and tell Herod that Jesus broke the law of the Sabbath. I know he really healed that man, 'cause I saw it with my own two eyes!"

"Oh, I'm not doubting your word, Tabitha. I'd never accuse you of lying! But sometimes things are not quite as they seem to be," Lucian reasoned.

"Tabitha, Lucian's right, you know," agreed Sarah, "I find it hard to believe he could change that man's shriveled hand. It must have been some sort of illusion."

"I'm sorry you feel that way, Sarah." Tabitha's joy left her. "I was hopin' he could touch you and make you well again. And I know if you could've heard him talk, you'd believe in him, too." She looked from one to the other. "I wish both of you would at least go hear him before you make up your mind about him. He talks other places, too, they say. Not just at the synagogue."

"Tabitha, I think my time would be better spent taking the baths. And incidentally, I'm planning to go to Tiberias next week. Will you go with me?" Sarah asked gingerly. "Lucian thinks I should go."

"Yes, of course, Sarah," replied Tabitha, plainly disappointed. "I guess I just get carried away sometimes. Maybe I'm too trustin', or just plain dumb!" She shrugged and got up. "I'd best get you two some food to go with your tea." She sauntered on into the kitchen, shoulders drooping.

"Poor Tabitha," Sarah said, after she knew the woman was out of earshot. "I'm afraid we were a bit blunt with her. Should we go hear the man, just to please her? To be so stubborn in some ways, she's terribly gullible in others."

"Yes, she is. You know, Sarah, if the man said the things that she remembers him saying, he might be very interesting. Of course, the healing story pretty well killed my interest. I've healed people before, myself, but I've seen that man's hand. He was born that way. There's no way that rabbi could restore a hand that was never even all there. No way!" He shook his head. "I wish he could heal people so easily. I'd give anything in the world to see you get well. I don't like for you to suffer, and besides, I think you might even consider marrying me if you had your health again. I just wish you could understand that I want you as my wife, anyway..."

"Lucian, please..." She broke off as Tabitha came back into the room with the tray of food. The cold meal was arranged attractively on the server—flat rounds of bread, fish, dates, and figs. She had also made little sweet cakes to eat with the fruit and tea.

"Tabitha, everything looks so appetizing!" Sarah tried to recover from the embarrassment of having Tabitha walk in on such an intimate conversation.

Lucian leaned over his tray, ready to attack the food. "Tabitha, if Sarah ever gives you any trouble, you can come and be my housekeeper."

"Lucian! Don't you dare try to take Tabitha away from me!" Sarah pursed her lips in a pout. "I couldn't survive without her!"

"Well, I'll just have to be content with the next best, I guess—eating here every time I can wangle an invitation."

"As if you needed an invitation to eat a meal with us." Sarah laughed. "But now I know you come just for Tabitha's food—not to see me."

But the old woman was not amused at their efforts to make her feel better.

CHAPTER 16

A loud banging on the front door shattered the quietness of the afternoon. Before Tabitha could set the tray of dishes down and go to the door, Tamar burst into the room.

"Where is he?" she screeched at Sarah, her face crimson and her hair tousled and flying.

"Where's who?" Sarah rose from her chair hesitantly.

"Oh, don't play dumb with me, you little harlot!" Tamar snapped, her black eyes darting around. "I know you—"

"Just hold on!" Lucian jumped up, raising his hand to stop her. "You've no right to barge in here like a maniac, calling Sarah names! Now suppose you just settle down and tell us what you want, in a civilized manner."

"Don't you tell me what to do! Elon is here somewhere. She's hiding him from me." She pointed her finger in Sarah's face.

"You're crazy!" Lucian was furious. "Either calm down, or get out!" As he reached for Tamar's arm, she jerked away, but he grabbed her and shook her. About that time Elon walked through the front door and rushed toward Lucian.

"Let go of my wife!" Elon drew back to hit him. "What do you think you're—"

"Stop it!" shouted Sarah. "Lucian's trying to calm her down!"

"Actually, I was about to throw her out." Lucian corrected. "She flounced in here calling Sarah a harlot, accusing her of hiding you. I can't imagine where she got that idea, but you'd better set her straight fast, Elon, because I won't stand for Sarah to be treated like that."

"What goes on here is none of your business." Elon retorted. You don't live here. Or do you?"

Lucian's answer landed the man on the floor, stunned.

Sarah turned pale, and just as she started to keel over, Tabitha grabbed her. "Now see what you've all done! You know Sarah's sick. She can't stand that kinda' thing. And on the Sabbath!"

Lucian took Sarah from Tabitha and put her back on her chair with a pillow behind her head. Tabitha brought a cool, wet cloth and bathed her face.

"I'm sorry, Sarah," Lucian said softly, holding her hand. "Want to go lie down for a bit?"

"No, I'll be all right in a minute," she replied, her voice barely audible.

"It's my fault, Sarah," Elon offered, his face flushed. "I'm afraid I jumped to conclusions before I listened."

"Ugh!" Tamar sneered. "You two make me sick! Well, I'm not sorry! This woman is after my husband and I hate her. I'll kill her!"

"Tamar, you idiot!" Elon grabbed her arm. "You don't know what you're talking about! Sarah has never—"

"Oh, don't give me that! She's been after you ever since Nathan died—maybe even before that." Her eyes narrowed. "You're always coming over here to see her, and giving her money. I know what's going on!"

"That's the craziest thing I've ever heard. And I'd better not hear any more of it." Elon yanked her around and started toward the door. "I'm taking you home where you'll stay until you learn to keep your stupid mouth shut." When she opened her mouth to reply, he jerked her through the door.

Sarah trembled all over. "Oh, Lucian, she was so wild! I believe she really intended to kill me."

"The woman's out of her mind." Lucian put his arm around her. "Sarah, I don't want you here by yourself—ever. She imagines things in that warped mind of hers, and there's no telling what she might do. Tabitha, you must make sure Sarah is with Deborah or with me when you leave the house, even for a little while."

"Don't worry! That woman scares me. And we'll keep the door latched, too." Tabitha shivered, shaking her head.

* * *

Lost in his troubled thoughts, Elon walked so fast Tamar could hardly keep up with him. His head throbbed and a sharp pain shot through the small of his back. The muscles were as taut as a bowstring. If he had to endure many more sleepless nights, he knew he'd be forced to have Lucian mix something for him. But he doubted the doctor had anything potent enough to make him forget what troubled him.

Should he start an investigation into Esli's murder? It was a well-known fact that the potter and his crew had been poisoned, but nobody had tried very hard to find out who did it. Should he tell the authorities what Tamar had said in her sleep? That would just about ruin him in this community. His own wife—a vicious killer? Surely not. Yet his suspicions continued to haunt him. Maybe this was the time to confront her with it. Of course, she'd only deny it, regardless of the truth. And if she were capable of such a heinous crime, what would his own life be worth?

If he kept quiet, maybe allowing a murderer to kill again sometime, could he live with himself? On the other hand, if he should reveal what she had said in her sleep, the authorities would look no further for a suspect. She'd be put to death, guilty or not. It was an impossible situation. And now he had another of her escapades to deal with.

As soon as they were in the house, he turned on her. "I can't believe you'd go over there and make such a fool of yourself."

"I thought you were there! And I had good reason." She pouted. "I know you sneak over there every chance you get."

Elon sighed wearily. "You don't know any such thing. I haven't been to Sarah's for quite some time. Besides, I don't have to sneak anywhere. When I want to go to Sarah's, I'll go. I don't find it necessary to account for my time to you or anyone else."

"Well, I'm aware of Sarah's game. The helpless little widow crooks her finger and you come running. She's got Nathan's money and now she's working on you. And you're dumb enough to fall for it." She turned toward the window for a moment and then whirled around toward Elon again. "I'm telling you this. She'd better leave you alone and stay out of my way."

"And you know how to take care of people who get in your way, don't you?" He regretted his words the moment they left his mouth.

"And just what does that mean?" She raised her eyebrows, staring at him viciously.

"Oh, nothing. Just forget— "

"Oh, no! I will not forget it. What did you mean?"

"I meant simply that you always make trouble for people who don't do everything to suit you." he said. "But as for Sarah, she isn't interested in me or my money. So let's just drop the subject." He picked up a scroll and unrolled it. "Right now I want to look over these figures again before the meeting tomorrow. There's a great deal of profit to be made here if things go as I plan."

"It's about time you got something going again. You've been neglecting your work lately." Before she could elaborate on her accusation, he grabbed her by the shoulders and shook her soundly. He let go of her by shoving her into a chair, where she sat limply.

Stepping back, he shook his finger in her face. "You'd better listen closely to what I'm about to say, Tamar! If you ever even go near my brother's widow again, I shall beat you! And then I'll divorce you! I hope that's clear, Tamar, because you need to think about how you'll have to live if you're not married to me. It certainly won't be as you're now accustomed to living." He turned and paced the room while she remained still.

"I've had it with you. Every time I turn around, you're doing something stupid. You'd better lay off the wine, so you can keep yourself under control." His breaths coming in short gasps, he stopped in front of her. "I can't stand you anymore, Tamar!"

CHAPTER 17

In twelve years and some three dozen trips to Tiberias, the routine seldom varied. The Seven Stones had become her second home. John and Anna even referred to one particular room as "Sarah's".

Nor was it any wonder that the spa treatments had become Sarah's panacea—her sanctum sanctorium. Basking in the swirling, soothing, warm water, with Iona always in attendance, she could lose herself in any fantasies of her choosing. The old apprehension and fear of potential danger in Herod's pagan city had been pushed long ago to the back of her mind, overridden by the restorative, tonic effect of the visits—as much psychological as physical.

On the last full day of this stay, Sarah woke to a rosy-fingered dawn, the sun's rays drenching the room in a delicate mauve. She lay still, dreading to disturb the tranquility of the moment. A cock's crow somewhere nearby, followed by the impatient braying of an obstinate mule in the stable yard, shattered the quietness and Tabitha stirred. "Are you awake, Sarah?" she whispered.

"Yes. That beast out there took care of that." She rolled over facing Tabitha's cot. "Truthfully, I was already awake, just enjoying the stillness of the morning, daydreaming, I suppose."

Tabitha yawned. "I don't know why I can't seem to wake up early here. Must be 'cause I don't have a thing to do. It sure makes a body lazy, but I'll have to own up to likin' it." She laughed. "These old bones can do with a rest now and then."

"I think these visits may be about as good for you as they are for me." Sarah remarked. "And I'm glad you enjoy the rest, Tabitha. I just wish we could stay for about a month. But even then I still wouldn't be ready to leave."

"And I don't wonder. If you could see the change a few days here makes in the way you look, and act. It's sure good for you. No doubt about that." Tabitha sat up, stretching her arms wide and yawning again. "I'd say it's just what the doctor ordered." She laughed.

"I wonder," Sarah mumbled, more to herself than to her companion.

Tabitha looked at her curiously. "Why do you say that? Lucian did send you here."

"Yes he did, but I can't help wondering what he would think if he knew that sometimes getting away from him..." Abruptly she rose and began straightening her bed covers. "Just forget I said that."

"Ah! Once you let words slip off your tongue, there's no use tellin' me to forget 'em." Tabitha stood with her hands on her hips. "Why, Sarah Amon! After all these years, you don't trust me enough to tell—"

"No, it's just that I shouldn't even think things like that about Lucian, let alone voice them."

"But that depends on who you're talkin' to. You can't help what you think. And maybe talkin' is better than keepin' it all bound up inside you."

"Maybe, but it's difficult to explain." Sarah took a deep breath. "When Lucian sends me down here to take the treatments, he thinks that the baths and the break from my work are what I need. And they are, of course. But to be perfectly honest with you, getting away from Lucian himself is probably good for me, too." Sarah dropped down on the bed again as a tear rolled slowly down her cheek. "Oh, Tabitha, if he knew that, it would really crush him."

"Child, I'm afraid I'm confused. The way you always ask him to eat supper with us... well, you act like you want him around all the time. I sure didn't know you felt that way about him."

"Oh, don't misunderstand me. The problem is that I do want him around. But he continually pressures me to marry him and—well, you know why I can't. What kind of a wife would I be, in my condition? I certainly couldn't be his—his mate!" Tears spilled freely.

"My lands, girl! If anybody in the world knows your condition, it's your doctor. And if he wants to marry you anyway, well he sure wouldn't be jumpin' into anything blind. Give him credit for knowin' his own mind, Sarah."

"But I'm not so sure he does know his own mind." Sarah sighed, spreading her hands in despair. "Oh, I know he could be happy and understanding for awhile. But sooner or later, Tabitha, he'd start feeling trapped, caught in a relationship which wouldn't satisfy his needs. And you know Lucian. He's far too kind to put me aside, once he had married me. I just don't think I could stand it, knowing he was miserable with me." Shaking her head, she wiped her eyes and blew her nose on the cloth Tabitha handed her. "I told him he should see other women, too. Maybe he'd find someone who could marry him and give him children and a home, like he needs—and deserves."

"Oh? And what did he say to that?"

"He was simply furious. He let me know in no uncertain terms that I wasn't ever to mention another word about other women!"

Tabitha opened her mouth to reply, but smiled, instead.

Sarah got up to finish making the bed. "I guess things will have to stay as they are now, unless by some miracle I get well. I tell you, Tabitha, if it weren't for these periodical trips down here, I couldn't take the pressure from him, and Deborah, too. She's just as bad. Says I'm crazy for not accepting his proposal." She turned to Tabitha. "Tell me, am I as unreasonable as those two think I am?"

"I don't think you're exactly unreasonable, dear, but in a way I can see what they're talkin' about. They both love you and they think the marriage is what's best for you. 'Course, they oughtn't keep at you about it. Maybe if they knew it bothers you so much, they'd let up." Tabitha hugged her affectionately. "You mustn't let 'em get you so upset. Just be thankful you've got people to love you so much, child."

"I am thankful, and that's why I feel so guilty. I'm just afraid that some of what Lucian feels is pity, more than love. I do love him, Tabitha, and I'd be so happy if I could have a normal life, as his wife." She sighed again. "But enough of this talk. I've got to get moving if I intend to spend time in that glorious bath today." She hugged Tabitha tightly. "Thanks for listening to me. You were right. It did help."

"I'm always here to listen." Tabitha patted Sarah's face lovingly.

"I'll bet Santimar's wearing a rut in those paving stones, pacing back and forth waiting for me." Sarah glanced toward the window as she finished washing her face.

"I wouldn't worry about that old man. He's got nothin' better to do. It won't hurt him to wait a few minutes." Tabitha laughed as she tied the sash on her drab, brown dress and started straightening her bed covers. "Sarah, I think you oughta' wear somethin' more cheerful today." She reached for the green tunic that Sarah was about to slip into and handed her the pink one.

"Tabitha, you're too much!" Sarah chuckled, knowing she might as well yield gracefully. "You never did like that dress, did you?" Tabitha's smug smile was her only answer.

As she put on the pink linen, Sarah was glad she had given in to the old woman's wishes, for this tunic really was her favorite. Remembering how Lucian had looked at her the first time she wore it, she smiled to herself. The pomegranate bark had produced exactly the shade of pink she wanted and she was secretly quite proud of the embroidery trim on the neckline and sash, done with a slightly darker tint. As she wrapped the girdle around her waist she smiled. "Tabitha, you were right. This dress does make me feel better. Whatever would I do without you?" She kissed Tabitha's cheek.

"You just keep thinkin' that way!" Tabitha beamed as she folded away the other tunic for Sarah and got out the white himation. The headpiece was loosely woven of the finest threads of linen, giving it the sheerness through which Sarah's dark hair showed.

* * *

"A vision of radiant beauty!" That's how John described her as the two walked into the dining room for breakfast.

"John, you sure know how to make a person feel good!" Sarah laughed. "No wonder you don't have any trouble keeping your rooms full. A little flattery here and there..." Sarah teased.

"But he's right," Anna chimed in. "You're especially lovely this morning."

"You're both very kind and I thank you." Sarah smiled as Tabitha gave her a smug I-told-you-so look.

Just as they had guessed, Santimar was waiting for her and after a hurried breakfast she was soon at the spa, chatting with Iona, and getting ready for the bath. Slipping into the warm water, she lay back and looked up at the white marble maiden. "You're good company, lovely lady. You continue to pour water for me from your pretty pitcher, but you never interfere with my thoughts," she said aloud.

"You like the goddess?" Iona smiled broadly.

"Yes, but she's not a goddess to me; she's more like an old friend, after all these years," Sarah replied. "And I've always loved the beautiful blues and greens of her pitcher."

As usual, Iona left her alone for awhile and Sarah settled back comfortably in the pool, determined to make the most of every delightful moment that was left of this visit.

These two hours now, a session in the afternoon, and another before she left in the morning would be all for awhile. She wondered just how many more trips she would be able to afford. When her savings were gone, that would be it. What she earned dressmaking certainly wouldn't cover expenses of this nature. It would barely take care of everyday living costs.

But maybe this would be her lucky trip. Perhaps this time the baths would make her well. She liked to dream about what it would be like, completely cured, married to Lucian. Maybe a couple of children. She wondered if Lucian ever dreamed of the same thing. She liked to think so.

When Iona came into the room just long enough to tell her she had a little over half an hour left, Sarah could hardly believe it. In such a slow-paced, lazy atmosphere it was incredible that time would dare go so fast.

Shifting to the other side of the pool, her back to the door, she started doing some of the water exercises Iona had taught her. Leaning back, her arms resting on the rim of the pool, she stretched her legs as far out as she could.

Suddenly the shrill, nasal voice gave Sarah such a start that she slammed the back of her head against the edge of the pool, trying to get turned around. Stars danced before her eyes for an instant before she was able to focus on the portly woman standing just inside the door, her bejeweled fists planted firmly on the two flabby bulges just below where her waist would have been, had there been a waist.

"The very idea!" the woman exclaimed in Greek. "Just what do you think you're doing in my bath?" she asked, glowering at Sarah, who had jumped up and grabbed her towel, wrapping it around herself.

A young attendant took the woman's arm. "Oh, Madam, I'm sorry! We've come to the wrong bath! Let's go back—I'll check the schedule again."

"Huh! She's the one in the wrong bath!" the woman screeched, jerking her arm away from the girl and pointing at Sarah. "I demand to know what this—this intruder is doing here!" She looked at Sarah contemptuously. "Aren't you a Jew?" Sarah's limited knowledge of Greek was being stretched to the limit. Hesitantly, not entirely sure she had understood the question, she nodded her head.

"I guess she's dumb, as well!" the woman snarled, staring stonily at Sarah. "But then, what could one expect of her kind?"

The attendant gently tugged on the woman's arm, turning her toward the door and saying things Sarah didn't understand.

Iona had entered in time to hear the girl trying to soothe the irate customer. She said something to the other attendant in Greek and laughed.

The matronly Greek glared at Iona. "I shall see that there is trouble here for this error! Someone will be punished! I shall not use the baths with filthy Jews!"

Iona shut the door behind the woman and began to laugh. "She is so funny!"

But Sarah could hardly see the humor. The old fears and shame of being an unclean woman engulfed her as she made her way hurriedly to the dressing room.

Iona pleaded with her to stay and finish the session.

"No! I'm leaving here as soon as I can get dressed. I didn't understand all she said, but enough to know that she was furious with me—and that she hates Jews." Sarah's hands trembled as she tried to dry herself. "Please, Iona, give me a hand with my clothes."

Helping her into the tunic, the therapist tried to comfort her. "You come back this afternoon. Things will be all right then."

"Iona, you've been so nice, as always, and you're a good friend. But I'm feeling better now, and I'm ready to go back to Capernaum. I just don't want any more trouble."

"But you already pay for all the baths—two more." She held up two fingers.

"That's all right. Don't worry about it." Sarah hugged her. "Goodbye, Iona, and thank you for everything." She left the room and hurried out through the atrium toward the front door.

Good old Santimar! He always came early, and she couldn't have been more relieved that this time was no exception. When she walked out the door and saw his carriage by the gate, she broke into a run. He smiled as he helped her into the coach. "You finished early today." Then he noticed the look on her face. "Wait a minute! What happened in there? You're shaking!"

"I'll be all right, Santimar." She shivered. "There was a Greek woman. She came storming in accusing me of using her bath. To tell the truth, I've never been quite so frightened. Please—I'd like to get back to the inn as quickly as possible."

Without further hesitation, Santimar complied. When he opened the door for her at the Seven Stones, Anna, John and Tabitha were in the dining area. "Better fix this lady something to calm her down. She's had a bad experience this morning." Santimar led her to a chair.

"Sarah! You're as pale as can be. What's the matter?" Tabitha jumped up and took her trembling hand. "Now tell us what happened, Sarah."

Sarah took a deep breath. "It's such a relief to get back here." She related the incident to them. "I'm all right now, but I think I'll stay away from that place."

CHAPTER 18

When Santimar walked into the doctor's office well before supper time, Lucian was more than a little surprised. "Are you back early, or have I lost a day this week?" he asked. "Or is something wrong?"

"Well, I guess you could say something was wrong. Sarah ran into a problem with a Greek woman at the bath house. I don't think it was anything serious, but she wouldn't go back, and wanted to come on home."

As soon as Lucian finished with the last patient, he left for Sarah's, arriving just as the two women were sitting down to eat. Well! Good timing once again!" He laughed, as Tabitha set a place for him at the table. "I see you're looking good, pretty lady." He leaned across the table and kissed Sarah on the cheek. "I was certainly not expecting to see Santimar drive in this afternoon. He told me you had a little trouble down there. I trust it wasn't too serious?"

"I suppose it wasn't," Sarah admitted, "but it seemed pretty terrible at the time." She filled him in on the details of her confrontation with the Greek woman. "Lucian, all of the old fears came back. Suddenly I was again an unclean woman, there in a public bath."

Lucian patted her hand. “If Apollonius had known about that, he’d have straightened her out. And, I assure you, he’ll be informed before you go again.”

“If you don’t mind, I’d rather not even think about going back. At least not yet.” Sarah shuddered. “At the moment, I’m just glad to be home, where I intend to stay.”

“Well, when you need the spa again, I’ll simply plan to go down with you,” he suggested. “But right now you look so healthy that there’s no need to worry about another trip for awhile. I must say, those visits really do you a tremendous amount of good.”

Sarah and Tabitha exchanged glances. “Yes they do, Lucian.” Sarah nodded, smiling.

* * *

When Sarah let Deborah talk her into walking with her to the marketplace to buy her week’s supply of oil, she had every intention of waiting on the steps of the oil shop until Deborah came out. She sat down in a shady spot on the top step. Her legs felt weak and perspiration popped out on her brow. She probably shouldn’t have tried to walk so far. *Deborah will have to wait for me to rest a bit before we walk back home.*

She noticed a crowd collecting in the square, around the village well. She wondered what the attraction was. Then she saw a man stand up on the low wall around the well. Sarah pulled herself up to see him better. She saw him holding out both arms, as if welcoming the people, but she couldn’t hear what he was saying.

Sarah left the steps and moved closer to the burgeoning crowd, which grew larger by the minute. Soon she could hear his voice. *It must be Jesus, the man Tabitha told us about! Maybe if I could hear what he says...* Sarah worked her way through the fringes of the mass. She saw the man reach down to someone near him. Then the words “you are healed” came to her ears. *Yes, it is Jesus! Tabitha said he healed people If only I can reach him, tell him I need to be healed.* But a dreadful fear flushed through her veins. She was unclean! She shouldn't be in this crowd! But she was here. She searched for a way out.

I've already come this far. If I can just get close enough to touch the bottom of his robe. Maybe I wouldn't have to call attention to myself! Her stomach clenched in a knot. She tried to steady her ragged breathing. Could she reach him? She had to! The heaving mass threatened to smother her. She'd surely be trampled, with no way out. Suddenly the mob shifted slightly, jostling Sarah closer to the rabbi.

He stood on the low stone wall surrounding the well. As she reached toward him, a large man stepped in front of her. Tears pricked the back of her eyes. She had been so close. Now she could see only the tassel on the corner of the rabbi's robe. Her gaze locked on the splash of blue.

If I can touch it—just the tip of his robe...Sarah squirmed forward, her arm reaching, stretching. *Only a finger's width*... Suddenly, a push from behind boosted her ahead and her fingertips tingled as they brushed against the coarse blue fringe. A surge of strength swept through her. Sarah knew she had touched absolute power.

A sweet sensation of euphoria enveloped her. The din of voices faded away. She touched her arm, her face. *Is it real?* She blinked. The crowd stood all around her, as before.

She heard his voice again. "Who touched me?" Though his question bore no hint of scolding, Sarah flinched.

One of the men with him laughed. "Master, with this crowd pressing around you, you ask who touched you?" Several others chuckled.

"I felt strength going to someone who touched my robe," Jesus insisted.

He turned toward Sarah, looking directly into her eyes. Her heart somersaulted and slammed against her chest. The crowd pushed back a little as she fell to her knees before him, barely breathing. Her pulse thundered in her ears in the dreadful penetrating silence. Slowly Sarah raised her face toward the rabbi.

She heard her own shaky whisper, "It—it was I, Rabbi." She bit her lips to keep them from quivering. "I have been ill for twelve years, and—and I thought—I hoped if I could only touch your robe, I could be healed. I—I'm so sorry." She hid her face in her trembling hands. *Is he angry? I didn't ask him first. Did I steal this healing?*

His hand felt warm, strong, gentle on her arm. Sarah lifted her eyes to his face and the kindness in those eyes drew her to her feet. "Daughter, your faith has made you well; go in peace, and be healed of your disease."

The tender pressure of his hand on her shoulder sent a wave of peace through her. She knew she was truly, completely well again.

"Thank you, Master," she whispered.

His warm smile, the slight nod of his head made her feel like a trusted friend, not a stranger.

She did not want to turn away from those clear, compassionate eyes. Her soul felt bare, clean—even beautiful. But when he moved to talk to another person, she let the crowd shove her back away from the master.

Deborah! She must tell Deborah!

Deborah waited at the edge of the throng. She grabbed Sarah's arm. "You could have been stoned, you know!" she muttered through clenched teeth, dragging Sarah past the gaping people on the fringe of the crowd. "You said you'd wait for me on the steps of the oil shop," she scolded.

Finally at a safe distance away, Deborah slowed her pace. Loosening her vise grip on Sarah's arm, she turned to face her friend. "Of all people, I should think you'd know how dangerous it is to go into that mob."

Deborah sighed, shaking her head. "I've known you since we were silly girls, but I've never before seen you do anything so stupid."

Sarah rubbed her upper arm and stopped, challenging Deborah. "And I've never seen you so angry."

"Well, why wouldn't I be angry? Sarah, I couldn't find you." Deborah's eyes filled. "I was so afraid you'd been dragged away and—and stoned." Tears spilled over.

"Oh, Deborah," Sarah wrapped her arms around her trembling friend. "I'm sorry. I didn't mean to worry you. I'm afraid I didn't stop to think. But I just had to go closer to hear what Jesus was saying. Tabitha had told me..."

Deborah stepped back, swiping at her wet cheeks. "Sarah, Tabitha is a superstitious old woman. You know she's been trying all sorts of ridiculous cures on you ever since she came to keep house for you and Nathan after you lost the baby." She laughed. "Remember how she bought an ostrich egg, burned it, and wrapped the ashes in a rag—"

"And insisted I carry them around for a month!" Sarah chuckled, recalling Tabitha's primitive attempts to make her well. She shook her head, smiling. "But I don't know what I'd have done without her these last ten years since Nathan died. She's like a mother to me."

"I know that, and I love her, too, but you must admit she's naive. I think any magician could sway her—"

"No, Deborah," Sarah shook her head. "that's where you're wrong. She tried all those so-called cures because that's what she grew up with, but Tabitha's pretty smart, and stubborn.

"And after she heard Jesus speak, Tabitha was different. She was sure the rabbi could make me well, especially when her cousin came to visit from Magdala, and said Jesus had healed her." Sarah sighed. "I wouldn't listen, of course, even after meeting Mary Hiram. I was as skeptical as you are."

Deborah stared at her for a long moment, then looked away, clenching her jaw.

"Anyway," Sarah continued, "I fully intended to wait there on the steps of the oil shop, just as we agreed. But when Jesus stepped up on the wall where I could see him, I really wanted to hear what he was saying. So without even thinking, I pushed through the crowd until I got close enough to hear him." Sarah took a deep breath, letting it our slowly. "And, Deborah, I don't know how anyone could criticize him. The things he said made perfect sense to me."

She laid her hand against Deborah's arm, slowing their pace. "Then he looked right into my eyes and—well, I've never seen eyes like his. At that very moment I was sure he could heal me."

Sarah stole a glance at Deborah, who looked straight ahead, her lips drawn firmly together.

"But when I started wondering how I'd tell him about my problem—that's when I almost panicked. There I was, people pressed against me on all sides—people who might know I was unclean. Believe me, Deborah, I was scared."

"You should have been!" Deborah snapped. "There must have been dozens who knew you—who could cause you serious trouble."

"Probably, but apparently everyone was too interested in Jesus to notice me. He was touching various ones on their heads and healing them."

"And just how do you know they were healed?" Deborah's voice held a sharp edge.

"Well, I—I guess I don't, but I assumed..."

"Oh, Sarah, I think you've been around Tabitha too long. You're as gullible as she is." She snickered.

"Yes, I suppose I am," Sarah responded, her words barely audible. She swallowed against the lump in her throat. Deborah tended to flare up instantly, saying things she didn't really mean. Just as quickly, she could overflow with genuine compassion. Over the years, Sarah had learned to be quiet and let her friend's emotions run their course.

After a few minutes of silence, Deborah turned to her. "Aren't you going to finish your story?"

Sarah shook her head, smiling. "I'll tell you about it another time. When you aren't mad at me. Or when you won't laugh at me."

"Oh, Sarah..." Deborah linked her free arm in Sarah's. "I'm not really mad. I was just so—so upset." She looked into Sarah's brimming eyes. "I'm sorry I laughed. I didn't mean to hurt you. But I really want to hear how you told the rabbi about your problem."

Captured by Deborah's pleading eyes, Sarah smiled. "Well, as I listened to him and watched his face, I had an idea." She hesitated. "Now you'll really think I'm crazy."

"No, I won't. What happened?"

"I decided his power could work just as well if I touched him—or rather, his clothes. And nobody would know."

"Oh!" Deborah's brows shot up. "So you just walked up and touched his robe?"

"No," Sarah laughed. "it wasn't that easy. Not with all those people in the way. Every time I got almost close enough, I'd get pushed back. I was about ready to give up, when a flash of blue caught my eye. It was the tassel on the corner of his robe moving back and forth as Jesus gestured." She made a swinging motion with her hand. "I waited until it was quite close, and then I stretched as far as I could, barely touching it."

She crossed her hands against her throat. "Deborah, I can't describe what I felt when I put my hand on the tassel. It was like I was in another world. And, believe it or not, the bleeding stopped immediately. I could feel it."

Deborah swung full around to confront her, looking directly into her eyes. "You mean—you're actually..."

"Yes, I'm well again, Deborah. I really am!"

Deborah looked away, biting her lower lip. "What happened next?"

"Then I heard him ask who had touched him and he turned and looked right at me. He might as well have pointed his finger."

"Oh, my goodness! I'll bet you were scared speechless."

"Yes, but then I had no choice but to confess. I thought I'd really be condemned for being there in that crowd. An unclean woman. But, Deborah, he reached down, took my hand and called me *daughter.* He told me to go in peace and be healed. Those eyes! I'll never forget them. So piercing, I was sure he could see into my soul. Yet they were so kind. And he didn't seem angry at all."

Dropping her head, she half-whispered, "I can't expect you or anyone else to believe something as far-fetched as this." They walked on in silence for a few moments.

Then Deborah gently slipped her arm around Sarah's shoulders. "I wish I could believe you're completely well. Permanently, I mean. I just don't understand how that could be. But I know something's different about you." She turned to look at Sarah. "You—you're absolutely radiant. And—well, I guess I'd like to know more about a man who could do that for you, even if it's only temporary."

"I'd like to know more about him too, and I intend to." Sarah clasped her hands together. "Now I can go for purification. And attend synagogue again!"

Deborah linked her free arm in Sarah's. "I hope you're right about all of this. I'd give anything to have things back to normal." Suddenly she stopped in mid-stride, turning Sarah to face her. "If you're really well, it means you and the doctor..."

Sarah's eyes shone with joy. "Yes, now I can accept Lucian's proposal. At last."

CHAPTER 19

"Do you think Lucian will believe you're healed?" Deborah looked doubtful after Sarah had exited the crowd in the marketplace and told her how Jesus had healed her..

"Why wouldn't he?" Sarah countered. "Oh, I know he didn't believe the story Tabitha told about Jesus healing the man's hand that had been withered since birth. As a doctor, he didn't think it possible." She laughed. "I didn't believe it either. But now I know better, and Lucian surely knows I wouldn't claim something untrue."

"Well, for years he's wanted you to be able to marry him. And has never treated you as if you were unclean, in spite of the law."

"Yes, I guess his being my doctor, he could visit me without getting us both into trouble." Sarah wrapped her arms around herself. "But, Deborah, if he still wants to marry me, I can say yes!" They both giggled, hugging.

A puzzling light flashed in Sarah's mind, like a candle brought into a dark room. She stopped walking. "Deborah, I remember Tabitha saying that Jesus had changed her 'inside'. I was confused by it then, but—but now I understand." She nodded with a satisfied smile. "I don't think my physical healing was the most important thing that happened to me today."

"How could you say that?" Deborah frowned.

"I can't explain it, but the rabbi made me a different person. I feel clean—in more ways than one." As comprehension charged her mind, an inexpressible peace swept through her.

They walked the sandy path to the edge of the city in silence. Then turning onto Tamarisk Way, with both their houses in view, Deborah eased her arm around Sarah's shoulders again.

"I can hardly wait to see Tabitha's face when you tell her." Her eyes sparkled, and Sarah knew then that her friend was on the verge of believing.

"I know Tabitha will be happy, but I'm afraid I can't expect the same from my brother-in-law or his wife." Sarah sighed.

"Oh? Why would Elon object? I know Tamar doesn't like you, but surely she wouldn't resent your health," Deborah reasoned.

"But Tamar's trying so hard to get herself established socially with the tetrarch's crowd. She's finally managed to get herself on Herodias' guest list, and if I did anything to embarrass her..."

"Oh, Sarah, don't worry about them. You haven't done anything wrong." Deborah took Sarah's hand and picked up speed. "Come on! Let's go give Tabitha the good news!"

* * *

"Tabitha!" Sarah's call brought the old woman from the kitchen, wiping her hands on a towel. Sarah and Deborah stood just inside the front door, grinning impishly at the obviously puzzled woman.

"Grown women, actin' like children," Tabitha muttered, turning away.

"Wait, Tabitha." Sarah reached out to her. "You've got to hear what happened! I..."

"You can tell me after supper." Tabitha shook her finger at Sarah. "Right now, I want you off your feet." Shuffling toward the kitchen, she grumbled to herself, "I try my best to take care of her, but what can I do, when she walks all the way to the market?"

Sarah and Deborah looked at each other and shrugged, following her.

"There's plenty of time for you to rest," Tabitha said, wiping the table needlessly. "We can't eat yet, anyway, 'til Santimar gets through fixin' that jasmine trellis in the courtyard. I don't know why Lucian sent the old man over so late in the day," she complained.

"But I don't need rest. I..." Sarah gently took Tabitha's wrinkled face between her hands. "Look at me. I feel better than I have for—for twelve years. Don't you understand, Tabitha? I'm well!"

The woman leveled her tired eyes at Sarah's. "Don't be talkin' foolish, child."

Sarah kissed her forehead. "You know I wouldn't joke about something so important."

Taking Tabitha's arm, she led her to the sitting room, Deborah following. "I know you've wanted me to hear Jesus speak," Sarah began, gesturing the old woman toward a chair. Sarah sat down nearby. "Well, he was in the marketplace today. And I managed to get close enough to hear him."

"Oh!" Tabitha's face brightened. "Well, you liked him, didn't you?"

Sarah laughed. "Yes, I did." She told how Jesus had looked into her eyes, giving her confidence that he really could heal her. "But I knew I couldn't tell him about my problem. Not in that crowd. I was really afraid."

"Oh, my poor little Sarah." Tears sprang to Tabitha's eyes.

Sarah reached to take Tabitha's hand. "I was about to give up, but then I noticed the tassel on the corner of his robe. It was the most beautiful hyacinth blue." Sarah clasped her hands against her chest. "So I stretched my arm farther than I ever dreamed possible, until I could barely brush my fingertips against it."

"Oh..." Tabitha's whispered as if she were holding her breath.

"And at that moment I knew I was well."

Tabitha gasped and jumped to her feet. "Oh, Sarah, you did it! You did it! I knew..."

"But wait! That's not all," Sarah broke in, lifting a restraining palm.

Dropping to the edge of her chair, hands clenched tightly in her lap, Tabitha waited.

Sarah described how Jesus knew she had touched him, and how she then had to confess. A worried frown crossed Tabitha's face.

"I guess you didn't know what he was gonna' do."

"No, but he pulled me to my feet, calling me 'daughter', and said I was healed."

A confirming nod from Deborah was all Tabitha needed to bring her out of her chair.

"You're—you're really... My little Sarah's well!" Tears wet her weathered face as she opened her arms to Sarah and Deborah. Locked together, the three women whirled about, laughing and crying at the same time.

Santimar bolted into the room, staring helplessly. "What's wrong?"

Wiping tears with the towel she had tucked in her sash, Tabitha answered, "Nothing in the whole world is wrong now. Our Sarah's been touched by Jesus and she's well again! Go tell the doctor to come and celebrate with us." She threw back her head and laughed. "I'm just so happy I might even hug you next, old man!"

Santimar backed out of the room in silence.

* * *

Sarah's miraculous encounter in the middle of Capernaum was hardly a secret, any more than were the other miracles performed by the rabbi. In the time it took a servant girl to walk home from the market, the story reached Elon's household.

When Tamar overheard Luci telling Hannah, the cook, what she had seen and heard, she grilled Luci and the other servants unmercifully, until she was satisfied they had told her everything about her sister-in-law's healing.

Delighted with the spicy bit of gossip about Sarah, Tamar eagerly repeated to her husband all she had heard and more, as soon as they sat down to supper.

"Why, I hear she even intends to follow the man around, witnessing to the healing." she told him, embellishing the story to her own liking.

"Sarah wouldn't do that," Elon protested. "Maybe the man did work some kind of magic on her, and she might even be taken in at first, as desperate as she is to get well. But I'm sure after she's had time to think, she'll pass it off for what it is." He shrugged. "I certainly hope so, anyway."

Tamar bristled. "Sweet little Sarah can do no wrong in your eyes, can she?" She scoffed. "Have you forgotten that your brother was barely in the grave when she got involved with her doctor? I wouldn't be surprised if they weren't carrying on before poor Nathan died."

"Now don't start that again," Elon scolded. "Nobody said Sarah was perfect, but she did love my brother. And Nathan liked Lucian as much as Sarah did. I'm sure there was no *carrying on*, as you call it. Lucian's merely a good friend." He sighed. "I don't know why you hate Sarah so much."

"Oh, you don't?" Tamar jerked her head up, glaring at him. "How would you like to be accused of causing her to lose that baby? I wasn't even near her when she caught her foot getting off the weaving stool! She shouldn't have left the yarn hanging loose, in the first place."

"Well, if I know you, I'm sure you said something to upset her..."

"I did not!" Tamar snapped. "Why do you always assume the worst about me? I was only trying to be friendly, and helpful. I certainly didn't intend—"

"All right! No use going over it again," Elon interrupted, dismissing the matter with a wave. "That's all in the past."

"No, it's not in the past. Not when you keep defending Sarah. After Nathan died, you even admitted you'd divorce me and marry her if she'd agree."

Elon flinched visibly. "I was simply angry with you when I said that, and you know it. You threw such a fit over my plans to give Sarah all of Nathan's money, as he asked me to..." Wrapping both hands around his cup, he exhaled wearily. His mouth tightened at the corners. "Regretfully, I let you talk me into cheating her out of a great deal of it."

Tamar sat quietly for a moment. She wanted to tell him what a fool he had been for giving that little twit anything at all. "Well, you did let Sarah keep the house, and most of the money."

"Hah!" he jeered. "For all that was worth. That pottery shop would still be earning money, if someone hadn't..." Elon set his mug down so hard the tea splashed on the table. "Hiring Esli was the smartest thing my brother ever did. The man certainly proved that Nabataeans are expert potters, and he was a good manager, as well. He made a great deal of money for us." He shook his head. "It makes me sick to think of Nathan, Esli and the whole crew murdered."

"But it wasn't your fault, Elon. You had no way of knowing their drinking water would be—poisoned."

"No, but I've never been able to figure out who could have committed the heinous crime. I didn't know our family had an enemy that vicious."

Tamar's heart beat quickened. A warning bell sounded in her head. "Elon, the murder probably didn't have anything to do with our family. Esli was a stranger here, and nobody knew anything about his past," Tamar offered. "He may have been the target instead of Nathan. Who knows how many enemies he might have had? The other men, of course, happened to take a break at the same time and—"

"Well, I'd like to get my hands on the culprit, whoever he is." Elon declared. "Surely none of them deserved that."

Tamar rubbed her damp palms together. How did Elon know what Esli deserved? Her heart pounded in her chest. Why, after all this time, did she still react like this? And why was Elon staring at her?

"Tamar, what's the matter? You look terrible." He reached to take her trembling hand.

She jerked away. "I—I just don't like to think of that dreadful day."

"Well, I'm sorry I brought it up. It was a horrible tragedy. And now that Sarah is out of money, I'll have to support her."

Tamar released a ragged breath. "It seems to me that if Sarah hadn't spent everything going to Tiberias to the baths, she wouldn't be broke. All that money for nothing!"

"Which makes it understandable that she'd be so willing to believe that charlatan made her well." He shook his head. "But when she comes down off her cloud, and sees—"

"Elon, I don't think you realize how much Sarah has changed since Nathan died. She doesn't like either one of us, and I know she talks about us to her unsavory friends. I wouldn't be surprised if she decides to take up with that—that radical, just to embarrass us. She'd find it amusing."

"Well, she'd better think twice about it. It certainly wouldn't be amusing to me. Not in the least."

Tamar smiled to herself, her hopes soaring. Was Elon actually beginning to think her way? She didn't honestly know why she hated her sister-in-law so much. Maybe because Elon was such a nitwit, when it came to Sarah. What a shame the woman hadn't been at the pottery plant when...

* * *

His curiosity sufficiently aroused, Elon knew he'd never sleep until he talked with Sarah. Why did she have to get involved with that bunch of rabble-rousers? Maybe he should just let her be. But if she started calling attention to herself by following that rabbi around... He couldn't afford that. As his brother's widow, she was somewhat his responsibility. If Nathan had lived, none of this would be happening.

Elon was tired. Tired of dealing with Sarah's problems. And tired, especially, of trying to appease Tamar.

He didn't expect a welcome at Sarah's, but all that mattered to him now was stopping her from doing anything foolish. She must be clearly reminded of her accountability as a member of his family. If it wasn't already too late.

CHAPTER 20

"Well, my friend, I trust you've put Sarah's trellis in good repair. Or were you too busy consuming Tabitha's famous cakes?" Lucian joked when Santimar walked into the empty room which earlier had overflowed with sick people. He noticed the puzzled look on the old Arab's face and sobered. "Is something wrong?"

"I wish I knew." Santimar scratched his head, his dark eyes troubled. "Strange things are going on over there. Sarah and Tabitha and the neighbor woman are all dancing around crying and hugging each other—and laughing, too." He frowned. "I think they've all taken leave of their senses!"

"Hysterical? Hm." Lucian lifted his brows. "Sounds strange. Did anyone come to the house while you were there?"

"Didn't see anybody. When I got there Sarah was gone and the old woman was busy in the kitchen. I went to work in the courtyard replacing the broken slats. After a while I heard a commotion and ran to see what was happening." He shook his head, heaving a sigh. "What Tabitha said to me is a little hard to believe."

"Why? What did she say?"

"I asked if something was wrong and she—well, she said something about everything in the world being *right*, and that Sarah had been touched by—somebody—and was well again."

Lucian stood silently for a moment, unconsciously stroking his short beard. "Jesus?"

"Yes! That was the name Tabitha called."

"Hm. The famous rabbi. I think I'll go see..." Lucian stepped uncertainly toward the door.

Santimar raised a hand. "Oh, yes! Tabitha said to tell you to come on over and help celebrate."

Lucian stopped long enough to glance at him curiously before lifting the latch. Santimar wasn't given to stretching the truth. The tough old former slave had come with him to Capernaum, as driver and handyman, over twelve years ago. He was the most level-headed man he knew. Lucian would trust his life to him. But whatever Santimar saw at Sarah's had shattered his usual composure. A sudden uneasiness drove the doctor more rapidly over the cobblestones.

In his single-minded haste, he opened the door without knocking. Sarah sat in the front room talking with Deborah and Tabitha. Halting just inside the door, Lucian stood staring at Sarah as if he expected something dreadful to have happened to her.

"Lucian!" Sarah jumped up, clasping her hands together. "I'm so glad you're here. I—" The strange look on his face interrupted her joy. "What's wrong? You look upset—and just when I have the most wonderful news."

"Santimar told me," he answered numbly, still unsmiling, "but I want to hear it all from you."

Deborah and Tabitha discreetly disappeared into the kitchen as Sarah sat down. Lucian took a chair near her.

Sarah eagerly related her experience at the square. "And, Lucian, I didn't even know Jesus was in the marketplace when Deborah and I went down there. I just seemed to be drawn that way, like I *had* to hear what he was saying. And I'm so glad I did force my way through the crowd, Lucian."

She clasped her hands together under her chin, a warm smile lighting her face. "It's so wonderful to be well again."

Fully expecting him to share her joy, Sarah beamed, certain that now he would feel free to ask her to marry him. And now she could say yes!

Her chest constricted as Lucian looked away, his eyes troubled, a peculiar tightness around his mouth. "Lucian..." She fought to keep her voice steady. "Aren't you happy?" Sarah exhaled a ragged breath. "You seem—angry, or maybe you just don't believe it."

"No, I'm not angry, Sarah. I *am* happy for you." He flashed a strained smile. "I guess—well, I don't really know what to say. It's just that I'm having trouble understanding it, of course, and..."

"I know. It's not easy for me, either, but I do have the advantage. I know how well I feel." She laughed.

"I'm glad you found someone who could help you, Sarah," he said quietly, looking down. Then he gave a pained sigh. "I tried everything I knew over the years, and then—then this man comes along and in a flash..." He snapped his fingers, frowning. "Instant healing." He shrugged. "It doesn't make sense to me."

"Lucian, I wish I could explain it to you, but I simply don't know how." Her eyes bright with tears, she reached to lay her hand on his. "But it's wonderful." With no response to her touch, she slowly withdrew her hand.

"I just hope you continue to feel well, Sarah." He stood. "And if you should ever need me again, I'll be around. I can cure a great many things, believe it or not." He forced another weak smile, but his eyes remained cold.

"I can't believe what I'm hearing." She rose uneasily. "It's as if you actually resent my being healed by someone else, though I can't imagine why, if you care for me."

"It isn't that, Sarah. I sent you to other doctors, didn't I?" He gave a barely audible groan. "To be truthful, I don't really know how I feel. But yes," he said, jabbing his fist into his other palm, "maybe I do resent that man, because I don't trust him. I'm afraid it won't last, and I don't want to see you disappointed and hurt." He turned toward the window. "And look at me—I'm the one hurting you most, by throwing cold water on your beautiful dream."

"Dream? Is that what you think it is? Lucian, I've depended on you for a lot of things, but even *you* can't tell me how I feel. And I know that I'm completely well right now." She twined her fingers to control their trembling. "But even if it's temporary, as you think, it's still better than nothing. I thought you'd be happy for me to feel well, even for a little while." The tears spilled over as she turned to leave the room.

She hesitated in the doorway. "If Nathan were alive he'd be the happiest man in the world today." She fled to her bedroom, sobbing.

Lucian stood for a moment, reaching lamely toward her retreating back.

"Lucian?" Deborah bolted from the kitchen, hands on her hips, as Tabitha went to Sarah. "What in the world did you say to Sarah to upset her so?"

"I didn't mean to! I—"

"Well, you *did*, anyway!"

"Deborah, you know a person can't be healed of her ailment so suddenly." He shook his head in exasperation. "I just don't want to see her hurt. When the spell wears off—whatever the man did—"

"If and when that happens, I'd think you'd want to be the one offering her the most support." Deborah's eyes shot daggers at him. "All that insistence that you wanted to marry her—it was all a lie, wasn't it?" Deborah spread her hands in frustration. "You knew she couldn't, in her condition, so you were safe, weren't you? But now that she would certainly agree to marry you, you have to find another excuse!"

"Deborah, that's not true! I wouldn't..."

Deborah leaned toward him. "Lucian, you said I know her ailment couldn't be suddenly cured. Well, I don't know any such thing, nor do you. You see, I was with Sarah at the marketplace. I don't understand it either, but I believe her—every word she says." She shook her finger in his face. "Face it, doctor, you may very well be wrong!"

"I hope so, Deborah—I really do. I'd give anything to see her well again. But—"

"But not if it comes from somebody else." Deborah whirled around and stamped toward the kitchen, hurling over her shoulder, "You're a selfish hypocrite, Doctor! And you don't know what love is!"

* * *

Lucian dragged himself home, wondering if Deborah was right. Had he actually wanted Sarah to be ill so she would have to depend on him? Did he have so little confidence in his own ability to make her love him? Surely he wasn't that cruel. He had worried about her and tried everything he knew to help her. So why, then, did he feel so much resentment for someone else who may really have helped her? Maybe he didn't love her as much as he thought he did. Otherwise, wouldn't he be celebrating with her right now?

Sarah was right about Nathan. Yes, her husband loved her so much he would welcome even a temporary cure—by anyone. He stopped, toying with the idea of going back, begging forgiveness and...

But, no, he couldn't pretend to feel something that he really wasn't sure about any more. Plodding slowly home, a miserable ache filling his chest, he failed to notice the man headed toward Sarah's house.

* * *

Elon squinted at the man hurrying in his direction, his head down, shoulders drooping. Elon stopped. "Good evening!" he said politely, offering his hand. But the doctor brushed by, apparently oblivious to his presence.

"Hm. Strange. Very strange, indeed!" He stood looking toward Lucian, who rapidly disappeared from his sight. "I wonder what happened at Sarah's to put Lucian in such a state."

* * *

"Come in, sir." Tabitha ushered Elon into the sitting room. "Sarah's resting now. I'll go tell her you're here."

"I'm sorry if it's a bad time, but I need to talk with her. Now." He paced around a bit before perching stiffly on the nearest chair, clenching and unclenching his hands in his lap.

Tabitha knocked gently on Sarah's door before opening it. "Child, I hate to bother you, but Elon's here. Says he wants to talk with you," she whispered. "Want me to tell him you don't feel like it now? Goodness knows you don't need any more upsettin' talk for tonight..."

"No, Tabitha. There's no use postponing the inevitable. I'm sure some of his friends saw me at the square." She got up, smoothed her hair and wiped at her red puffy eyes. "I must look a fright," she said lamely.

Her brother-in-law stood and stared at her face as she entered the room.

"Good evening, Elon," Sarah greeted him with reserve, expecting the worst. "What brings you here this time of day?" She motioned to his chair and sat down across the room.

Hesitating, Elon continued to gaze at her intently. "Sarah, is something wrong? You've—been crying."

"It's all right, Elon. Please tell me why you're here. I'm sure this isn't purely a social visit."

He winced. "I guess I deserve that, after what happened last time I saw you. You thought I had cheated you, but, as Nathan's older brother, I was not required to turn any of his money over to you."

"Not by law, of course." Sarah leveled her eyes at him, unsmiling.

He averted his gaze, grimacing. "I ran into Lucian on the way here." He cocked his head, as if expecting an explanation.

Sarah looked away. "So?"

"The doctor seemed very distraught—didn't even appear to see me at all, though I spoke to him. I assumed he had been here." Elon lifted one eyebrow, then the other. "I suppose he had something to do with why you're crying."

When Sarah refused to look at him or respond to his probing, he cleared his throat. "Anyway, I've received a bit of unsettling news about you, and I thought it best to speak to you face to face." His arrogant tone made her cringe inside.

"I can't think of anything you might have heard about me, unless it's about my healing. But why should that upset you? I should think that no matter how you feel about me, you'd be happy that I'm well again. Surely you wouldn't begrudge even an enemy his health."

"Now, Sarah, you know I don't consider you my enemy. And I would be glad if you were well again, of course. But I've heard that you've involved yourself with a radical rabbi who is going around saying things that could get him and all of his followers in trouble with Herod. I hope you remember what happened to that other preacher who condemned Herod's private life."

"How could you possibly have heard I'm involved with the man, when I met him for the very first time this afternoon, and only for a few minutes?" She shrugged. "All I know is that I was ill—have been, as you know, for twelve long years—and now I'm completely well."

She folded her arms. "Surely someone who would do that for me must be good. And, yes, I <u>do</u> believe in him. But I'd hardly call that being involved—"

"Well, from what I heard, you were right there in front of him—even *kneeling* to him!" Elon's face reddened all the way to his receded hairline. "Sarah, the man blasphemes, and breaks the law of the Sabbath—and talks against Herod." He clenched his jaw.

"Have you heard him do those things?"

"Of course not! But I know people who have!"

"Well, I don't know anything about that. I've heard him speak very few words, so far. And he said nothing that would be displeasing to Herod or anybody else. The man told me not to be afraid, and that I was well."

She unfolded her arms and fingered the end of her sash lying in her lap. "Elon, can you even imagine what that meant to me? I don't see how anyone could fault him for doing good. Before you accuse him of being so bad, you should at least hear him."

"Forget it!" He raised a cautioning hand. "I want no part of his kind. All I need is for someone in Herod's court to connect me or someone in my family with that bunch of rabble-rousers." He shook his finger at her, narrowing his eyes. "So you, Sarah Amon, are *not* to get involved!"

"I don't even know any of the people you call 'rabble-rousers'."

"You'd do well to keep it that way." He got up to leave. "Just remember that whatever you do reflects on my family, and affects my reputation," he admonished, walking out.

* * *

More than a little upset, Elon walked fast, nervously twisting the heavy ring on his finger. He wished he could believe that Sarah would stay away from those people, but she was obviously convinced the man had healed her. Maybe Tamar was right. Sarah might start going around with that crowd, doing whatever the radical rabbi asked her to do. And if she were seen in that group by the wrong people... Elon shuddered. "She could ruin me in the community. I can't afford that," he whispered, clenching his fists. "I can see right now that I've a major problem on my hands."

* * *

"What did I do wrong?" Sarah asked Tabitha after Elon left. "Elon's accusing me of associating with 'rabble-rousers', as he puts it, and Lucian..." She buried her face in her hands.

"You poor child." Tabitha sat down next to her. "You didn't do anything wrong, Sarah."

"I would have expected Elon to take that attitude, of course. But Lucian?" She wiped her eyes with the clean handkerchief Tabitha handed her. "I could hardly wait to tell him I was well. I just knew he'd be so thrilled, and say we'd get married right away! I—I really thought he loved me, Tabitha."

"Oh, Sarah, I think he just needs some time. You know he tried to make you well, and it's hard for him to think somebody else could help you..."

"Tabitha, you didn't see his eyes. He looked at me as if I'd betrayed him. He was a stranger to me." She twisted the cloth in her hand. "I guess I'd be better off ill, than for everybody to turn against me."

"Now you just stop that kind of talk!" Tabitha shook her finger at Sarah. "I haven't turned against you, and neither has Deborah. You probably didn't hear Deborah fussin' at the doctor. She told him she believed every word you said!"

"She did?" Sarah's face brightened.

"Yes, she did!" Tabitha nodded triumphantly. "And I'll tell you another thing, Sarah. You'll have new friends now."

"But that's what Elon warned me against." She spread her hands. "If I have anything to do with any of Jesus' followers, Elon will be furious."

"I know, dear," Tabitha said quietly. "But I do want you to get better acquainted with my cousin Mary. Elon won't have to know. He can't keep you from going to the synagogue."

CHAPTER 21

Sarah tingled with anticipation. Her feet barely touched the ground on the way to the synagogue. She had complied with the instructions to obtain purification. On the eighth day after her healing, she had taken two doves to the synagogue door. The priest had interceded for her and pronounced her clean. Oh the joy of those words! After twelve years of existing as an unclean woman, she was now free—clean! She wanted to run, and skip, and dance, and sing!

"Sarah, I think you might take off flyin' like a bird, any minute!" Tabitha teased.

"I just might, at that!" Sarah's bubbly laugh caught the attention of a group of her friends waiting for her at the women's door of the synagogue.

They took turns hugging her, and were still whispering about how wonderful she looked as they all entered the women's balcony. Sarah saw Lucian scanning the women's area more than once. But when his eyes found hers, he blushed and turned away. Surely he could see the difference in her. She searched his face for some sign of the old Lucian, the one who wanted her well so he could marry her. The one who told her over and over how much he loved her. Instead, she saw a clenched jaw. A coldness in his eyes. Her heart ached.

Was her health was worth the price? Would she be required to deny what Jesus did for her? But how could she do that?

* * *

Sarah gawked at the imposing stone structure. Her knees shook so hard they threatened to buckle. She wanted to turn and run, but it was too late. Mary had already pulled the bell rope.

Why had she let Mary and Tabitha talk her into visiting the steward's wife, anyway? She had no business in Herod's palace. The fact that the tetrarch had never lived at the Capernaum fort was little comfort to her. His business manager did, and for all she knew, Chuza could be as formidable as Herod.

Mary Hiram had insisted Chuza's wife would love meeting someone who had been healed by Jesus, as she had.

"Joanna had a problem similar to yours," Mary had told her, "and she was touched by Jesus, too." Mary had gone on to suggest, "Talking with Joanna might help you with the difficult choices you're facing."

Sarah couldn't imagine the steward's wife caring about her problems. Tamar often spoke of Joanna, claiming to be her friend, which hardly made Sarah eager to meet the woman. She couldn't imagine having anything in common with one of her sister-in-law's cronies.

Sarah jumped when the heavy door swung open. The uniformed servant ushered them up white marble stairs through a colonnade entrance into the main hallway. The elegant room looked like a banquet hall, with its smooth cedar floors, intricately carved wooden chairs and tables, and ornate hanging lamps.

When Sarah stepped into the courtyard, she inhaled deeply of the fragrant air, relieved to be out of the dark, cavernous building. Colorful flower beds and hanging plants with trailing vines decorated the terraced yard, creating a homelike ambience.

The place reminded her of the bath house grounds in Tiberias.

Joanna walked near the oblong pool with her little son, who squealed with delight over the fountain's cool spray. She smiled and headed toward the women, as a maid took charge of the child.

Mary and Joanna embraced. "Joanna, I'd like you to meet Sarah, the woman I told you about," Mary said, taking Sarah's arm.

"Oh, yes, the one who suffered for twelve years!" Joanna exclaimed, clasping Sarah's hand in both of hers. "My dear, I found only a few months of it quite debilitating." She led the way to a couple of white marble benches near the pool.

"I spent a great deal of time in Tiberias taking the baths," Sarah replied. "Of course, they helped only temporarily and were needed more and more often."

"It was the same with me. But isn't it marvelous that we don't have to rely on those things any more?" Joanna folded her hands against her chest. "We're so blessed to know Jesus."

"I'm afraid I can't say that I really know him. I met him for a very few minutes," Sarah responded.

"Oh! Then you haven't heard him speak?" Joanna asked.

"No, he left the city before my purification. Naturally, I'll be glad when he returns to Capernaum so that I can learn more from him."

"I'm sure he'll be back soon," Mary assured her. "He went to Nazareth for a few days to see his family. I don't think he'll be gone long. I hear his brothers are quite upset with him at the moment."

"I'm afraid they're not alone in that." Joanna shook her head. Her face took on a somber expression.

Mary raised her brows. "Sounds like you've run into some trouble," she remarked. "Has the tetrarch heard about your connection with the rabbi?"

"I don't think so, but it's only a matter of time. Chuza says Herod will probably insist that he force me to deny all interest in Jesus. It really puts me in a hard place." She sighed audibly.

"Chuza is so good to me and fully supports my desire to follow the man who gave me back my health. I love my husband dearly, and can't bear the thought of his suffering on my account. On the other hand, how can I denounce the Master?" She shrugged. "But Chuza insists that he can handle Herod, so I guess we'll just have to wait and see. Meanwhile, I'm trying to stay quiet."

Sarah shook her head. "And I thought I had problems. My friend's rejection, and my brother-in-law's threats seem insignificant compared to the consequences you're facing." Sarah clasped her hands in her lap. "When Tamar spoke of you, I never thought..." Sarah dropping her head and felt the heat rising to her face.

"Oh, my dear," Joanna laid her hand on Sarah's arm. "I can imagine the picture you must have had of me." She smiled. "How well do you know Tamar?"

"My late husband was Elon's brother."

"Oh! I had no idea you were related." Joanna sobered. "Sarah, I really feel sorry for poor Tamar. She loves being part of Herodias' elite group. And I'm afraid she doesn't understand what that means. Herodias can be...." She frowned as if searching for the right word. "Well, I'll just say Tamar could find herself in a web from which there's no escape."

Joanna took a deep breath. "But enough depressing talk! I see Delmia bringing a tray of refreshments. She must have read my mind." She laughed.

* * *

Sarah's opportunity to hear Jesus speak came only three days later, when he returned to Peter's house. She and Tabitha went with Mary to an evening meeting. Rebecca had saved space for them at the edge of the crowded atrium.

When Jesus spoke about the kingdom of heaven, someone asked him which of his disciples would be greatest there. The question clearly disturbed him. He called one of the small boys to him and placed the child at his feet.

Then he said, "Unless you turn to God from your sins and become as little children, you will never get into the kingdom of heaven. Therefore, anyone who humbles himself as this little child, is the greatest in the kingdom of heaven. And any of you who welcomes a little child like this because you are mine, is welcoming me and caring for me. But if any of you causes one of these little ones who trusts in me to lose his faith, it would be better for you to have a rock tied to your neck and be thrown into the sea."

He went on to talk about other ways of living right, and about how important each person is to God.

Sarah was so interested in everything he had to say that she could hardly take her eyes off him. But in this roomful of people, several men obviously had a different kind of interest in the rabbi.

Three men dressed in rich-looking robes, their tassels hanging much longer than those of the average Jew, made no attempt to hide their displeasure. Sarah recognized them as friends of Elon.

At one point, after seeing his critics whispering among themselves, Jesus said directly to them, "A divided kingdom ends in ruin. A city or home divided against itself cannot stand. And if Satan is casting out Satan, he is fighting himself, and destroying his own kingdom. And if, as you claim, I am casting out demons by invoking the powers of Satan, then what power do your own people use when they cast them out? Let them answer your accusation!" He apparently knew that they were talking about his healing, earlier that same day, the blind and dumb man who was said to be demon-possessed.

Jesus continued. "But if I am casting out demons by the spirit of God, then the Kingdom of God has arrived among you. One cannot rob Satan's kingdom without first binding Satan. Only then can his demons be cast out! Anyone who isn't helping me is harming me."

Sarah thought he handled himself admirably with his self-righteous adversaries. But it bothered her when they stomped out, pulling their robes close, as if they would be contaminated if they touched anyone. She wondered how much their influence could jeopardize Jesus' work.

She would have liked to thank Jesus for healing her, but wouldn't dare interrupt him as he spoke with his friends. She and Tabitha expressed their appreciation to Rebecca and slipped out.

On the way home they talked about the good people they were getting to know.

"You know, Sarah, we're mighty blessed to be invited there tonight," Tabitha marveled.

"Yes, and everything Jesus said made so much sense to me." Sarah sighed. "But, Tabitha, I'll admit that I'm more than a little nervous. I'm sure those three men who obviously came to criticize, are friends of Elon. And one of them looked right at me. I'm sure he knew me." Shivering, she wrapped her arms around herself. She had really sealed her doom tonight. Elon would be furious. And Tamar...

CHAPTER 22

"I thought, Sarah, that I made my position clear about your involvement with that radical group." Elon scowled, ignoring Sarah's feeble attempt at hospitality. "But you've shown total disregard for your family. You were seen right in the middle of one of that—that—blasphemer's little meetings. Now, Sarah, I simply cannot allow this to continue."

Tamar stood in the middle of the room with her hands on her hips, glaring at Sarah. "You're bringing disgrace to our family! I should think you would be more grateful for all we've done for you!"

Wondering what great favors she was supposed to be grateful for, Sarah met her sister-in-law's stare, unblinkingly. "Tamar, I've done absolutely nothing to disgrace you. I'm sorry you think I have. But it isn't your place to select my friends."

"Well, it seems *somebody* needs to, after you showed such poor taste in friends just last evening!" Elon bellowed. "I've been warned that if a member of my family continues to associate with those rabble-rousers, I shall be put on Herod's list!" He wagged his finger at her. "Now if you think I'm going to stand by and let that happen, you're mistaken! I'll publicly swear severance with you!" He clasped his hands behind his back and paced.

"In other words, if I don't choose my friends according to your liking, you'll disown me as your sister-in-law." Sarah nodded her head. "Fine! That will relieve you of the responsibility for my actions." She shrugged. "And it will release me from worrying about approval from you. I can survive disgrace."

Elon sneered. "If you understood the consequences, you wouldn't be quite so ready for that. Disgrace will be the *least* of your problems. Anyone who associates with you will suffer the same, including your dear doctor friend."

"And do you really think you can survive long with no clients for your sewing business?" Tamar smirked. "Just remember that you'll be a virtual leper in this town, if Elon disowns you!"

"There's no reason for you to ruin my business, Tamar. It has nothing whatsoever to do with your social standing. That would be *revenge*, pure and simple." Sarah sighed, lowering her head sadly. "I'm glad Nathan can't see what you're threatening me with, Elon."

"Oh, don't talk to me about my brother! He would be very angry with you if he could see what a fool you've turned out to be!" Elon's eyes snapped with anger.

"You really didn't know Nathan at all, did you, Elon? If you had, you'd know he would be grateful that I've been healed, and would want to know more about the healer."

"I didn't come here to argue with you about what my brother would think," Elon countered. "I'm the one you have to answer to now, and this is your last warning, Sarah."

"I guess I'll have to live my life as I think I should and you'll have to do the same." She looked him in the eye. "I won't deliberately do anything to cause trouble for you, but neither will I turn away from my friends just for the sake of my own welfare."

For a moment, Sarah thought she caught a glimpse of sad admiration in Elon's eyes. But glancing at his angry wife, he straightened, as if gathering strength.

"Sarah, you've made your choice. I wish you hadn't gone in that direction, because I know Nathan would not approve. He wanted you to live comfortably. And, Sarah, as Nathan's brother, I would be willing to take responsibility for your welfare the rest of your life, if you'd only cooperate."

Sarah sensed some regret in his words. He was trying hard to exonerate himself for what he surely knew in his own mind was wrong.

"Elon, I wish the two of you could meet Jesus, as I did, and find the peace that comes with knowing him."

"No, thank you!" Tamar snapped. "We want nothing to do with such rabble and that includes you, my ex-sister-in-law!" She raised her sharp chin higher, bouncing the brassy, curled tendrils against her cheeks. "I hope your friends will be willing to support you, for you've just made yourself very poor with your stupid decision. They'll probably have to take you in, since you may not be able to pay rent on this place!"

Sarah's head shot up, as did Elon's. "Now, Tamar, let's not get ahead of ourselves..." Elon put out a cautioning hand to his wife.

"Rent?" Sarah jumped to her feet, crossing her arms. "Tamar, I own this place. Nathan built it with his own hands—for me!" Sarah looked at her brother-in-law. "Elon, you know..."

But he only dropped his head sadly, for after Tamar had suggested that he possess the house, it was obvious he didn't have the nerve to back down.

The two left, Tamar huffily and Elon shamefully, or so it appeared to Sarah.

Having heard the whole thing from another room, Tabitha came in and sat quietly for a few moments. Sarah stared numbly into space.

"Daughter, are you sure you're doin' the right thing?" Tabitha finally ventured. "Maybe you ought to be a little quieter about your new beliefs."

Sarah looked at her solemnly. "Tabitha, Jesus said last night that anyone who isn't helping him is harming him. Until then, I thought I could try to hide my belief in him. But now..."

Sarah smiled through tears welling in her eyes. "Tabitha, I wouldn't give up this peace in my heart for the entire Roman Treasury. I still have some money left and we'll get by for a while. When that's gone, we'll have to make different arrangements."

She looked into Tabitha's eyes. "Please understand that I speak only for myself and my own commitment. You'll have to decide for yourself." She reached over and placed a loving hand on Tabitha's hands folded in her lap. "I don't expect you to suffer because of my stand. I release you now, Tabitha, to leave me, with my eternal love and respect. You won't be harassed, because you aren't related to Elon. Many people would love to have you work for them—including Lucian."

"Oh, Sarah!" Tabitha pulled Sarah into her arms. "I'm with you all the way. I'm so proud of you." Her voice trembled with emotion. "I love you like my own daughter—I wish you were."

Touched deeply by Tabitha's loyalty and affection, Sarah was unable to speak for a moment. She swallowed hard. "I'm sure my mother would be very pleased for you to be her stand-in, Tabitha, and I'd be honored to be your daughter. We'll simply adopt each other." She pressed her cheek, wet with tears, to Tabitha's.

"Child, as long as we have each other and Jesus, and our friends—we'll be fine." Tabitha set her jaw defiantly.

"I hope you realize what you're asking for." Sarah stepped back, her hands on Tabitha's shoulders. "It's easy to talk about how we're going to be all right as long as we have each other, but I'm afraid things are much worse than you think."

Sarah walked over to the window, looking out toward the lake. "Maybe our situation isn't hopeless, but it's bleak, at best. The last time I looked at the savings record Lucian keeps for me, there was far less than I remembered." She shrugged. "I haven't paid much attention to it, since I only used it for the trips to Tiberias. Fortunately, we've been able to get along quite nicely on what I get from dressmaking."

"But we can expect that to stop." Tabitha shook her head.

"Tamar made that quite clear. And on top of that, I'll have to pay rent on my—my own house." Her shoulders sagged in despair. "I don't know how we'll survive, Tabitha. When I called Elon's hand, I probably ruined us both." Tears poured as she turned to face Tabitha.

The old woman slipped her arm around Sarah's shoulders. "Don't worry, child. We'll figure something out. You know Lucian won't let you..."

"Tabitha, Lucian doesn't want me to have anything to do with Jesus, either. Besides, you heard Elon say that anyone who is my friend will suffer, too. And I wouldn't think of letting Lucian's work be ruined because of me. He'd be out of business in one day, if Tamar so decided." She shook her head. "No, I won't do that to him—or to anyone else."

"I'll just bet Elon won't really carry out his threats. Don't give up your dressmaking till you're forced to. Let's go on like always and see what happens," Tabitha suggested, trying to be the optimist and postpone the inevitable. "Don't forget I can bring in some money working as a midwife."

"Don't count on it! Elon said I'd be like a leper, so I doubt if anyone will be having much to do with us, for any reason. You'll have to leave me to be treated any differently."

"Well, I'll not do it, I can tell you that!" Tabitha stomped out of the room.

Sarah picked up a gown she had been working on for Sephorah, the banker's wife. It was almost finished and she knew the woman would be pleased with it. She had seemed so happy to find a dressmaker. Sarah finished the dress before bedtime.

* * *

Sarah waited quite a long time in Sephorah's sitting room before the woman appeared. She nodded curtly and quickly turned her gaze away.

"I'd like you to try this on, for I believe it turned out even better than we thought it would." Sarah smiled at Sephorah, approaching her with the garment. "Your choice in fabric was an excellent one."

"I-I'll try it later, Sarah." Sephorah backed away a bit, avoiding Sarah's eyes. "I'm quite busy right now. If you'll just tell me how much I owe you..."

"But I thought you would want to put it on while I'm here, so that I could make any necessary adjustments."

"I'm sure it's fine. Please—let me pay you." The obviously flustered woman handed Sarah what they both knew was far more than the asking price.

"I see. Tamar works fast." Sarah looked into Sephorah's startled face. "I suppose this is the last dress you'll be needing me to make." She laid the garment across a chair and turned toward the door, her shoulders drooping.

"Sarah, I—I'm so sorry!" Sephorah took several hesitant steps toward her. "I don't like what's happening, and if it weren't for my husband..."

Sarah looked back at her with pity as she walked away, knowing that Sephorah was the more miserable.

* * *

Weary and discouraged, Sarah told Tabitha what had happened. "There's no use asking anyone else to let me sew for them. Tamar has wasted no time making good her threat.

I see no other way except to leave here and start over somewhere else—where Elon and Tamar have no influence."

CHAPTER 23

Sarah tried to swallow around the lump in her throat. Her fist poised to knock, she hesitated at Deborah's door. Bracing for the difficult task ahead, she rapped lightly.

The time had come to release Deborah, her best friend who had stood by her when Sarah was considered unclean, and who would probably support her even now. But she would not ask Deborah to choose between her and David. David's careful avoidance of Sarah and Tabitha, and Deborah's sudden coolness had clearly revealed her husband's attitude.

"Sarah." Deborah looked surprised as she opened the door. "Why so formal? You usually come to the kitchen door. I..." She motioned toward a couple of cushioned chairs.

"I know, Deborah," Sarah interrupted. "I—I guess I wasn't thinking."

"Oh, Sarah, I don't like what's happening, and I don't know what to do about it." Deborah's eyes filled.

"Deborah, I'm the one who has to do something about it," Sarah leveled her eyes at her friend. "And there's only one solution. I'm leaving Capernaum. Tabitha and I have to move." She spit out the words as if they were poison.

"You—you *what*?" The tears Sarah would have predicted didn't come right away. Deborah stiffened, her hands clenched together in her lap. She stared at Sarah, her eyes reflecting a mixture of hurt and anger. "I can't believe you're really doing this."

She got up and walked to the window, her back to Sarah. "What will you do? Just you and Tabitha in some strange place?"

"I don't know yet. You surely know I'm not going because I want to. I have no choice."

Deborah whirled around, her face flushed. "Yes, you do! For one thing, you could marry Lucian!"

"Do I need to remind you that he turned his back on me the day I told him Jesus healed me? And hasn't been around since." Sarah dropped her head. "I'm not sure he was ever really serious about my marrying him. When he knew I couldn't, or wouldn't, it was safe for him to keep asking me."

Deborah was quiet for a moment, her forearms resting on top of a chair back. "Yes, I accused him of that, myself. But, Sarah, I think he feels as David—that maybe you're not really healed. Could they be right?"

"Don't you think I know if I'm well or not?" Sarah asked indignantly.

"But you might not know if it's temporary." Deborah sighed. "Good gracious, Sarah, you could save yourself a lot of grief if you wouldn't insist on being involved with that group!"

Deborah subconsciously stroked the smooth, dark wood of the chair. "You're putting a lot of people on the spot, you know. If anyone takes your side, he jeopardizes his own livelihood." Her eyes pled with Sarah. "I believe in your healing—I really do. But David..." Tears rolled down her cheeks. "David doesn't even want me talking about it. It's not that he thinks Jesus is evil. He just can't afford..."

Sarah stood, her eyes fixed on Deborah's. "Now do you see why I'm leaving? I would never expect anyone to throw away everything because of my personal decisions."

She swallowed against the huge lump in her throat. "I don't know how to explain why I have to make this commitment. But please remember, dear one, I love you and always will, no matter where I go. And in spite of your anger with me right now, I know you feel the same way." Sarah ran to Deborah, hugged her tightly for a moment, and ran out of the house, leaving Deborah weeping uncontrollably.

* * *

Alone in her own house, Sarah yielded to all the pent-up hurt, guilt, anger, and every other emotion that had been building up inside her. Looking upward through her tears, she cried, "Oh, God, why do I have to give up even Deborah?"

* * *

Sarah was embarrassed when Tabitha brought Mary Hiram home with her, to find her still crying.

"You must have told Deborah," Tabitha said quietly, smoothing a lock of damp hair from Sarah's brow.

Sarah could only nod, unable to stop an occasional spasmodic sob.

"Mary's going back to Magdala tomorrow, Sarah." Tabitha motioned her cousin to a chair. "I'll fetch us some tea."

"I'm sorry things are so hard for you, Sarah," Mary said softly. She cleared her throat. "Tabitha told me about your decision to leave, and I've come to invite you to stay with me in Magdala."

Sarah's head shot up. "Mary, you're so kind. We haven't even discussed where we'd go. Frankly, I've had no idea what direction to take."

"Coming to my house won't take away the sadness, but it might solve one problem." Mary smiled at Sarah.

"I know this move is stressful, to say the least, for both of you. And at my home you'll be able to relax for awhile, get your thoughts together, and make plans for the future," she offered. "I have some dear friends in Bethany, near

Jerusalem. They're close friends of Jesus, as well, and could help you get situated there."

"You're a Godsend, Mary—literally." Sarah gave a big sigh of relief. "I guess my faith is very weak. I was about to come to the conclusion that everybody was against us."

"Jesus' friends will never be against you, Sarah," Mary assured her. "We take care of each other."

"I'm finding that out. God must be leading us in the right direction."

"Always! Even when it seems you're all alone. When you doubt, just remember how he made you well."

Tabitha came into the room with a tray. "I hear that lots of people are touching the tassels on Jesus' robe and being healed, too." She set the tray on a table near the two women. "Some folks think the tassels are magic."

"But it isn't magic, Tabitha!" Mary exclaimed. "Jesus uses God's power—nothing else!" She took a cup from the tray. "Yes, many have been healed by touching his clothes, but only because they believed.

"Unfortunately, there are some in high places who not only don't believe in him, but would like to see him dead! Herod, in particular. From what I've heard, he seems to be cursed by the death of John, and thinks maybe Jesus is John come back to haunt him." Mary shuddered. "That poor man. He needs Jesus more than anybody, but thinks he has to destroy him, instead."

"He's a dangerous man." Sarah frowned.

"Yes, and I'm worried about the Master. He has been telling his disciples that he's going to die soon. Nobody knows quite what to make of it. I'm afraid he expects Herod to have him killed."

"But doesn't he have the power to stop the tetrarch?" Sarah asked. "Surely he won't stay here and let himself be killed!"

"It looks to me like it's very dangerous to be a follower of Jesus, Mary," Tabitha remarked soberly. "Now don't look at me like that! I believe in him, too, but I've been thinkin' about what some people have to go through if they dare say they believe! Take Sarah..."

"No, Tabitha, don't worry about me," Sarah broke in.

"But I do worry! Mary, she's lost the man she—the man she thought loved her. Her business, her dressmakin', is gone. And now she has to give up her home and move away from Deborah, who's been like a sister to her, to some place where nobody knows her. That's a mighty big price to pay for believin'. Where will Jesus be when she needs him?"

"Tabitha! You shouldn't..."

"It's all right, Sarah." Mary held up her hand. "Tabitha's questions are valid. It *is* a high price to pay, but I really believe that God will go along with both of you. The complete joy we receive from following Jesus is simply priceless. If one is allowed into the Kingdom of Heaven by following the teachings of Jesus, then no price is too great." Mary turned to Tabitha. "Tell me, cousin, if Sarah gave in to Tamar and Elon, denouncing what she truly believes in, what would she really gain? Would the money, prestige, or anything else be worth the selling of her very self?"

"Well—no—I guess—not." Tabitha dropped her head. "I'm ashamed I even questioned the price."

"Oh, but you mustn't ever be ashamed of thinking, Tabitha! The Master's teachings can withstand our questioning. And if you don't ask the price, how are you going to know if you can pay it?" Mary smiled. "Sarah, don't let me, or anyone else, pressure you into a decision. It has to be what you feel..."

"Don't worry, Mary." Sarah laid a hand on her arm. "I've counted up the cost, and I've made up my mind to follow Jesus."

"I know you're right," Tabitha agreed. "But I can't help wondering how soon Tamar will find out where you are, even when we move far away."

"Oh, I doubt if she will even care where I am, as long as I'm out of her way!" Sarah laughed.

"Don't be too sure of that, Sarah." Mary held up a cautioning hand. "She could make points with Herod if she could use you to get to Jesus."

"I hadn't thought of that." Sarah frowned, shivering inside. "I must never leave a clue for her."

* * *

"God will be with us," Sarah whispered, running her fingers over the smooth olivewood chest. "Tabitha keeps reminding me." With the end of her sash she wiped the satiny surface where a tear had dropped.

She could still see Nathan's strong hands as he planed the wood for their furniture, and rubbed each piece until he was satisfied with its smoothness.

"Nathan could have been as good a carpenter as he was a potter," she said aloud, going from one piece of furniture to the next, caressing each chair, table and chest lovingly. Very few dwellings of their contemporaries were so well-equipped.

How she dreaded leaving this house and its precious contents to Elon and Tamar! But she could take only the necessities.

In her bedroom she raised the lid of a small chest beside her bed. Lifting out the beautifully carved ivory box, she took out the alabaster vial of perfume. "I'll never part with you," she said, clasping the treasure to her heart.

She'd never forget the first time Nathan took her to Tiberias to the Greek physician. They had been so sure a week of soothing mineral baths would cure her. When that didn't happen, Nathan had tried to ease her disappointment by surprising her with the costly fragrance.

She rubbed her finger over the alabaster. "At least I can take you with me to remind me of Nathan's love. You're the most precious possession I own." She pressed her lips to the yellowed jar, placing it carefully in the box. A rap on the door pulled her reluctantly away from the past.

It was Lucian.

CHAPTER 24

"David told me you're leaving Capernaum," Lucian said abruptly, his voice strained. "Please don't go, Sarah."

"I'm sorry, Lucian, but I have no other choice."

"But where will you go?" A deep frown creased his forehead. "Do you have any idea what an unmarried woman alone is apt to face, off in some strange place? There's no telling what might happen to you!"

Sarah could see that he was on the verge of panic. "Please, Lucian, come in. And calm down." She closed the door behind him as he walked on in and took a seat. "I'm not just going off without a plan in mind. Do you think I'm a complete fool?"

"No, but I didn't know..."

"Probably because you haven't spoken to me lately," she reminded him.

He blushed, dropping his head. "I know, Sarah. I'm..."

"I have a friend in Magdala. Tabitha and I have been invited to visit her for awhile. She has some ideas that I'm not at liberty to discuss at the moment. But I assure you, Lucian, that I'm not totally helpless. And Capernaum isn't the only place in the world that I can live."

"Well, I want to know where you are—always."

"I don't know yet exactly where I'll be. And I don't want Tamar and Elon to know my whereabouts, so it would be better if you could honestly tell them you don't know either."

She shifted in her chair. "Oh, by the way, I'll have to ask you to get the rest of my money from the bank, what little there is. I'll need all of it." She looked at him affectionately. "I really appreciate your keeping it safe for me. You've been a wonderful friend."

"Friend?" He slumped, shaking his head. "I can't believe this is happening. You know there's a better way than this. You don't have to leave your home. I love you and you love me! It's as simple as that!"

He got up and walked around. "You wouldn't marry me because you had a problem that you thought I couldn't cope with. Well, now you say you're cured. So why can't we be married? You wouldn't have to worry about not having customers for your dressmaking business—I'll make a living for us." He sat back down on the edge of his chair and leaned forward. "What about it? Will you marry me, Sarah?"

Her heart pounded, and for a moment no words would come. Swallowing hard, she took a deep breath, letting it out slowly. "Lucian, I've longed for the day when you would ask that and I could accept. And I thought that when you found out I was well, you would want us to get married right away. But instead, you resented my healing and walked away from me. So naturally, I thought you had changed your mind." She fingered the hem of her sash.

"And you don't believe I'm well. I've accepted that fact, and also that you resent Jesus. But if you could just meet him..."

"Sarah, I'm not interested in meeting the man. In fact, if I want to continue practicing medicine in Capernaum, I would be foolish to get mixed up with him or his group."

"Well, since I've chosen to be one of them, you have just made the decision for us. If you have anything to do with me, you jeopardize your career. And I certainly don't want that to happen!"

"It wouldn't, if you didn't get involved with them!"

"I'm already involved." She closed her eyes for a moment, sighing. "Don't you understand? The man *healed* me!"

"So—is he going to *unheal* you if you don't run around to all his meetings? You can appreciate him. Respect him. Without going all out, can't you?"

"Lucian, you're asking me to compromise my beliefs. You can't accept me as I am. I've changed more than you think, not just physically. You see, Jesus touched me inside, too. I'm a new person."

She shook her head. "If I gave up my belief and turned my back on the man who healed me, I'd be so miserable that you wouldn't want me." Tears spilled down her cheeks. "Any way I go, Lucian, I'd be bad for you, so there's nothing else to talk about."

He took her in his arms, hugging her tightly against him. Then holding her shoulders at arms' length, he spoke softly. "I guess it's an impossible situation for now. Maybe you're right. Maybe I should meet the man. Please don't give up on me, Sarah. I'll try to believe—and if you'll let me know where you are, well, maybe things can work out for us someday." He dropped his arms, turned and walked slowly toward the window.

"Sarah, what about this house? I hate to see you walk away from it. Nathan built it for you."

"You've no idea how it hurts to think of leaving it, but Elon has already let me know he's taking it, anyway. It's his right as Nathan's only brother. I wouldn't be able to live in it if I stayed here. He has said that I'll have to pay him rent—more than I could ever afford." Her voice broke as she choked back a sob.

"I'm sorry. I shouldn't have mentioned it. I know you're right. He'll hurt you any way he can! But Sarah, don't give him the pleasure of taking all of these things that Nathan made for you. He can't confiscate them!"

"I have no way to take anything but the necessities."

"If you'll let Santimar take you in the carriage, the storage compartment can be packed full. And I can keep the furniture for you. When you get settled I'll find a way to get it to you," he offered.

"You've already been too kind to me, but I'll take you up on that offer. Tabitha and I will be staying in Magdala for awhile, and having Santimar take us that far will be such a relief! We'll probably take a caravan to the next place."

"Better yet, Santimar can go back to Magdala and take you wherever you decide to go. He'll just need to know when you want him."

Her plans didn't include telling Lucian where they were going, but she saw no need to break that news now. She'd rather he would have the furniture than for Elon and Tamar to sell it.

"I plan to go to Magdala in about a week, so you could have the things moved to your house the day before I leave. I'll let you know the exact day, of course. Or maybe I should ask you when it would be convenient for Santimar."

"He can go anytime," he assured her. "But why don't we set next Wednesday for me to pick up these things?"

"Tabitha and I will have them ready," she promised.

His hand on the door latch, Lucian turned to look at her as if he were going to say more, then slowly walked out.

The pain in her chest was crushing. The temptation to run after him, ready to accept his proposal on any terms was extremely hard to fight.

"Tamar should be very happy now," Sarah muttered through clenched teeth. Her sister-in-law had turned their lives into a shambles! Sarah wondered bitterly if Elon and his wife would ever have to pay for what they had done to so many people!

* * *

Sarah climbed the stairs to the rooftop to help Tabitha fold the last of the laundry. She paused to look at the potted plants her companion had placed beside the staircase. One of the ivies had completely covered the strings that stretched to the rooftop, its dark, shiny leaves contrasting beautifully with the sand-colored stone. Tabitha had contributed a tremendous amount of work and love to help make the place attractive. Sarah knew Tabitha would hate to leave it almost as much as she would.

Lost in her thoughts, Sarah didn't notice the man standing at the edge of the yard holding his horse's rein, until Tabitha moved to the top of the stairs and stared at the man suspiciously.

When Sarah turned in the direction of Tabitha's gaze, the man addressed her pleasantly. "Good afternoon, Madam."

"Good afternoon," she replied, courteous but distant. When he didn't move on, she turned and continued up the steps.

His swarthy skin and turban headdress marked him as an Arab, no different from the thousands she had seen traveling through Capernaum. But the fact that he was off the main road, alone, aroused a wariness in her.

Just before she reached the top of the stairs, she heard him clear his throat. "Begging your pardon, Madam, I'm looking for someone who can take care of my lame animal."

"Sir, it would have been easier on the main road into the city," Sarah responded.

"I realize that now, but when I found that my horse was getting much worse, I unwisely cut across the countryside, hoping to shorten his walk. Now I don't really know where I am. Could you kindly direct me to the nearest inn, where I can get treatment for the animal and lodging for myself? I would be forever grateful," he pleaded, bowing at the waist.

Sarah couldn't hold back her smile. "If you'll just follow this street on around," She pointed east to where the street turned. "and continue straight to the north, you'll come to the market square. There are provisions for both of you there. But perhaps you should water your horse first—it's still quite a walk to the inn."

"Madam, you are truly a kind person! I hate to trouble you, but the animal certainly could use a drink." His weathered face crinkled when he smiled.

"I'll fetch it," Tabitha offered, starting down the stairs. As she passed Sarah, she whispered, "Let him stay out at the road. We don't know anything about him."

"Tabitha will bring the water for your horse," Sarah told him.

Before the man could answer, Elon's carriage pulled up in front of Sarah's house. As Elon helped his wife from the coach, Tamar saw the stranger. Halfway out of the vehicle, she stopped.

Sarah saw the man stare at Tamar's ashen face. When his lips curled into a brief smile, Tamar turned back into her seat in the carriage.

"What's the matter? Aren't you getting out?" Elon asked.

"I—I feel a little dizzy," she replied weakly. "Please—I'll wait in the coach. And draw the curtain. I have a vicious headache. Don't be long, Elon."

Elon nodded to the stranger as he pulled the carriage curtain shut and looked curiously at Sarah, who was still standing near the top of the stairs, where she had watched the mysterious exchange with curious interest.

Ascending the steps toward her, Elon said sternly, "I need to talk some business with you."

"Of course, Elon. Tabitha is getting some water for this man's horse. The poor animal is lame and needs a fresh drink before he goes on to town."

Elon barely glanced at the man. "I'll state my business briefly. Tamar isn't feeling well—nor am I, for that matter," he complained. "On our last visit, we mentioned to you that if you stayed here, we would have to charge you rent. I've been very generous up to now, but since you've forced me to disown you, I'll have to ask the same of you that I would of any other tenant. I've set the monthly rate for your rent at twenty-four denarii, starting immediately," he informed her, hands on his hips.

Sarah couldn't believe it. "Elon, you know I can't pay that much, and neither will anybody else pay such exorbitant rent for a house this size."

"Oh, but you're wrong about that! I know any number of other people who would jump at it. Perhaps you'd better look for another place."

"Elon, I'm planning to leave Capernaum next week, anyway. Will you at least allow me to stay here that long? I need time to get my things together."

"Where do you intend to go?"

"Away—where I won't be a bother to you again." She looked him straight in the eyes.

He lowered his gaze for a moment, blushing. "Very well. I suppose we could work something out. Tamar and I are going tomorrow to Caesarea Philippi for a few days. I'll let you stay until next week for five denarii—in advance."

"But I don't have that much here now. What time will you be leaving in the morning? I could..."

"Oh, never mind!" He crossed his arms impatiently. "I'll extend that much more charity, I guess! But when I return from Caesarea, I'll expect you to be gone. And don't look for anything else from me!" He shook his finger at her hatefully.

"Thank you, Elon. I won't ask for more, I assure you."

Watching him strut back to the carriage with his chin in the air, she could hardly contain her anger. The very idea that being allowed to spend a few days in her own house should be considered charity!

The stranger had stood quietly listening to the unpleasant exchange between Sarah and Elon, while his horse drank thirstily from the tub Tabitha had brought.

"Somehow, that's just the kind of man I'd have expected Jeda to team up with," the man remarked, watching the carriage roll away down the dusty road.

"Who?" Tabitha asked.

"Jeda—the woman in the carriage." He pointed in the direction of the departed vehicle.

"But her name is Tamar. Elon is my late husband's brother," Sarah corrected, coming down the steps. "You've undoubtedly confused her with someone else."

"So that's what she calls herself now! He laughed. "I assure you, though, that she used to be Jeda. Even dying her hair didn't change her that much. I'd know her anywhere. She knew me, too. Didn't you see how pale she turned when she looked up and saw me standing here? It didn't take her long to feign a headache and get out of sight."

"But why? I'm afraid I don't know what you're talking about. And—and I don't think I want to know. Perhaps you'd better go on now..."

"I'm very sorry, Madam. But I hesitate to leave without telling you that I've probably caused trouble for you."

"Trouble?" Tabitha frowned. "What kind of trouble?"

"You see, I've known Jeda for many years, and I'm a real threat to her. I guess you could say I'm her past come back to haunt her."

"But I'm not the least bit interested in Tamar's past. We're leaving here, anyway, so what has any of this got to do with us?" Sarah frowned.

"Madam, do you really think Jeda will believe that I just happened to stop by here to get directions and water for my horse?" He laid his hand on the animal's back. "She won't know what I've told you and will probably assume the worst."

"Sarah, it sounds bad to me." Tabitha's face showed alarm.

"I don't believe this!" Sarah raised her hands in dismay. "I haven't had enough trouble already, so you have to come along and make more for me—for us! How dare you involve us in something we know nothing about and had nothing to do with!"

"Madam—please! I know this is an unfortunate coincidence. But, believe me, that's exactly what it is." He shook his head. "I had no idea I was stopping at the house of a relation of Jeda, or that she would happen along!" He shook his head.

"But of course you'd never believe that. A chance encounter such as this would be one in a million. However, no matter what you think about why I'm here, it doesn't lessen the danger for you. I strongly suggest that you leave here as quickly as you can, without telling a soul where you're going." he urged. "If you really know Jeda, then perhaps you know that she would stop at nothing to get rid of anyone who might be a threat to her. And right now you two are on that list. I assure you, Madam, she has everything at stake this time!"

"And how do I know that you're not the dangerous one?" Sarah countered.

"You don't." His eyes met hers. "But if you stay here, you'll find out. The hard way. I'm terribly sorry I've put you two nice women in such a spot." He took the rein and walked off toward town.

CHAPTER 25

They stood numbly watching him go. "Tabitha, what in the world do you suppose that man has on Tamar?" Sarah's shoulders slumped as she forced her weak, trembling knees to move toward the house.

"I don't know, but whatever it is, it must be bad." They finished folding the linens and went inside.

Each absorbed in her own thoughts, they worked silently, Sarah sorting their belongings into piles, some for taking with them and some for leaving with Lucian. Tabitha bundled them, ready for moving. The two worked for more than an hour.

Finally, Tabitha broke the silence. "I think we ought to get out of here before night, Sarah. I don't mind telling you—I'm scared stiff!"

"I am, too, and I've been thinking the same thing." Sarah shuddered. "Tamar won't waste any time, if that man was telling the truth. And for our own safety, we'd better assume he was. She can't possibly afford to go off to Caesarea Philippi with him in town, thinking we know about her past, whatever it is!"

"I'm wondering if she might come over here in the middle of the night. Tonight." The fear in Tabitha's eyes alarmed Sarah even more.

"I know what you're thinking, Tabitha. We don't dare stay here tonight." Sarah shivered. "I can't believe we're sitting here talking about being murdered! If this is a nightmare, I hope..."

"Well, talking about it won't get us out of here!" Tabitha got up. "We need Santimar to get us to Magdala fast—before too late tonight!"

"Yes, suppose you go to Lucian's and see if Santimar will come over here. But don't tell Lucian what's going on, whatever you do. For his sake!"

As Tabitha opened the door to leave, she came face to face with the turbaned stranger again. Hearing her startled gasp, Sarah came running out of the kitchen.

"A thousand pardons, both of you. Please don't be afraid of me. I warned you to flee for your lives. But I couldn't live with myself, knowing that you had no transportation. If you could bring yourselves to trust me, I can get you out of here within the hour, to wherever you wish to go," he gestured toward the street. "I've rented a carriage, which is right now at your disposal. I owe you that much."

The two women looked at each other. "We wouldn't have to get anybody else mixed up in this, Sarah," Tabitha urged.

"We don't even know you." Sarah's heart hammered her chest. "But I suppose we have no choice but to trust you." She caught Tabitha's eye. "I hope we're doing the right thing. I can't even think straight at the moment."

"God will be with us, Sarah. I believe it," Tabitha offered. "If we can get to Mary's, she'll take care of sending us to a safer place."

"Yes, she has promised that," Sarah agreed. "Will you just take us to Magdala, uh—sir?"

"Why don't you call me Sashi? That's not my name, but it will do for now," he said, smiling. "And, yes, I'll be glad to take you to Magdala, Sarah."

She flinched slightly hearing him call her by her first name. But, after all, it was more convenient that way. She and Tabitha were at his mercy now, whoever he was! The thought filled her with an almost paralyzing terror.

Within the hour the carriage was packed and the two women were ready to leave. As they walked out the door, the lump in Sarah's throat grew larger by the minute. Climbing into the carriage, she turned for one last look.

"Don't do it, Sarah. Don't look back." Tabitha put a comforting arm around her shoulders.

Tears were streaming when Sarah took her seat in the enclosed coach. As they pulled away, she cracked the curtain and looked toward Deborah's house. She had seen her leave right after lunch, probably to spend the afternoon with her mother. David must have gone there after work, too, for nobody seemed to be at home now. At least that part had timed out right. It would have been very puzzling to them to see her and Tabitha leaving with this stranger, without saying a word to anyone. It was better this way. Lucian would be hurt, but he was better off not knowing. Sarah's heart sagged.

As the trio started down the road toward Lake Galilee, dusk had settled over the countryside, like the curtain that had closed on Sarah's and Tabitha's past. Before them was a frighteningly uncertain future.

* * *

Tamar paced her bedroom like a caged animal. Why did Shamri have to turn up now? She should have guessed he was the one keeping track of her for Aretas. She remembered him as the king's number one agent, and there was no doubt in her mind that he had been on her trail since the very day she ran away from Aretas. King Aretas didn't let her go free all these years for nothing! But then—what about the agent in Herod's palace?

She must find out what Shamri was up to. Her only hope was his greed. Every man has a price, and he would be no exception. But was that price within her reach?

Unfortunately, there were Sarah and Tabitha to deal with first. They had to be stopped at once. Tonight! She had hoped to use Sarah to lead her to the group of Jesus' followers who would interest Herodias. But she couldn't take a chance now on what Sarah could tell Herodias if she were cornered. She and Tabitha had to be stopped before they blabbed Shamri's story to Lucian. Or Elon! Or was it already too late?

She paced faster. Even if she eliminated the two women tonight, she still didn't dare go to Caesarea tomorrow. She had to find that Arab and buy him off. It wouldn't be hard to feign exhaustion in the morning, the way her head throbbed now.

If she could only convince Shamri that her whole life was centered on her effort to set Herod up for Aretas. If he only knew how she hated the sight of the tetrarch!

Every time she saw him she remembered with disgust the first time she actually met the savage beast. But King Aretas was partly to blame. He shouldn't have married off his daughter to Herod! Poor little Rafi. She was so young to be taken away to Livias to be Herod's queen.

Aretas did send Tamar to be Rafi's companion. But when she ran away, back to Aretas, and told him she'd been raped, he shouldn't have tried to send her back. That's why she left, and she deserved the things she stole!

But she still wanted the same thing King Aretas did—Herod's head. Would Shamri buy that story? Probably not. She wasn't even sure she believed it any more herself.

She had become accustomed to the "good life", and sometimes revenge didn't seem as important as it once did. As much as she had told herself she wanted to help Aretas, she wondered if she could ever be satisfied in his palace again—especially as a servant. And she had no reason to believe he would trust her in any other way!

Her motives were immaterial now, anyway. She was caught between Herodias and Aretas, and saving her own neck was paramount!

Lucian's medicine had relieved Elon's stomach pain and he retired early. "Tamar, I hope you'll get to sleep soon, too, for we must leave early in the morning." He said drowsily, crawling under the covers.

"Don't worry. I'm totally exhausted. In fact, I'll have to feel much better in the morning or I won't be able to go with you." But his snoring already echoed through the chamber.

Well after midnight, she donned her black robe and tiptoeing first to the kitchen, slipped quietly out into the darkness. The entire city seemed deserted at this time of night.

She tried Sarah's front door, expecting to find it barred. Surprised when it opened with a squeak, she stopped dead still in her tracks. Then confident that the sound had not awakened them, she slipped the blade from her sash and started first toward Tabitha's room. She would be the lighter sleeper, and most dangerous to her. Moonlight through the undraped windows made it easier. Tabitha must have already packed the curtains.

When she reached the bed, ready to smother the woman's face as she stabbed her, she found it empty! Jolted by this turn of events, she sat on the side of the bed. Ah! Tabitha had to be spending the night with someone else, a complication she'd have to deal with later.

But when she found Sarah's bed unoccupied as well, panic seized her. Where could they have gone since this afternoon? Or had they heard her and crouched somewhere, waiting for her to come near?

Clutching the knife handle tightly, she stood still for a moment to contemplate her next move, listening carefully for one of them to make a sound. That's when she noticed there was no cover, no linens of any kind on the bed. She crept to the chest where Sarah kept her clothes. Empty! Rushing back into Tabitha's room, she threw open the closet. Nothing! They were gone. They had run away. Away from her!

"They can't do this to me!" she hissed. "No! No! No!" Her voice grew louder as she jabbed the knife into the bed with each word. Suddenly realizing what she was doing, she drew in her breath sharply, clasping her hand over her mouth. "I will find them!" she vowed, whispering through clenched teeth. "But I must not fall apart!"

In a daze, she skulked back across town. Shedding the robe, she slipped back into the bedroom.

CHAPTER 26

"What are you doing?" Elon asked thickly, turning over in bed. "Is it time to get up already?"

"No, Elon. I was just getting a drink of water. I'm feeling worse and can't rest. You go back to sleep."

It was true that she couldn't rest, for she had to find out where Sarah and Tabitha went. Lucian would know. Sarah wouldn't make a move without telling him. Somehow, she'd get it out of him.

Tamar's mind raced on and on until Hannah called at their door. "Time to get up, Sir!"

"All right, Hannah," she answered. "Elon, get up and get ready, dear." When he grunted and sat up, she whined, "Do you mind too much if I don't go, Elon? I hardly slept last night. My head aches and I'm very weak." She laid her arm across her forehead. "I must get some medicine from Lucian. Maybe a few days rest..."

"But I had counted on having you with me when I talk to that property owner. From what I saw, his wife has quite an influence on him and you could..." He shrugged. "Oh well, just take care of yourself. I'll handle things in Caesarea Philippi."

As soon as Elon left town, Tamar was ready to go out. To establish her innocence and set the stage, she first went to Sarah's. Hoping that Deborah might be watching, she knocked at the front door for quite awhile, even calling Sarah's name loudly several times.

Then she rapped on Deborah's door. After the third knock, Deborah came.

"Good morning!" Tamar said brightly. "I was at Sarah's and nobody answered the door. Is she here?"

"No, she isn't." Deborah frowned as she began closing the door. "I haven't seen her."

"Really? Do you know where she could have gone? She and Tabitha were here yesterday afternoon when my husband and I stopped by. Do you think they might both be at the market?" Tamar probed.

"I've no idea," Deborah replied.

Tamar didn't believe for a minute that Deborah wouldn't know Sarah's whereabouts. But that didn't matter. Now she could go to Lucian's and tell him that Sarah was gone.

* * *

Tamar arrived at the clinic just as Santimar entered the front door. "I hope the doctor can see me soon, for I'm terribly ill." She clutched her throat dramatically.

Hearing her voice, Lucian came out of the back room. "Why, Tamar! You're the last person I'd expect to see this early! Don't tell me you've got the same thing that was troubling Elon yesterday! By the way, did the medicine help?"

"Yes, he slept like a baby all night, Lucian, and has gone to Caesarea Philippi today. But I was unable to go with him. My head aches and I'm terribly exhausted. It doesn't help, of course, to be so upset and worried about Sarah."

"Oh?" He raised his eyebrows. "Why would you be so worried about Sarah?"

"Well, Elon was rather hard on her when we stopped by there yesterday, and I thought I'd go over this morning and try to smooth things over, even though I was feeling so dreadful." She put her hand to her forehead. I knocked on her door for the longest time, calling out to her, but nobody answered. Lucian, there was no activity there at all." She took a deep breath.

"I went next door to Deborah's and she said she hadn't seen her. I just don't know what to make of it!" She shook her head. "I'm afraid something has happened to her! She told Elon yesterday that she and Tabitha were going away next week. But it seems she's gone already! Do you have any idea where she is, Lucian?"

"No, I'm afraid I don't. I know she planned to leave next week." He had no intention of giving Tamar what little information he had. Her story didn't ring true, at all. If Elon was giving Sarah a hard time, Tamar would hardly be trying to smooth things over with her.

"Oh, surely she was at home," he said. "Maybe you didn't knock long enough, or maybe they were busy and didn't hear you. Or perhaps both of them went to the market this morning."

"Lucian, I have a dreadful feeling about it. Would you go over there with me?" Tamar wrung her hands. "I'm afraid something has happened, and I'd rather not go back there alone."

"Oh, don't worry about Sarah. I'll check on her myself. Suppose I just give you something for your headache and you go on home and stay in bed today." He had an idea that Sarah and Tabitha had simply refused to answer the door when they heard Tamar's voice. Still, a nagging concern made him want to check things out for himself.

After Tamar left, he had Santimar drive him over there.

* * *

After knocking several times with no response, Lucian tried the latch. To his surprise, the door opened. "Sarah? Tabitha?" Everything was quiet. Too quiet.

He walked through the house. The kitchen looked strangely empty, and then he noticed that most of the jars and cookware were gone. Looking through the rest of the house, he saw that only the bare furniture remained.

As he started out of Sarah's room, something about the bed caught his eye. The pad was badly torn. Closer examination revealed that it had been slashed. When Santimar came to see what was going on, Lucian showed him the mattress.

"What do you think caused that?"

The old man scratched his head, puzzled by what he saw. "A knife of some kind." He frowned.

"Sarah would never do such a thing! And where is she? And Tabitha?" Lucian straightened up, looking all around.

"Everything's gone! Santimar, she left without a word to me. But how do you suppose she took all of these things? She and Tabitha couldn't have carried all that stuff by themselves!"

"I thought I was to take them to Magdala." Santimar scratched his head.

"So did I." Lucian walked outside.

Deborah came out of her house, walking toward him. "Lucian, what's going on? Where's Sarah?"

"I was hoping you could tell me!" He spread his hands. "Tamar came to my office claiming to have been by here. Said Sarah wasn't here and she was worried about her. I..."

"She did come by asking about Sarah. I told her that I hadn't seen her," Deborah replied.

"You didn't know Sarah and Tabitha were gone."

"No, but—but we don't see each other much anymore," she reminded him. "Maybe she and Tabitha went to the market, or to visit some of their new friends."

"Deborah, they've packed up and moved. Everything's gone but the furniture."

"That can't be! She wouldn't go away without saying..." Deborah looked stricken. "When I left the house a little after noon yesterday, Tabitha was folding laundry on the roof." She looked toward her neighbor's house. "Sarah was on the stairs the last time I saw her. She waved to me..."

She swallowed hard, turning back around. "Oh, but there was a man standing by his horse out at the edge of the road. Looked like he was asking her something." She shrugged. "I didn't get back until after dark. David met me at my mother's and we had supper there. Sarah and Tabitha must have packed up and left while I was away!"

"About this man—what did he look like? The man you saw talking to Sarah."

"I really didn't pay much attention, Lucian. All I could think about was how painful it was for Sarah and me, having such a gulf between us." She shook her head sadly. "But let me think—he was a dark-looking man...and he was wearing a bright turban. Several colors, as I remember."

"None of this makes any sense." Lucian climbed into the carriage. "They were supposed to go to Magdala. Santimar was to take them." He shook his head in despair. "I can't imagine what could have changed her plans so drastically that she'd run away without a word!" He was angry, but also worried.

* * *

Tamar waited anxiously at the clinic until Lucian and Santimar returned. "I just couldn't rest at home, Lucian, until I found out about Sarah. Did you find her?"

"No such luck." He shook his head. "It's as if Sarah and Tabitha just vanished into thin air, along with all of their things." He slapped the table top in frustration. "It seems they had a visitor yesterday. A stranger. Whether he's involved in their disappearance, I don't know. But it worries me. He could have..."

"Oh, yes!" Tamar raised her hand. "A man was standing out near the street with a horse when Elon and I stopped by. Sarah told my husband that the man's horse was lame, or something, and Tabitha was getting water for it before he went on to town. I stayed in the carriage and hardly saw the man at all. I did notice he wore a turban, but didn't see his face," she lied, wondering if Shamri really did take Sarah and Tabitha. Her heart almost stopped as she imagined what the three of them might be up to and what they could do to her.

"I find it very strange that a traveler would be on Tamarisk Way on his way to town." Lucian rubbed his chin absent-mindedly. "I'm afraid his presence and their disappearance is no coincidence. He must be involved in some way."

Santimar raised a cautioning hand. "Now, Lucian, don't borrow trouble. Let's try to keep our thinking positive—without panic."

"That's right, Lucian," Tamar agreed. "You'll find them, I'm sure. And when you do, will you please let me know? I'll be worried until I hear, and I'm sure Elon will, too!"

* * *

When Tamar was gone, Lucian sat down at the table. "Santimar, do you know who it is that Sarah was planning to stay with in Magdala?"

"Of course I do, but you didn't think I was going to let on to Tamar, did you?"

"Man, you always know what's going on, don't you?" Lucian laughed. "I'd like you to..."

"Way ahead of you, doctor! I'll be in Magdala as soon as my horse can get me there."

"I can always count on you, my friend." He patted Santimar's shoulder. "And if they are there, just tell Sarah that her safety is very important to all of us, but that we're not intending to intrude on her privacy."

"I shall. And try not to worry, Lucian. I'm certain I'll find them safe and sound. There's surely a very logical reason for their sudden departure and she's probably already preparing to let you know where they are." He turned to leave the room, but hesitated, facing Lucian again. "About the slashed bed—there was no blood..."

"Yes, I noticed that, too. And I saw nothing else to indicate violence, or struggling." Lucian sighed heavily. He had an uneasy feeling that there was more to this than any of them could imagine. Sarah would never have run away like that unless she were desperate or forced! And he'd never rest easy until he had an answer!

CHAPTER 27

A loud banging at the front gate jarred Mary Hiram out of a sound sleep. She lay still as she heard Jude shuffling toward the outer courtyard.

"Who's there?" he growled.

"I bring visitors from Capernaum, sir. Tabitha wishes to see her cousin, Mary Hiram, on an important matter!" Sashi shouted.

"Jude, let them in at once! I'll meet them in the entry hall," Mary called to the old servant from her upstairs bed-chamber.

"Must be mighty urgent to be coming at this hour!" Jude grumbled as he opened the gate and let the party inside the courtyard. Then reluctantly opening the main door, he announced, all the while eyeing them suspiciously, "Here they are, Miss Mary—your night visitors."

"Tabitha! Sarah!" Mary, still tying the sash of her robe, rushed excitedly down the hall toward the unexpected guests. "I'd have waited up for you had I known you were coming tonight!" She hugged her cousin.

"Mary, please forgive our rudeness, dropping in unannounced, in the middle of the night!" Sarah reddened, turning her gaze to the floor. "We've surely disrupted the sleep of the entire household."

"Oh, please don't apologize!" Mary embraced her new friend. "Joel and Dinah are away for a few days. Besides, I invited you here. Remember? And you're welcome at any hour!"

"But you know we wouldn't come barging in here like this without good reason!" Tabitha interrupted. "The fact is, we're in big trouble! And we didn't know what else to do!"

"Tabitha, my dear, what in the world..."

"Mary, she's absolutely right," Sarah broke in. "Had we not left hurriedly, I don't know what might have happened."

A worried frown crossing her face, Mary took Sarah's arm. "We needn't stand in this drafty hallway. Let's go in here where we can sit down and talk." She ushered them into the dimly-lit sitting room nearby. "Marla, please make tea for our guests," she called to the girl who had slipped quietly into the hall. "I can see that they're exhausted." She pulled a chair closer to the two women who had seated themselves on a couch. "I want to hear what happened to cause you to flee in such a state."

"Mary, involving you in our problems is the last thing we wanted to do, but as Tabitha said, we have no one else to turn to who might understand our situation." Sarah sat up on the edge of her seat as she related the events that had caused their quick exit. "So you see our options were few." Tears gathered and spilled over. "I'm so sorry to impose this on you."

"Please—I'm so glad you felt you could come to me, that the two of you trust me that much." Mary reached over and laid a hand on Sarah's hands, clasped tightly in her lap. "Now we'll get you to a safer place. My friends in Bethany will take care of you." She smiled. "I assure you, it certainly won't be the first time they've handled something like this, and believe it or not, it's not the first time for me!" She laughed at their startled looks.

"When you made a decision to follow Jesus, you let yourself in for this sort of thing—not that the problem with Tamar has anything to do with that. But it may not be quite as unrelated as it looks. And this may not be the last time you have to pick up and move on a moment's notice. People in high places feel threatened by Jesus and that doesn't make his followers exactly popular with them. So, you see, we simply must be ready and willing to help each other."

"But we can't stay here long, for some of the people in Capernaum knew we were planning to come here for a visit. They might come here looking for us!" Tabitha shivered.

"I hate to see you start out again before morning as tired as both of you are," Mary said, "but if Tamar is as much a threat as your driver has told you, we mustn't take a chance." She rang a bell. "I want you to eat something first, though."

A maid appeared almost immediately. "Marla, these people will be going on before dawn, so we must have a meal for them. If you..."

"Mistress, I took the liberty to prepare something. It's about ready." The girl bowed, smiling at the guests.

"Bless you, Marla." She laughed. "I'm so fortunate to have her," she told Sarah and Tabitha, "and incidentally, you needn't worry about any of this household. After you leave here tonight, they will have never seen you at all! You see, everyone in this house is a friend of Jesus and his disciples!"

Tabitha sighed with relief. "God is truly with us." She looked at Sarah, nodding her head.

Mary rose, gesturing them to follow. "Come let's go to the dining room and see what Marla has come up with. And while you eat I'll tell you all about the friends you're about to meet."

She led the way down the wide, mosaic-tiled hall, through a lovely atrium with a beautiful fountain in the center, and into the dining room on the other side. Marla was bringing a tray of cold sliced lamb, warmed lentil soup, bread and fig cakes.

Though the food looked tasty, Sarah was too tired and nervous to be hungry. Aching all over, she sat down with Tabitha and began sipping the warm, soothing tea. Soon she relaxed enough to eat a bit.

"Lazarus and his two sisters, Mary and Martha, live in a lovely house in Bethany and you'll find that their household, too, will be sympathetic to your problems," Mary told them. "Jesus is a close friend of theirs and has visited them many times. Martha does most of the cooking, though she has plenty of help.

"Lazarus is a sickly man—has been all his life. So you may not see much of him. But he's a kind, gentle person and will welcome you, I promise! His sisters dearly love having guests and their beautiful estate surely lends itself to entertaining."

"It sounds so wonderful." Sarah smiled. "But I hope Tabitha and I won't have to impose on them for very long. We want to make our own way as soon as possible."

"And they'll do everything possible to help you do that." Mary got up. "While you finish eating, I'll write a note to them." She left the room.

Returning, she handed a small scroll to Sarah. "Just give this to Mary or Martha. My driver has explained to the man who brought you how to get to Lazarus' estate from the main road through Bethany. By the way," she added, "he has been fed, too, and told about a caravan that you can catch before they get very far. It's easier to travel with a group. And safer!" She walked with them out to the carriage.

"I wish I could tell you how much we appreciate what you're doing for us. Sarah's eyes filled with tears.

"I told you what a wonderful cousin I've got, and now you know it was true." Tabitha hugged Mary tightly.

Marla was smiling when she brought the large basket, handing it to Tabitha. "Now you must eat some more as soon as you feel like it," she said to Sarah. "There's plenty of food for the whole journey."

"Thank you, Marla. I promise I will." Sarah smiled warmly at the girl. She turned to Mary. "We were just about at the end of our rope, when you rescued us. God bless all of you!" Sarah hugged Mary and Marla and climbed into the carriage with Tabitha.

Sashi cracked his whip lightly and the horse surged forward. A faint light was visible on the eastern horizon. It would take some fast traveling to catch the caravan, which very soon would be heading out again.

"This horse is sure faster than Santimar's mules," Tabitha remarked, leaning back in the speeding carriage.

"Sashi must have traded his lame animal and rented this rig," Sarah mused. "He went to a lot of trouble for us."

"He could have stolen the horse and rig both, for all we know!"

"Oh, don't say that, Tabitha! We have enough problems without being chased by an irate owner." Sarah scolded, both of them managing a laugh as they sped through the countryside. "At this rate, we'll catch the caravan before noon."

In less than an hour the carriage slowed as they turned onto a road going almost due east. Pink streaks rising from the tiny sliver of sun peeking over the horizon radiated the glow of dawn over the eastern sky.

Sarah pulled back the curtain to see the splendor. "Look, Tabitha! This is a new day—our first day, because we must put all the old ones behind us."

"Yes, I guess we are starting over. But, Sarah, we mustn't forget all the other times. The good days are worth remembering, and even some of the bad ones, because sometimes we learn more from trouble than any other way." Tabitha reminded her.

"True." Sarah looked into Tabitha's face and squeezed her hand affectionately. "You're a wise woman, Tabitha, and you're always here when I need someone to get me back on the right track!"

Before long, the driver pulled over and stopped at another intersection. Sarah opened the curtain between them. "What is it, Sashi?"

"The caravan was camped here last night." He got down and looked the place over. "They haven't been gone much more than an hour. We'll catch them before they slow for the midday meal. They won't stop for long, though. Just time enough for a cold snack."

"I'll give you the money to pay the leader to let us join them," Sarah reminded Sashi. "I would like to reimburse you for your time and rig, too."

"No, I can't take your money. Had I not come along at the wrong time, you wouldn't be joining this caravan. For my own peace of mind, getting you to a safe place is my responsibility."

"But not the entire cost..."

"Please—I must do it this way!" He turned and spoke to the horse, cracking the whip.

Sarah sat back in the seat, looked at Tabitha and shrugged. "Stubborn one, isn't he?"

Tabitha chuckled, wondering what else they'd learn about this stranger.

By the time they finally caught up with the caravan, the travelers were taking a break for lunch. When Sashi pulled up some distance away, so as not to cover their food with grit, the savage-looking caravan leader walked toward them.

"You'd better move on. This is a private caravan! Only payin' customers can ride with us!"

"I'm quite familiar with the rules of the road, mister!" Sashi snapped back at the man. "And we wish to join you."

He climbed down from his seat. The two men walked a few paces away, and after a bit of haggling, Sashi paid the fee.

"Hey! What's your name?" Sashi called back as he neared the carriage again.

"Minez!" someone nearby answered.

"And he's a bloody bully!" another voice added, not too loudly.

They barely had time to eat from the basket Marla had fixed for them, before Minez yelled for everyone to mount up. He obviously enjoyed intimidating anyone who would let him. But when he came back and shouted at Sashi to move on, slapping the horse, he found he had met his match.

"Keep your hands off my animal!" Sashi ordered, and the startled man stepped back.

Sarah smiled to herself, thinking that when Sashi was riled, he was every bit as mean-looking as Minez. She wouldn't want him mad at her, and she sincerely hoped that other people, including the leader, found her driver as formidable.

An odd mixture of people made up the band of travelers, all heading for Jerusalem, according to what Sashi could learn. The group had originated in Tyre, on the Phoenician coast.

Several families were among the crowd, and a group of distinguished gentlemen, who Sarah guessed were business men. But it was the few unsavory-looking characters who didn't seem to fit any particular category, who worried Sarah.

CHAPTER 28

"You can relax now, Doctor. Sarah and Tabitha are all right," Santimar told Lucian, who slumped over his desk concentrating on the small scroll in front of him.

"You found them! Did you tell them...?

"No, no." Santimar held up his hand. "I didn't see them. They're already gone. And don't ask me where." He sat down across the table from Lucian. "But I finally got to talk to Tabitha's cousin. She wasn't eager to talk to me at all."

"Start at the beginning, Santimar. I want to hear all you've found out."

"Well, I never would have got any answer at all, if I hadn't known an old fellow that works for Mary Hiram, the cousin. He finally talked her into seeing me. When she found out who sent me, and that we were really concerned about Sarah's and Tabitha's safety, she reluctantly told me enough so we'd know they were being taken care of. But you won't believe why they ran out so fast!"

"Oh?"

"The man that was here—the Arab—knew something about somebody here in Capernaum, something that could be very damaging to him. Or her. And it seems that while he was stopping to water his horse at Sarah's, that person saw him there."

"Tamar!"

"But I didn't let on, and if Mary knew who it was, she wasn't about to say." He leaned back in his chair. "Anyway, the man, whoever he is, knew he had endangered Sarah and Tabitha, so he came back and took them away to Magdala." He shrugged. "Mary wouldn't tell me where they went and she said if you or I told anybody else that we even know this much, we'd be in trouble, and Sarah would be in further danger."

"You're talking about real danger, aren't you?" Lucian paled at the thought. "Santimar, you never made that trip to Magdala. Understand?"

"What trip?" The old man sighed. "I don't know what that Arab has on Tamar, but apparently he was certain she'd do away with Sarah and Tabitha for learning about it!"

"I hope and pray she never finds her!" Lucian shook his head. "Now I know why she was looking for Sarah this morning. She must have been there during the night, and when she found them already gone..."

"She was so angry, she took the knife she had in her hand and jabbed it into the bed!" Santimar slapped his thigh.

"You're right." Lucian put his hands over his face for a moment. "Santimar, we'll continue to express our worry about what might have happened to Sarah and Tabitha. And I'll even pretend to be angry that she didn't say goodbye."

"It'll be our secret," Santimar solemnly pledged.

* * *

Traveling east of the Jordan River, the caravan passed through the city of Pella and before dusk had crossed through three towns in the province of Peraea. Twilight caught them just south of Succoth, where their road split, one fork going to Samaria, and their route straight south. Minez stopped the group for the night.

Sleeping mats were unrolled, fires started, and the people settled down for supper and rest. Minez placed the families and groups traveling together around the outer circle, putting the single passengers in the middle. Sashi wasn't too happy with the spot assigned to their carriage.

"I tell you, I don't like the looks of those three." He nodded in the direction of the rough-looking party a few yards away. "I'd just as soon they'd have been put at the other side of the camp."

Sarah had already noticed them staring at her with ugly grins more than once, which made her nervous. She assumed, though, that the people were watched over during the night by the leader, or guards.

She and Tabitha wrapped their covers tightly around them on one side of the fire, while Sashi made his bed on the opposite side. He took the outer area, putting the women next to the center of the circle. The cover felt good to Sarah, and although the ground was hard, she was tired enough to rest anyway. Before she dropped off, she heard Sashi's snoring and decided that he must not have been too worried about the men. Tabitha's hard breathing told her that she, too, was asleep. The crackling fire and the warm cover lulled Sarah into restless slumber.

She was awakened several times by her fragmented dreams. Tamar was chasing her. Lucian was always there, but just out of reach.

Then another nightmare, far worse than the others, invaded her sleep. But this time, she couldn't wake up. It was when the man pulled the blanket from around her that she realized she wasn't dreaming. It was terrifying reality! As she started to jump up, he roughly pushed her back down, his hand clamped over her mouth. As he tore at her clothes, she tried desperately to scream, only to have his hand cut off her breathing. When she tried to bite him, she tasted the blood of her own lips mashed against her teeth.

She was able to make out the form of Sashi coming toward them, but the wave of relief was short-lived, when she saw another man hit her would-be rescuer from behind. When Tabitha stirred, turning over, the man hit her, too.

She was sure that both of them had been mortally wounded, and fully expected to be next. The man laughed hoarsely as he tore the rest of her clothes from her. When she tried to squirm out of his clutches, she felt a fist in her side. Momentarily, she blacked out. When she came to her senses, one of the men was holding her arms outstretched, while the one who undressed her brought his huge, heavy body down on her. She closed her eyes, gritted her teeth, ready for the inevitable. But suddenly he groaned and fell to the side, partly on her leg. Simultaneously, the grip on her arms was suddenly loosened.

In the dim light of the smoldering fire, Sarah saw the forms of two others pulling both her attackers away. She lay still, afraid to make a sound, assuming these newcomers would take up where the others had left off.

"Woman, get up," she heard someone whisper coarsely. "You're all right—they'll never bother you again." He squatted, gently pulling the blanket over her.

"W-who are you?" She sat up, struggling to wrap herself in the cover.

"Just a friend, madam."

"I think Tabitha and Sashi were badly hurt. They may even be..."

"Nah! They'll be all right." The stranger stood up as Minez came rushing toward them with a lighted torch.

"What in Caesar's name's goin' on?" He brandished a vicious-looking dagger at the strangers, having it knocked instantly from his hand. "W-what do you want? You won't get much gold from this lot!"

"We don't want your money, old man!" The big fellow's deep bass voice was quite a contrast to the high-pitched, nervous screech of Minez. "We just stopped a couple of your crew of filthy vermin from violating this decent woman."

"Since when are the Sicarii interested in defending women?" snarled Minez. "And how do you know what kind of woman this one is?"

"Anytime we find one of God's people, man or woman, needing defense, that's when! And how we know about this woman is none of your business. We're strangers to her, but she's not unknown to us."

As dawn began to break Sarah counted five men dressed in coarse robes, each with a long dagger in his sheath. She was shaking so hard she could hardly breathe, even wrapped in the blanket. Others from the caravan had been awakened by the noise and were standing back looking on in fear for their own lives.

Minez got a blanket from the dead men's camp and spread it over the two bodies. Seeing the color drain from Sarah's face, Tabitha went to the carriage for a cloth. "Child, just try to relax and don't look at them." She moistened the rag and wiped Sarah's brow with it.

Sashi stooped down and took her hand. "I'm sorry I didn't stay awake to look after you. I was under the impression that a caravan leader was responsible for the safety of his passengers." He glared at Minez, who stood by awkwardly. "Why wasn't there a guard?"

"There was! How was I to know they weren't trustworthy!" Minez gestured toward the two dead men.

"Do you mean to tell me that these people who attacked us were your guards?" Sashi got up and faced the leader. "And who was supposed to protect people from <u>them</u>?"

Minez shrugged. "I'll take care of all of you tonight. Myself!"

"You'll do nothing of the kind!" Sashi contested. "We've all paid for one night in an inn, and that's where we'll stay! And furthermore, you'll refund our money. After what this woman's been through, it's the least you can do!" He rubbed his head. "And Tabitha and I didn't fare so well either."

Minez shrugged and ambled away sheepishly, prodding the on-lookers to go back to their places.

Sarah looked up at her rescuer, who stood with his men, watching Minez trying to regain some authority.

"I don't know how to thank you, sir. I would like to pay you something, and we have food we can share with you."

"We didn't do it for pay, Madam. You've suffered enough, both here and in Capernaum. You don't need us taking your money, too. Besides, seeing that trash destroyed is ample reward."

The other four men nodded wholehearted agreement, muttering remarks about the badly organized caravan.

"But we won't refuse on your offer of a bit of breakfast." Their leader told Sarah, laughing.

Tabitha got up immediately. "We've got a basket full of food some kind people gave us. I'll be happy to get it." She smiled as she turned toward the carriage.

"I'm curious. Why did you help me?" Sarah asked the man, blotting her bleeding lip on the cloth Tabitha had used to wash her face. "You indicated that you knew me. How could that be?"

"I'm Manahem, son of Judah, Madam. The main concern of my associates and myself is the way Godly people are forced to bow to Caesar. We're trying to remedy that." He looked down. "And though aiding women in distress is not our usual job, we knew that we couldn't let that happen to a friend of Jesus. We don't know much about the rabbi as yet, but he's apparently teaching the things we believe in, too. At this point, at least, we're on his side."

"But how did you know I was friendly with his people?"

"Let's just say we try to keep up with what goes on," he answered, and when Tabitha brought the food and handed it to one of his men, he bowed graciously to both women and shook Sashi's hand. "I'd be a little more careful, if I were you. One of those snakes got away. Watch out for him." The five men waved as they mounted the horses they had retrieved earlier, and rode away.

"Oh, I forgot about that third one!" Sarah looked at Tabitha. "I don't think I'll sleep again until this trip is over!"

CHAPTER 29

"Women!" Minez snarled hatefully, as he and another man attempted to move the bodies of the slain men. "That's all they're good for—causing trouble! Now I've got a couple of dead men on my hands! They weren't much, but they did work for me, and now..."

"Minez, shut up your whining!" Sashi snapped. "You hire people like them, so what do you expect? They're your problem, so don't blame these women! They didn't provoke the attack."

Minez growled and went about moving the corpses as Sashi smothered the fire.

In the carriage, Tabitha dug around in the food basket for breakfast for the three of them while Sarah looked for fresh clothes. She took one look in the storage box and gasped. "Tabitha! We've been robbed!"

"Well, now we know what that third man was doing." Tabitha turned toward the campfire. "Sashi! That other man was robbing us when all that other was going on!"

The driver leaped into the coach and inspected the compartment. "I think he must have only started to get into things when the Sicarii came. Looks like everything is just rumpled a bit—he probably didn't have time to take anything."

"Thank goodness!" Sarah sighed, putting her hand to her heart. "I'd hate to arrive in Bethany with half my clothes gone."

"We'll have our breakfast as soon as you're dressed." Tabitha pulled the curtain closed and went with Sashi to gather up the rest of the sleeping mats and blankets.

Sarah dressed and combed her hair as quickly as possible. The pain in her side where the man had hit her made it hard to move freely in the small space. As she straightened the clothes that the robber had pulled out, her hand automatically went in search of her alabaster jar. Surely it was there somewhere. Frantic searching failed to turn it up.

When Tabitha came to see about her, Sarah was sitting on the floor, sobbing. "It's gone," she cried. "My perfume—it's gone!"

"Are you sure?" Tabitha searched the bag to no avail.

Sashi came back carrying the bedding, ready for a quick breakfast. "We'd better hurry. Minez will be ready soon. And he..." He stopped short when he saw Sarah's face.

"The robber took something, all right," Tabitha told him, "something pretty valuable." She explained about the perfume.

"That's too bad, Sarah. I'm sorry. But at least you can survive without something like that."

Sarah burst into tears again.

"Sashi, it was a special gift from her late husband, not long before he died," Tabitha offered. "It's very expensive, but that's not why she treasures it. It's because of Nathan."

Sarah was too upset to eat and her lip was beginning to swell too much, anyway. When they got on the road again, she said nothing. But when she kept crying off and on for awhile, Tabitha finally became exasperated with her behavior. "Child, I know it hurts you something terrible, but you must be thankful we all got out of that mess alive!"

"I am, Tabitha, but you've no idea how much that jar of perfume meant to me!"

"No, I guess I don't. I didn't know anything could be that important," Tabitha replied sadly.

They rode on in silence for awhile, except for Sarah's quiet crying. Then Tabitha could stand it no longer. "How do you think Sashi feels about what happened? He blames himself, but he can't do a thing about it! He could buy you another jar of perfume, but it wouldn't be the same."

"I—I don't want him to do that. It isn't his fault."

"Then what do you expect us to do? Carrying on like that sure won't bring it back!" Tabitha shook her head.

Sarah sat quietly, hurt that nobody seemed to understand. Tabitha had never been so insensitive. But as she continued to think about it, she began to feel ashamed. Tabitha was right. Crying and pouting would not bring back her treasure.

She sheepishly reached for Tabitha's hand. "I'm sorry. Will you forgive me for acting like a spoiled child?" She wiped her eyes on the cloth Tabitha handed her. "Sashi was right. One can survive without perfume!"

Tabitha patted her hand lovingly. "At least you're human!" She laughed. "I'd hate it if you were perfect all the time." She looked closely at Sarah's mouth. "You really took a beatin' back there, child!"

"What that man was about to do to me was much worse than this!" Sarah shuddered. "And I wasn't hurt any worse than you and Sashi. I thought they had killed both of you."

When they stopped for lunch, Sarah said to Sashi, "That man that came to our rescue said his name was Manahem, the son of Judah. I think I've heard of him. Wasn't Judah the one who led the revolt that destroyed Sepphoris?"

"Yes, and I've heard Manahem is filling his father's shoes quite well. The Sicarii are mostly Zealots, determined to see that the Jews don't have to serve any master but God. But some of them have become quite violent. They don't like the taxes that Herod and the Romans inflict on everyone. They do have some very good ideas, but they carry it to extremes. I hear they go into the crowds at Passover time in Jerusalem and knife people they want to get rid of. And of course, there's no way to catch them."

"How awful." Sarah shivered. She had been so naive when she had attended Passover in Jerusalem. Little had she known about such crimes being committed in the crowd.

"I've heard they like Jesus because he speaks up about the sins of people in high places. But I've also heard that he doesn't approve of their tactics." Sashi laughed. "Of course, I'll have to say—killing those people last night was strictly in defense. Your defense! They did what I should have been doing, myself."

"Do you think they had been following us all the time?" Sarah asked.

"It's hard to say. Obviously, they know who you are and how you've been treated in Capernaum. Who knows? They may never come around again or they might be nearby when you least expect it."

"That's a little frightening. I'm glad we're staying at an inn tonight." She breathed a sigh of relief. "God is surely with us. We know that."

"I'm sure of it," agreed Tabitha. "He works in some strange ways."

Sashi remained silent on that subject, looking down pensively. Tabitha and Sarah exchanged glances.

In mid afternoon the caravan turned straight west at Livias, province headquarters of Herod Antipas. The sun was low in the sky when they crossed the Jordan River, heading toward Jericho where they would spend the night at an inn. This would put those going to Jerusalem in the city by mid-morning the following day.

Arriving in Jericho just before sunset, they barely got a look at the beautiful resort city with its lush greenery, before dark. A veritable oasis!

The inn was a caravansary, with accommodations for the entire company, including animals. A mediocre meal was served and soon Sarah and Tabitha were sharing a small room in the middle of the building.

Hoping to get more sleep than had been possible the night before, they retired early. Sarah lay awake for awhile, listening to the foreign sounds of an unfamiliar city. But exhaustion soon caught up with her and she slept soundly until Tabitha aroused her at daybreak.

"Wake up, Sarah," the old woman whispered. "Time to get ready to go again. We'll be in Bethany before midday."

Sarah dressed, and reaching into the bag for her comb, she stopped, drawing in her breath sharply. Her fingers encircled the box. She looked at Tabitha, her hand still in the bag.

"W-what is it, Sarah?" Tabitha stared at her, wide-eyed.

Sarah lifted the alabaster box barely out of the bag and peeked inside with uncertainty. Sure enough, the jar was there as if it had never been removed.

Tabitha's mouth dropped open in surprise. "How did *that* get in there?" Her question was barely audible.

Sarah could only shake her head, dumbfounded.

"Are you thinking what I'm thinking? Maybe Manahem found that robber. But how on earth could he have got in here without either of us..." Tabitha's hand flew to her mouth. "Oh, my goodness!"

"I don't know what to make of it!" Sarah took a deep breath, letting it out slowly. "Both of us searched this bag, and the vial just wasn't there. Even the box was gone." She went quietly to the small window, pulling the curtain back only enough to peek out. "I guess Manahem or one of his men could probably creep in here without making a sound. They're experts at stealth, I'm sure. But..." She looked at

Tabitha with fear in her eyes. "The only other thing I can think of is that Sashi could have taken it and then thought better of it."

"I guess that's one of the first things that entered my mind. But, Sarah, I just don't believe he's that kind. The other things he does don't fit with somebody that'd steal perfume."

"No, and I still think it had to be replaced by the Sicarii. Somehow I feel we have a guardian angel watching over us. With a dagger!"

Tabitha shook her head in amazement. "It sure does look like it."

They waited until after they had eaten breakfast and were in the carriage before they mentioned the mystery of the perfume to Sashi.

"It's downright hair-raising, Sashi!" Tabitha exclaimed after Sarah had described how she found the box.

"Well, we know the robber wouldn't have brought back what he stole, so I'd say it had to be Manahem," Sashi agreed. "I can tell you this—whoever replaced it is a top-notch spy!" He shook his head, smiling. "Nobody else could do it!"

"Well, there's another possibility," mused Tabitha, "It could be that an angel brought it back. Sarah, maybe you're supposed to have that perfume for something special sometime. Who knows?"

"Now, Tabitha, you're getting moonstruck!" Sashi laughed. "You'd best stick to believing that Menahem brought it!" He climbed up into the driver's seat, shaking his head and chuckling to himself.

As far as Sarah was concerned, Menahem and an angel were one and the same. She was so glad to get her precious treasure back.

* * *

The morning sun was high in the sky when Sashi turned the carriage south, away from the rest of the caravan, and headed toward the house of Lazarus. It was the last short leg of a very eventful journey for these two women. And it was here that their lives would begin anew.

Sashi hoped they would be safe here. At least, he had done his very best to get them far away from Jeda! It remained to be seen if the god whom they trusted would be faithful to them.

CHAPTER 30

A twinge of anxiety crept through Sarah as the carriage jolted along the narrow, dirt street on the edge of Bethany.

Things had happened too fast. She had not made the decision to come here; it had been made for her. Descending upon these total strangers, unannounced...Begging—that's what it was! Wasn't there some other way?

As she toyed with the thought of shouting to Sashi to take them to an inn, the carriage slowed, turning into a lane through a grove of ancient, gnarled olive trees. She was committed.

When the trail turned sharply to the right, the travelers suddenly found themselves before a splendid, palatial residence, whose immaculate grounds and gardens were surrounded by groves. It was as if the town of Bethany had been left many miles behind, instead of only a few yards back, at the end of the lane.

Pulling back on the reins, Sashi slowly brought the carriage around to the flower-bordered path at the outer courtyard's black iron gate. Before Sarah descended from the carriage, she saw a woman coming toward them across the garden.

The petite lady opened the gate and greeted them with a broad smile. "Good day! May I help you?" She stood in the open gate. "I don't believe I've seen you in Bethany before."

"No, we're from Galilee," Sarah answered nervously. "We're friends of Mary bas Hiram of Magdala, and..."

"Mary Hiram?" The woman's smile spread wider. Her eyes twinkled. "A dear friend!" She hurried out to meet them.

"I'm Sarah, and this is Mary's cousin, Tabitha," Sarah said, climbing down and offering her hand.

"And I'm another Mary," the woman said laughing, as she grasped Sarah's hand firmly.

Sarah nodded. "I think I'd have known you anywhere, from Mary Hiram's description."

"Well, I won't pursue that." Mary laughed again. "There's no telling what that teaser said about me!"

Taking Sarah's arm, she led the way back into the courtyard. "You've had a long trip. Come on inside. My brother and sister will be surprised to have guests from Galilee." She led the way through the courtyard to the heavy front door.

"Sarah, have your driver set your luggage inside the gate and I'll have someone bring it in later. Just come on in, when you're finished." Mary smiled and went inside.

Sashi carried everything from the storage compartment, setting it where Mary had instructed. When Sarah looked at the meager pile of things, a lump rose in her throat.

"Tabitha, look at that. The sum total of our possessions."

"But, child, we're still on our feet. Just be glad of that." Tabitha set her jaw, determined not to be defeated.

"Sashi, what will you do now?" Sarah turned to the man whose identity and purpose remained a mystery.

"I'll be out of the province before tomorrow, and out of your lives, at last." He wiped his brow. "I'm just sorry my timing was so unfortunate. I can't undo anything, but I hope you'll find a good life for yourselves here."

"Thank you, Sashi, for everything. And who knows? Perhaps your timing was right after all. Things were going from bad to worse for us back in Capernaum. It was probably better that we got out when we did, which incidentally, would have been just about impossible without you! We'll be fine here." She took his hand in both of hers. "God be with you. You're a good friend."

He squeezed her hands gently. "Don't ever let your guard down. It may seem that you're completely out of danger now, but that may not be true. Jeda will be desperate to find you two, and please understand—she's no amateur."

"We'll be careful, Sashi, I promise." She shivered, folding her arms tightly. "But from what Mary Hiram told us, these people have quite an underground protection system going, so don't worry about us."

Tabitha reached out to shake his hand, too. "God bless."

They stood watching as he climbed upon the seat and rode away, as he had said—out of their lives.

Tabitha straightened up the little pile of belongings, trying to make it look neater. "Sarah, I wonder who Sashi really is. I know God sent him to us." She held the gate open for Sarah. "And these good people here—he sent us to them."

"Then why do I feel so nervous and humiliated? I hate begging and that's what we're doing." Sarah's knees felt weak as she and Tabitha walked toward the door.

Mary came down the hall as they entered, and gestured toward another room. "Do come on into the sitting room. Martha and Lazarus will be in shortly." She fluffed the pillows on a couch for them. "Please sit down and rest while Luci fetches tea for us."

Sarah lifted the small scroll from her sash pocket. "Mary, we've brought a note from Mary Hiram. Perhaps it will explain why we've so rudely dropped in on you, with neither invitation or even previous arrangement." She handed the letter to the puzzled woman.

Breaking the seal, Mary walked toward the window, unrolling the paper as she read. "Why, you poor dears!" She turned back toward the two and dropped down into a chair, shaking her head.

"Well, Mary, introduce us to our guests!" Martha said cheerfully, coming into the room with Lazarus right behind her.

"Martha, Lazarus, this is Sarah," Mary said as Sarah stood and reached her hand to Martha, "and this is Tabitha, Mary Hiram's cousin." Lazarus shook Tabitha's hand.

"I just read a letter they brought from our friend in Magdala. Here, brother, you read it." She solemnly passed the scroll to him.

Martha waited silently, her gaze fastened on her brother's face. Soon he handed it over to her, remaining quiet until she, too, had finished it.

"Oh, my!" was Martha's only comment as she lowered herself into a chair.

"Sarah, Tabitha..." Lazarus gestured for them to take their seats again. "From what Mary has written, you two have been through quite an ordeal! But I assure you that you'll be safe with us. We'll see to that." His eyes, slightly sunken into the thin, pale face, were moist.

"Sir, if you only knew how it distresses us to impose ourselves upon you, with our burdens. We didn't know what else to..." Sarah buried her face in her hands.

Tabitha put her arm around her shoulders, tears brimming her own eyes. "Go ahead and cry, Sarah. You've been brave long enough. If you people knew what she's gone through, even on the trip..."

"No." Sarah put out a hand to stop her. "Please..." She shook her head at Tabitha, who reluctantly complied, shrugging.

"My dear, you mustn't think of your coming as an imposition," Martha contended. "It gives us an opportunity to help a couple of other believers, friends of Jesus."

"Indeed!" Mary agreed enthusiastically. "Sarah, Mary Hiram wouldn't have sent you here had she not known we would be glad to help." She smiled warmly. "Mary told us in the letter that you had been miraculously healed by the Master." She clasped her hands together against her breast. "My, what a wonderful experience for you to think about!"

"My sister is right, Sarah," Lazarus agreed. "You must try to think on the blessings."

Martha handed her a soft, white handkerchief and she wiped her eyes, embarrassed that she had fallen apart so completely. "Yes, I know she's right. And I'm sorry for my behavior. I'm usually more stable."

"But you're only human, my dear." Martha laughed. "We've all had times like that. I think what you need right now is a nice warm bath and a good rest. Let's have a bit of bread and tea, while Luci sees that your bath is made ready.

"Mary told us that you people would be kind and generous, but that was a gross understatement!" Sarah said, managing a wan smile.

After the pleasant snack and soothing bath, she stretched out on the cot, relaxing for the first time in what seemed a century. She and Tabitha had adjacent rooms, comfortable and cheery.

Rousing late in the afternoon, Sarah dressed hurriedly and went down to the kitchen, where Tabitha was helping the women prepare supper.

"Well, Tabitha, I see you've found a way to help out, while I've slept the entire day away."

"And that's exactly what you needed." Mary spoke up. "I'm so glad you were able to nap. Besides, if one stays around this kitchen, my sister will work her to death!" she teased.

"Would you listen to that?" Martha complained. "It's a major effort to get Mary within shouting distance of this area! She's always puttering around with her flowers or gabbing with someone. The only reason she's in here right now is to glean from Tabitha all the news of Galilee!" Martha winked at Sarah.

"I'm afraid I'll have to admit to that," Mary confessed. "Tabitha has been filling me in on Jesus' meetings there. She tells me she just recently learned of the change in her cousin Mary. What a wonderful example of how Jesus can change a life!"

"I've only known Mary Hiram a short time, but I find her to be very warm and kind—so much like her cousin, I might add." Sarah smiled at Tabitha, who blushed and turned away to set the table.

Martha wiped her brow with her sash. "Mary, you may call Lazarus to supper now. Tabitha has the table ready." She led the way into the dining room.

The two Galileans had never been in a home where dining was so luxurious. Around the large, rather low table, long padded couches were arranged like spokes on a wheel, Roman style, so the diners could recline, leaning on one elbow, or sit upright on the end of the couch facing the table. Lazarus reclined, but his sisters chose to sit up to eat. Sarah and Tabitha followed their lead.

Lazarus was eager to hear all about his friends in Galilee, and how Sarah and Tabitha got to know Mary, Rebecca and the others. Sarah told them all about the meeting they had attended at Peter's, and about Joanna's healing.

When Lazarus asked about what route they had taken to Bethany, Sarah could see from the way Mary and Martha looked at Tabitha that they knew the whole story. But Tabitha began telling them all about the cantankerous Minez. The more they laughed at her amusing story, the more she embellished the tale.

"Sounds as if you had a very interesting journey, in spite of your hurried departure," Lazarus said, still chuckling as he pushed himself up from the couch. "You ladies will please excuse me now. I have again consumed too much of my sister's good cooking and must get up and move about." He raised a hand in protest as Sarah and Tabitha started to stand. "Just stay where you are and have a nice visit." He looked pale and tired as he hobbled out of the room.

After her brother was out of earshot, Martha said, "My poor Lazarus. He eats so little, as you could see, but it hurts his stomach as if he had eaten ten times as much. He isn't at all well these days. Doesn't even feel up to talking much. But there's no kinder man in the world than my brother. You see how he has us all sit at the table with him, unlike many men. Of course when there are other men here for a meal we choose to sit in the women's dining room, adjoining this one."

She reached over and patted Tabitha's hand. "Tabitha, thank you for those funny stories. The laughter did Lazarus more good than you could know."

"Sometimes it's pretty good medicine," Tabitha replied. "I'm glad if I helped."

Sarah thought how much this good man reminded her of Nathan and Lucian. She remembered with fondness how they, too, disliked the old ways of treating women.

"Martha, I haven't enjoyed a meal so much in a long time." Sarah sipped her tea. "Everything is delicious."

"My sister is an expert cook," Mary agreed. "I always stuff myself too much when she makes her special stew." She rubbed her stomach, laughing.

"That girl always eats like that and look how thin she stays!" grumbled Martha. "And I can just taste, and get fat!"

* * *

Sarah found the hospitality of the first evening to be an everyday thing. All was going so well in Bethany that it frightened her. The sooner she and Tabitha could find a place of their own, and be independent, the better she would feel.

But she remembered Sashi's warning. Tamar would never give up the search for her and Tabitha. Would this new-found security and happiness be snatched away again?

CHAPTER 31

"It's a far cry from your house in Capernaum, Sarah," Tabitha noted, stepping back to inspect her new arrangement. "You can only do so much with three chairs and a table," she muttered, looking around the scantily-furnished room. "But I'll have to say, it beats livin' with other people."

"It certainly does." Sarah agreed, putting the last of the bowls in the small cabinet. "I can't believe Anna offered you a job with a cottage so soon after she met us. And with Mary and Martha telling everyone coming and going at their house, I've already lined up several customers for dress-making."

Tabitha chuckled. "It's really somethin', the way people come in bunches to have supper with Mary and Martha and Lazarus."

"Yes, and it took me a while to realize the meals were actually secret worship meetings. And the fellowship is wonderful, no matter how different the people."

Sarah walked to one of the two windows in the room, pushing back the short curtains. "I think I like this place, Tabitha," she said, smiling. "Everything is nice and clean. So light and cheerful. What else do we need?" She made a sweeping motion around the room. "This room is big enough for cooking, eating and sitting, and each of us has a bedroom. It's actually rather cozy." She hugged her arms to herself.

* * *

Tabitha loved working in the big house for Anna and Jacob, who were kind and generous, and treated her and Sarah as good friends.

Thanks to liberal advertising by her new friends, Sarah soon had almost more happy customers to sew for than she could handle. She became familiar with import shops in nearby Jerusalem, where she could buy beautiful Babylonian silk fabric. It took an entire day to walk to the city on the narrow dirt road skirting the Mount of Olives, do her buying, and walk back to Bethany. On the advice of Jacob, she always chose her trips when the road was full of other women walking.

The luxurious fabrics were quite expensive, but her more wealthy customers who had heard of her talents by word of mouth, were frequent guests at parties in Jerusalem when Pontius Pilate was in residence in the Palace Antonia. Cost was no object for them, and Sarah loved designing fashions for them from the lovely material.

She was able to buy all the things she and Tabitha needed now. The money came in better than she had imagined it would. Anna wouldn't hear of her paying rent, saying that the house was a supplement to Tabitha's meager earnings.

Sarah happily contributed a good portion of her money to help fund the supper meetings, though with her many sewing jobs, she rarely had time to attend. She was thankful for the work, but she missed the fellowship. Tabitha went several times a week and told her all about them just before they said their bedtime prayers together.

As difficult as it was to put the frightening events of her past behind her, Sarah had stopped cringing at every unfamiliar sound. Fear of Tamar had been pushed to the back of her mind.

* * *

One day in the fall, one of Sarah's best customers unknowingly shattered her tranquil world. Looking at Sarah's latest purchase of fabric, she exclaimed, "Oh, if I had worn a gown made from that to the party in Tiberias, they really would have made a big fuss!"

"T-Tiberias?" Sarah's heart skipped a beat at the name. She felt the blood rush to her face.

"Yes, we spent last week there. Oh! I almost forgot to tell you!" She put her hand to her throat. "I ran into someone you know, Sarah. Why didn't you tell me you were from Galilee?" She pouted.

A gasp caught in Sarah's throat. She swallowed hard to gain composure. "Oh, I..." she stuttered shakily, "uh, couldn't you tell from my speech that I was one of those country girls?" Sarah struggled a weak laugh. Her heart slammed against her ribs.

"I guess I did notice a little accent. But anyway, I attended a gala affair at the palace there and was wearing the blue silk tunic you made for me. Several women remarked about how lovely it was, but one in particular was very interested in it. She asked me where I found a dressmaker with such talent. Of course I knew it would be of no help to her, so far away, but I was happy to tell her about you.

"When I told her your name was Sarah, she asked me to describe you. Well, my dear, you'd be pleased to hear my description," she teased. "And then, surprisingly enough, she said she knew you! In fact, she said that you were once her sister-in-law!" She fingered the brocade.

Sarah dropped the fabric she was holding. "T-Tamar?"

"Yes, that was her name! Tamar. And she seemed so pleased to find out where you're living now. She asked me exactly where you're located, so she could visit you." She held up her hand. "But you mustn't tell her I told you, for she asked me not to. Said she'd like to surprise you on her next trip to Jerusalem." She giggled. "But I thought you'd want to know. Now you must act surprised when she comes!"

Tabitha, bringing tea just as the Tamar's name was mentioned, almost dropped the tray in the woman's lap. Apologizing, she hurried out of the room before her trembling caused a real catastrophe.

After the customer left, Sarah dropped weak-kneed into the nearest chair. "Tabitha, I feel as if the ground just fell out from under me."

Tabitha sat down. "What in the world are we goin' to do?"

"We must leave, of course, immediately." Sarah held her head with both hands. "This involves our friends here, as much as us. If she finds us here, not only will she kill us, but she'll tell Herodias where she can find this group of Jesus' followers!"

"Yes, and soon, I'm afraid." Tabitha shivered.

"The woman said she saw Tamar last week." Sarah suddenly paled. "Tabitha, she could be on her way here now!"

"We must tell Anna and Jacob right now." Tabitha stood. "They'll know what to do."

Sarah pulled herself out of the chair. "Tabitha, when you teamed up with me you really got yourself in deep, didn't you? And it gets worse all the time." Tears trickled down her cheeks.

"Well, if I'd known then what I know now, I'd still have made the same decision, I can tell you that! I've had more happiness with you than I ever dreamed of, and if I died this night, it would be worth it." She hugged Sarah. "We'll get through this together, child. Remember—God will be with us!"

God will be with us, Oh, how Sarah was counting on that.

CHAPTER 32

The tiny cottage behind Nahum's house looked dismal in the night shadows. Every creak and thump of the carriage was magnified in the quietness. Sarah could hear her own heart pounding.

Jacob and his driver helped unload their belongings, all of which fit in the middle of one room, with ample space left over.

"Nahum and Elizabeth will see you in the morning. Most of their servants are day workers, as ours, so they won't arrive until sun-up," he told them in hushed tones. "Incidentally, when our household help finds you gone this morning, they will be led to believe that you had to go back to Galilee. That's for their good, as well as yours."

Sarah nodded. "Of course. We wouldn't want them involved in any danger because of us."

Watching the carriage pull away, Sarah was suddenly aware of intense exhaustion. The dread of pulling up stakes again, fleeing Tamar's clutches to another set of total strangers, had consumed her thoughts the night before, robbing her of sleep. Parting with the wonderful friends they had made in Bethany was almost as painful as leaving Capernaum. And just when things were going so well.

Tabitha touched her shoulder, jarring her from her musing. "Sarah, I see the lady has made our beds for us. Let's try to get some sleep." They walked toward the bedrooms. "It's not as nice as our little cottage in Bethany, but we're safe here. And I thank God for making these folks here in Jerusalem willing to give us a place to live. And they're even giving me work." She smiled, though Sarah saw the tears about to spill. "I know you'll have some customers for your dress-making, too, as soon as..."

"No, Tabitha, I'm not going to do that any more."

Tabitha took a step back, raising her eyebrows. "Why, Sarah, we might not be able to live on what I..."

"Shhh," Sarah cautioned. "Jacob said Elizabeth wished there were two of you. Well, she'll have her wish." Sarah walked on into her bedroom and sat down on the edge of the bed. "I think I'd rather have a job of that sort."

"But—your dressmaking!" Tabitha whispered hoarsely.

"Just think about it, Tabitha. If anyone comes looking for me, what do you suppose they'll be looking for? A seamstress, that's what." Sarah shrugged. "So I think I'll be an inconspicuous servant woman, and very happy and thankful for the opportunity."

Tabitha sat down beside her, taking her hands. "I'm so proud of you, daughter!"

But Sarah went to bed with a heavy heart. "Dear God," she whispered, "when I touched the tassel I thought being healed would make my life perfect. I thought it was worth everything. But now I don't know. How much more must I pay? Is there ever an end to the running? The fear?" She buried her face in the pillow and sobbed until she fell asleep.

* * *

Awakened by the morning brightness, Sarah lay in bed for a moment, dreading to face another day of uncertainties. It was when she finally pulled herself to a sitting position that she noticed the view from her window. The rich orange-pink and gold tones of a magnificent sunrise bathed the world in brilliance. Even a gnarled old olive tree behind the garden, unable now to produce anything but a few faded-looking leaves, took on a look of sheer beauty in the glow of the morning sun. It stood proudly in its elegant soft mauve mantle. Sarah's distress suddenly lessened and she felt a warmth envelop her as she observed the majestic spectacle before her.

"Oh, God, forgive my self-pity! You're still with us, just as we've asked so many times. You're all around us. Please give me strength. Strength to deal with adversities with more faith and patience."

"Sarah, did you call me?" Tabitha came out of her room rubbing the sleep from her eyes. "I heard you talking."

"I was speaking with the one who will see us through this difficult time, Tabitha. Come over here and look at the sunrise. It has painted the entire earth in rose-gold!" Humming, she went to the kitchen.

Tabitha looked out the window, shrugged, and shuffled after Sarah.

"Tabitha, let's unpack these baskets. There'll be no breakfast until we find our utensils and food!"

"I guess we do need to eat a bite before we get started." Tabitha started a fire in the little brazier. "I don't know how early the woman will want to see us."

"And we certainly want to be finished breakfast when she does." Sarah stopped for a moment, looking at Tabitha. "I am so amazed at the underground system the believers have. You know, Tabitha, they are people of considerable means and good reputations in the community. Yet they're still willing to risk their lives not only for their own faith, but to protect other believers." She went back to her task.

"I've been feeling quite sorry for myself, I'm afraid, thinking that I had paid a great price for touching the tassel. Actually questioning the wisdom of my commitment. But without the hardships we've had to face, we'd probably never have seen what power truly dedicated people have, and what wonders can be performed. Maybe there's good reason..."

"Child, I believe there's a good reason for everything. I'm not smart enough to figure out how these folks work, but I trust them. And I know things'll work out for us as long as we're together." She hugged Sarah tightly.

* * *

When Elizabeth came early to welcome them, clasping their hands warmly and flashing the friendly smile that lit up her round face, they knew they had found another new friend.

"I do hope you'll find the cottage adequate," she said, looking around as if inspecting the place for the first time. "We had a couple living here for years. He was our gardener and she worked in the house, but both of them have been gone for some time." She brushed a bit of dust from the table top. "We've been getting by with day servants except for Amos, our trusted driver and all-round handyman. He takes good care of us—has a room in back of the kitchen. Since our son and his family moved away, the two of us have been able to get by without much help."

"Tabitha and I want you to know how grateful we are to be allowed to stay here." Sarah smiled at the woman. "We're aware of the danger our presence brings, but we hope to be assets, perhaps offsetting that burden somewhat..."

"Why, whatever are you talking about? Burden?" Elizabeth laughed, waving her hands in protest. "My dear, you mustn't think that!" She was a woman of some years, though her full face evidently stalled the arrival of wrinkles, making it difficult to guess at her age. Her hair was lightly frosted with silver, giving her a distinguished elegance.

"You're very kind, Elizabeth," Sarah replied as she pulled out a chair for their guest. "Jacob indicated that you would be willing to take Tabitha as a housemaid."

"Yes, indeed. When I said that we'd been getting by without live-in servants, I meant just that. Getting by," Elizabeth admitted. "The girls we have coming for day work aren't very dedicated to their job. Things have been shamefully neglected."

"I promise you they won't be neglected any longer. Not with Tabitha around." Sarah looked at her companion proudly.

"I know. Jacob told us how much they hate to lose her." Elizabeth smiled broadly.

"Jacob also quoted you as saying that you wished there were two of Tabitha." Sarah smiled nervously. "I realize, of course, you may not have been serious, but if you really could use another maid, I'm available," she offered timidly. Then raising her hand, she added quickly, "But please don't feel obligated. I'm sure I can find work in the area."

"Oh, well, I was under the impression that you were a dressmaker by trade, and I know you will be able to get a very good clientele among our friends here. You'll be meeting all of them soon. You see, we assemble as often as possible without arousing suspicion."

"Yes, it's true I've made my living as a dressmaker for years, but it was my sewing that forced us to flee Bethany. So, I really think it would be wiser to lose myself among the servants." She sighed. "And really, I would find it a pleasure to serve you and your husband in any way I can. My room and board would be more than enough pay. I already owe you so much!"

"You may be right about your dressmaking going against you," Elizabeth conceded. "but you don't owe us anything, dear. You'll be paid a fair wage."

"Sarah, I hate to see you give up your sewing," Tabitha chimed in. "I can see why you want to and I agree that it may be the smart thing to do, but child, you've never been a maidservant."

"Oh! You don't think I can do it?" Sarah teased, winking at Elizabeth.

"Now I didn't say that!" the old woman argued. "I just know how much you love your needlework, and you're so good at it."

"Well, it's not as if I'm going to quit sewing altogether. I'll do all of ours and anything Elizabeth needs, too," Sarah assured her.

Elizabeth clasped her hands against her chest. "I can see right now, Sarah, what your job here is going to be." Her eyes lit up as she talked. "I want you to take complete charge of the household linens. They've been scandalously neglected for so long! And perhaps I could get you to do something about my clothes..."

She threw back her head and laughed heartily. "And we need new curtains, too! And—and, Sarah, do you know how to embroidery?" She asked sheepishly.

"Does she know *how*?" Tabitha laughed. "Why, you've never seen embroidery 'till you take a look at some of hers."

"Oh, Tabitha..." Sarah blushed, shaking her head.

"I'd give anything to learn how to do fancy needlework for my own enjoyment," Elizabeth said seriously. "You see, I didn't learn those things as most girls do. My mother died when I was very young and I was brought up by a cranky old aunt who taught me just the necessary chores. She wasn't very good with the needle and hated doing it."

"I'd love to teach you, Elizabeth, that is, if you're not just trying to spare me from doing housework. You see, in spite of Tabitha's insinuations, I used to do all of my own cooking and housekeeping for my husband."

"No, no, my dear. I have a selfish motive behind all of my suggestions," Elizabeth confessed. "You see, when I heard you two were coming here, I was hoping so much that you'd be the kind of people I'd enjoy having around for company." She looked down. "I'm not too well these days, and I get terribly lonely when Jacob is busy doing his own things. He insists on overseeing the work himself, and keeping his own records.

"And since I don't know how to do needlework, I have nothing to occupy my time." She put her hand on Sarah's. "Do you think you could put up with trying to teach this old woman, and listening to her incessant babbling?"

"Elizabeth, you're a dream come true." Sarah hugged her new friend.

Elizabeth's eyes filled with tears. "And you two are an answer to my prayers."

* * *

When Elizabeth left, Sarah sank into a chair, her shoulders sagging. "Tabitha, do you have the feeling we've come this way before?"

The old woman looked at her sadly. "Yes, child, I do. But we'll just have to do like we did last time. Trust. God..."

"I know," Sarah interrupted, "God will be with us."

CHAPTER 33

In the two years with Elizabeth, Sarah had settled contentedly into a pleasant routine, sewing, mending and doing fancy needlework with Elizabeth.

Tabitha loved it there, too, and had become the favorite servant, with her funny stories and sense of humor.

More than any other of her tasks, Sarah enjoyed fashioning dresses for Elizabeth. Dressmaking still her true love, she still had the tendency to get carried away with it, unable to put a garment down until it was finished.

As in Bethany, Sarah and Tabitha found the small community of believers friendly and devout. Their meeting place was usually an inn run by Mary Asher, a widow. Since her husband, a successful exporter, had left Mary and her young son financially comfortable, the "inn", well off the beaten path, was hardly a source of income for her. At each dinner meeting the so-called customers dropped whatever coins they could afford in a basket, for their share of the meal.

Also, as in Bethany, Sarah was too busy most of the time to attend the meetings. One evening when she was working unusually late on a dress, Tabitha rushed into the cottage.

"I nearly forgot about the meetin' tonight! We'd better get goin' soon." She bustled around, getting herself ready.

When Sarah made no move to put her sewing away, Tabitha prodded, "It's gettin' late. Aren't you goin'?"

"No, I'd like to finish this dress, if you don't mind. Elizabeth would like me to start on the draperies tomorrow." She saw the disappointment on the old woman's face. "I'm sorry, Tabitha. I guess I could finish this later. I don't like you going alone..."

"Don't worry. I won't be by myself. I told Adah she could go with us." Tabitha shrugged. "You know, Sarah, someone told her she looked like you, with her pretty dark hair and slender build, and she was just thrilled to pieces!" She laughed. "And she does resemble you, except she's younger."

"Don't remind me how much younger!" Sarah teased.

After Tabitha left, she put the dress down and made a light supper for herself. Then she worked until the garment was completely finished.

Stretching her arms, she went to make tea for her and Tabitha. Surely she would be home soon and would tell her all about the meeting. She smiled, thinking it would be more interesting to hear Tabitha's account than to have been there herself. How fortunate she was to have that dear old friend with her. She couldn't imagine what her life would have been like had she not been blessed with Tabitha.

When the tea was ready and still no Tabitha, Sarah began to worry. But at the sound of footsteps, she breathed a sigh of relief.

"Sarah, are you still up?" Elizabeth called to her.

"Yes—please come in." She opened the door.

"We just got home and I saw your light. I told Nahum I'd come see why you two weren't there tonight. I hope neither of you is ill."

"Elizabeth, Tabitha went with Adah, the girl down the street. Didn't you see them?" Sarah's chest suddenly constricted. "Adah came by and they walked off toward Mary's."

"Oh..." Elizabeth put her hand to her throat. "Neither of them were there." She grabbed Sarah's hand. "We'll get Nahum!"

In only seconds Nahum met Sarah outside. "Let's try to be calm. Maybe they went somewhere else. But we'll find her." He motioned to Amos, who had heard the commotion and come outside. "You two women stay right here, in case they come back. We'll go back toward Mary's."

Before his torch was completely out of sight, both she and Elizabeth, standing near the house helplessly, heard a faint groaning. They grabbed each other and stood motionless, listening. The second time it sounded more like a cry, coming from the orchard near the road.

"Nahum! NAHUM!" Elizabeth yelled breathlessly, running with Sarah toward the source of the noise.

Sarah reached the orchard first, trembling with dread. Her fears were realized when she saw Tabitha lying face down, motionless.

"Is it Tabitha?" Nahum ran up to her. "Move back, Sarah. Let me get to her." The two men started to pick her up when Elizabeth gasped. "Here's Adah." She whispered weakly, pulling back a bush.

When Nahum found that Adah was not breathing, he and Amos carried Tabitha into the big house, laying her on a couch in the sitting room.

As Elizabeth gathered and dampened cloths, Nahum sent Amos for the doctor, doubtful that Tabitha would be alive when he arrived. "And when you get back, Amon, please go for Adah's family," he instructed, his voice trembling.

Tabitha was pale and cold, barely breathing. As Sarah looked into the still face, she realized just how much she loved this woman. This one who had been like her own mother, always there when she needed her, always considering Sarah's needs above her own.

Tabitha opened her eyes and looked into Sarah's, which were brimming with tears. "S-Sarah." Her voice was a whisper, barely audible. "He—he called her—Sarah..." And Sarah knew she was gone.

She held Tabitha close, weeping as she had never wept before. Rocking back and forth, she held her dear friend until Nahum and the doctor came and forced her to let go.

"You must try to get hold of yourself, Sarah," Nahum said gently, his arm about her shoulders.

The doctor examined Tabitha and stepped back. "The lick on the head...She didn't have a chance." He shook his head.

"Doctor, the dead girl—go to her family. They may need you." He walked the doctor out the door as Adah's parents arrived.

When he returned, Sarah was still sitting on the floor beside the couch. "Even the one I loved more than anything." She buried her face in her hands. "And Adah. So innocent. It was all my fault."

"Sarah! How can you say such a thing?" Elizabeth helped her up into a chair. "You had nothing to do with what happened to her. You were always so good and loving to her."

Sarah look up through her tears. "But don't you see? The murderer thought I was the one with her." She shivered. "Tabitha said just before she left that someone told Adah she looked like me! And before Tabitha died," Sarah stifled a sob. "she said the murderer called her Sarah!"

"My dear, Tabitha chose to take that chance. She told us you tried to get her not to stay with you because of the danger, and she made the decision to remain with you, at any cost."

Nahum sat down, leaning forward in the chair. "There are only two people to blame—the one who committed the crime and the one who hired him to do it, if that's the case."

The doctor had left a sedative for Sarah and after persuading her to take it, Elizabeth put her to bed there in the main house.

"You know what this means, don't you Elizabeth?" Nahum stroked his short white beard thoughtfully. "The murderer will report the mission accomplished."

"Oh! Yes, it probably means Sarah is no longer in danger from her sister-in-law." Elizabeth dropped her head. "But what a price to pay!" she whispered.

CHAPTER 34

Standing at the bare work table, Sarah looked around for the curtain material she had left folded, ready for sewing. Had she imagined leaving it there?

Turning to the chest that normally stood at the end of the table, she searched. It was gone. Steadying herself against the table, Sarah looked all around the room. Except for the table and chairs, the room was vacant.

"I'm loosing my mind," she whispered, dropping into her usual work chair.

Sarah had resumed sewing for Elizabeth the day after Tabitha was buried, less than a week ago. She couldn't bear to be in her cottage without Tabitha. But her heart was no longer in her work.

Sarah couldn't be comforted by anyone. Life had no more meaning to her. In one way or another, she had lost everyone who had ever been close to her. Everyone!

And now this—this *what*? What on earth was going on? Where was Elizabeth? She was always there every morning to have tea with her. Was this Elizabeth's way of letting her go? Maybe they didn't want her, without Tabitha. Without Tabitha. Would there ever be *anything* without Tabitha?

Sarah stared vacantly at nothing. She had cried all the tears she had.

"Good morning, Sarah," Elizabeth greeted her brightly, coming into the room.

"Elizabeth," Sarah started, pulling herself to her feet. "Is this a joke, or..." She dropped back into the chair. "I left my work here and..." She swept her hand over the table.

"Sarah, in your frame of mind, you're in no condition to work on anything. I..."

"I know I haven't done my job very well lately." She looked up at Elizabeth with tears welling in her eyes. "I certainly don't blame you for letting me go. I'm just sorry I haven't been..."

"Now, Sarah, before you jump to such ridiculous conclusions, let me explain." She pulled another chair to the table and sat down. "You're not being dismissed. Why, I couldn't ask for anyone to do half as well as you, my dear. But you do need to get away for awhile, even if it's for a few days." She smiled at Sarah. "I've arranged for you to go to Bethany for a visit with Mary and Martha. They'll help you get things in perspective. Would you do that? For me?"

Sarah looked into Elizabeth's pleading eyes. "I'd like that very much," she replied softly. "I know how Mary and Martha loved Tabitha, and I'd like to tell them in person about what happened."

"Good." Elizabeth clasped her hands together. "We're sending you in the carriage. This close to Passover, you can never tell who might be coming from Galilee. And you really should stay out of sight while you're there," she cautioned.

Sarah leaned back in her chair. "You are the kindest, most understanding..."

"Oh, now don't give me credit for too much. The truth is, I can't stand seeing you hurt so badly, and I'm hoping Mary and Martha can help you cope with your grief better than I've been able to."

"I promise you I'll come back ready to do my work properly." Sarah stood. "But you don't intend for me to leave today, do you? Shouldn't I finish the curtain I was working on?"

"Amos is ready to drive you as soon as you get your things together," Elizabeth said, waving off Sarah's question. "We'll send him back for you in about three days, so you won't need much." Elizabeth rose, giving Sarah a hug. "That way you'll be home before too many people arrive for Passover."

As Sarah put a few things into her satchel for the short stay in Bethany she took out the vial of perfume, caressing the beautiful alabaster. She had handled it so often its creamy surface had darkened. It never failed to make her feel close to Nathan. She would keep it forever. She wanted it near her, even when she went away for only a few days. So she laid it carefully back in the box and slipped it into the bag with her clothes.

* * *

When Luci opened the door to Sarah, she squealed with joy, and promptly shut the door.

"Luci!" Sarah called out, laughing at the maidservant's absent-minded excitement.

Lucy opened the door again, grabbing Sarah around the neck, almost knocking her down. "I'm sorry, Sarah," she said breathlessly. "I'm so glad to see you. I'll go and bring the mistress!" She was off toward the back of the house as Sarah walked on into the sitting room.

Soon Mary and Martha came running, both hugging her at the same time, crying.

Martha stepped back, wiping her eyes. "We heard the terrible news, Sarah. I can't believe Tabitha's gone."

"But we didn't hear how she died. Was she ill, Sarah?" Mary held Sarah's hand in both of hers.

Lazarus entered the room before Sarah could answer. He shook her hand vigorously. "We're so glad you came, my dear." He sat down, gesturing for the others to do the same.

"We want to know what happened, if you can tell us without too much pain."

"Yes, I wanted you to hear it from me." She sat down and took a deep breath. "Mary, you asked if she was ill." She shook her head sadly. "It might not be quite so hard to part with her, if that had been the case." She told them all about Tabitha's and the servant girl's murders.

"Oh, Sarah, if Jesus had been there, she'd still be with us. I know she would!" Mary declared, wiping tears.

"There wasn't time and, of course, I wouldn't have known where the Master was, anyway." Sarah dabbed at her eyes. "But there's more," she said, as the three listened intently for the rest.

"The last time I spoke with Tabitha, just before she left that evening, she talked about how much the girl, Adah, looked like me. Others had told her that, as well." Sarah swallowed hard. "Tabitha's last words were, 'He called her Sarah.'" Her voice broke and tears rolled down her cheeks.

Mary drew in her breath as she, Martha and Lazarus exchanged surprised glances. "The man wasn't a robber, then, or..."

"Obviously he was sent." Lazarus shuddered. "And whoever hired him must think he succeeded."

"Yes, apparently he was sent to kill me." Sarah covered her face with both hands. "If it were not for me, Tabitha would be alive, and so would Adah." She sobbed, as both women tried to comfort her.

Suddenly she raised her head, wiping her eyes with the cloth from her sash pocket. "I'm sorry. Tabitha wouldn't want me to behave like a child."

"Tabitha would understand, my dear, for she knew how you loved her." Lazarus spoke softly, with sympathy. "But I must tell you, Sarah, that not too long ago someone was in Bethany looking for you. It must have been the same man."

Sarah paled. "Tamar must have sent him, after that woman told her where I was."

"Yes, because he asked Sephorah if she knew where he could find the seamstress named Sarah," Martha told her. "Sephorah told him that someone fitting the description had lived there briefly but had gone back to Galilee somewhere. He talked to some of the servants and they told him the same thing."

"That's what they honestly thought, of course." Mary added.

Sarah stiffened. "I wish Tabitha had never been close to me. And I wish I had never involved *anyone* in my problems with Tamar. I hate what she did to Tabitha, and I'll never forgive her. Never!" She spoke the last word through clenched teeth. She sat rigid, no longer crying.

Mary, Martha and Lazarus were too shocked to speak for a moment. Never had they seen such anger in Sarah.

Lazarus cleared his throat. "Sarah, it is much more difficult to forgive someone for harming a loved one, than if he harmed us. But Jesus has said that we must, or our heavenly Father will not forgive us." He leaned forward in his chair. "My dear, you must trust God to help you forgive. You must not carry around this bitterness in your heart."

"But you don't know Tamar. She caused me to lose my child. She forced me out of my own home, away from Capernaum. I lost my friends there. She forced me to leave Bethany. And now she has killed my dear Tabitha!" Tears rolled down her cheeks. "How can you possibly think I could ever forgive such a monster? Even Jesus could not help me with that!"

CHAPTER 35

Mary went to Sarah, kneeling beside her chair. "Even he who made your body well again? Could he not soften your heart?" She looked at her brother. "Did you know that Lazarus actually died, was in the grave for four days, and Jesus brought him to life again?"

"Wh-what?" Sarah put her hand to her throat. "No, I—I didn't know."

Lazarus smiled. "Yes, it's very true. And how I praise him for the good health that has been restored to me!"

"Sarah," Martha spoke up. "Jesus will be speaking at Simon's house tonight. You remember the little old man who had the leprosy? Well, Jesus healed him, too."

"And it will surely be safe for you to go with us to hear Jesus, for Tamar won't be looking for you now." Mary reminded her.

"But she must still be careful not to go out on the streets," Lazarus suggested. "If someone from Capernaum in is town for Passover, Tamar might get the word that Sarah is still alive."

"I will be pleased to go with you this evening. And, yes, I'll be careful, Lazarus, during Passover in particular." Sarah dropped her head. "I feel so ashamed for my unforgiving spirit. I'm so thankful for what Jesus did for me, and I won't turn away from my faith. Maybe he *can* help me to forgive some day." Her eyes glistened as she looked at her friends. "I'm so blessed to have friends like you and to have had Tabitha, who stayed with me to the death." Her voice broke. "I shall not forsake the God she trusted so totally." She smiled through the tears. "Dear Elizabeth. She knew I needed to come here, and what a good time to come, when Jesus is here."

* * *

At Simon's house, Sarah was reunited with Sephorah and Jacob and the other friends who had been so wonderful to her and Tabitha.

After the meal, as everyone clustered around Jesus, ready to hear him talk, Sarah wondered if she would have the chance to thank him personally for her healing.

Reaching into the deep pocket at the end of her sash, Sarah's heart beat wildly. She had made up her mind what she wanted to do. If only she had the courage to approach the Master. As she wrestled with her shyness, Mary came and sat beside her.

"Mary, would you do something for me?" Sarah whispered.

"I'll try, dear. What is it?"

Sarah slipped the vial of nard into Mary's hand. "Would you please anoint the Master with this? It's very precious to me, and I must give it to Jesus."

Without answering, Mary quietly rose and went to the Master. She poured the contents of the alabaster jar on his head, whispering to him.

He looked toward Sarah and nodded, smiling. "Bless you," he said.

"Thank you, Jesus," she whispered, dipping her head shyly. She felt her heart would surely burst with joy.

Then one of Jesus' disciples spoke up, "Woman, why are you using that expensive perfume? Don't you know that our Master has taught us not to waste things like that? Why, you could have sold that for enough money to feed the poor for a long time!"

Embarrassed, she dropped her head. And then looking up at Jesus, she opened her mouth to tell him she was sorry if she offended him.

But he raised his hand. "Let her alone!" he said to the man who complained. "Why berate her for doing a good thing? You always have the poor among you, and they badly need your help; and you can aid them whenever you want to; but I won't be here much longer. She has done what she could, and has anointed my body ahead of time for burial. And I tell you this in solemn truth, that wherever the Good News is preached throughout the world, this woman's deed will be remembered and praised."

Everyone grew very quiet and the man who had criticized her was now the embarrassed one. Sarah felt a little sorry for him, but she was so happy that she hadn't displeased Jesus. It was like floating on a cloud! She could tell that he recognized her, even though it had been almost three years. And once again, his eyes had seemed to look into the depths of her soul. She believed he remembered healing her.

She wished Tabitha were here to see Jesus, too. And maybe she was. Oh, how she hoped so. Then she remembered that Tabitha had told her there must be something important she would need the perfume for.

She thought also about how pleased Nathan would probably be that she had used the gift in such a special way. Now, when she looked at the alabaster vial and the beautiful little hand-carved box, she'd think of how Nathan had provided a way for her to thank the Master.

* * *

"You idiot! Why on earth did you wait until now to tell us this?" Herodias shrieked, pacing furiously. Malchi flinched, wishing desperately that he had followed his first instinct to keep quiet until he could talk directly with Herod Antipas.

"But I tell you, my lady, I didn't know until today that the man was a spy for Aretas!" The assistant steward crossed his arms defensively. "When I saw him talking to the Capernaum landowner's wife, I had no idea he was more than a servant that had been hired to help with the banquet! Surely you're aware, Lady Herodias, that there were many extra servants working at Fort Macchaerus that night."

He shifted nervously. "But when I noticed the same man here at this palace, I naturally became suspicious and began watching his every move. Only today did I catch him listening outside the steward's door. And my immediate action almost got me killed. Thank the gods for the soldier who came around the corner just as the man pulled his knife on me!" He drew a shaky hand across his forehead.

"Anyway, the scoundrel's in the dungeon now, my lady, and I would like to report this matter to King Herod, only I can't seem to locate him. Is he in the palace?'

"Never mind. I'll report it to my husband. But first, I have some questions of my own for the man. What is his name?"

"I believe he's called Nimri, my lady."

"So take me to Nimri, this instant!" She flounced past the guard, Malchi following reluctantly, certain now that it had been an error to mention anything about this to her.

Her angry voice echoed through the damp corridors of the dungeon long before the guard stopped at the cell, where Nimri stood eyeing his visitor through the narrow slit. When the heavy door swung open with a rusty groan, the prisoner bowed low.

"Guard, search this man thoroughly, so that I may speak with him privately!" She barked, stepping back.

"But, my lady, he has already been..."

"Do as I say!" She crossed her arms impatiently while the guard complied.

In the cell with Nimri, she looked him over, sneering. "So this is an example of Nabataea's finest!" She laughed mockingly. "I wonder if old Aretas had any idea how quickly you would admit to spying for him."

"Lady Herodias, I have served my king well. He'd have no complaint about me." He lifted his chin proudly. "So I got caught." He shrugged indifferently. "I could deny what I was doing here, make up some kind of tale. But what would that get me? My head, that's what!" He slashed his finger graphically across his throat. "And that would be stupid—something I'm never accused of! A little careless, maybe, but not stupid. Not when I can bargain with you."

"What makes you think you're in any position to bargain?" She sneered.

"Oh, dear queen, I thought you were smarter than that." It was his turn to laugh. "Surely you know I'd never have placed myself in the enemy camp without insurance, if you get what I mean."

"No, I don't get what you mean! Why don't you just save both of us a lot of time and come right out and say what you have to say!" she snapped angrily. "I've had about enough of your childish games!"

"I'm disappointed in you, Herodias. I had counted on more of a challenge." He scoffed hatefully, plopping on the bare cot. "Don't you think the tetrarch might be just a bit upset to learn of his wife's little escapades? You wouldn't want him to know how you spend some of your evenings when he's away from the palace, would you?"

"You filthy snake! It so happens that Herod doesn't know that you're here, and death quiets the most dangerous of tongues," she threatened.

"You just keep forgetting, don't you?" He chuckled. "Like I told you, I'm not stupid. Death might quiet my tongue, but it sure won't quiet the scroll that describes the small but numerous discrepancies. Even the gentlemen's names. The evidence will never reach your hands before it gets to Herod, unless I'm safely out of the country," he bandied, savoring each moment of watching her composure slipping away. "See what I mean? Insurance."

Reddening, she snarled through clenched teeth, "All right! I'm listening. Tell me the names of those disloyal people, and I'll arrange for your safety."

CHAPTER 36

"Oh, I think it would be better if I told the tetrarch himself," Nimri replied, strutting around the cell, his hands clasped behind his back.

She struck at him with her fist, but he grabbed her arm before she connected with his face. His eyes narrowed as he twisted the flesh on her wrist. "I wouldn't do that, harlot!"

"How dare you!" She wrenched away from him, stepping back toward the door. "You'll tell *me*, not my husband! I have good reason..."

His hostile laugh reverberated through the dungeon. "Yes, dear Herodias, I don't doubt that for a minute! Why, I do believe that the gracious lady has got herself into trouble with His Majesty in more ways than one!" He laughed again. "It wouldn't do for Herod to find out how you've maneuvered things to suit your evil purposes, would it now?"

"Oh, shut up!" She turned away, rubbing her wrist which had turned very red. "I don't know how you know every move I make, but..." Whirling around to face him, she sighed impatiently. "Are you going to tell me what I asked of you?"

"Sure. Why not? You'll be interested to know that we've acquired most of our information from the very woman that you thought was spying for you—Tamar, wife of Elon ben

Amon, of Capernaum," he informed her solemnly. "One more example of your poor judgment of people. She took a great deal of pleasure in telling us a few important tidbits about Herod's military plans. You see, she has no aversion to sleeping with a few loose-tongued soldiers. You get a man drunk enough and excited over a pretty woman, and he'll tell her anything she wants to know."

He laughed insolently. "But then, nobody knows more about that than you, do they?" He shrugged. "Anyway, those trips Tamar made down here to give you little pieces of information to satisfy you have been delightful little trysts for her, right under her stupid husband's nose, and under yours, as well. And you thought she was tickled pink with your boring parties."

"But she didn't expect you to betray her, did she?" Herodias had a far-away look in her eyes. "I would almost feel sorry for her if I didn't hate her so much for what she did."

"Oh, don't think she wouldn't do the same to me, if the tables were turned."

"I've heard quite enough for now." Herodias summoned the guard. "I'll be back in an hour to make the arrangements for our swap. Your freedom and safe passage, for the scroll, you despicable blackmailer!"

He cackled. "Call me what you like, my lady! But if I were you, I wouldn't let too many minutes lapse before I got back down here. It would be a shame if my cohorts decided you had reneged on your promise."

* * *

In Jerusalem the atmosphere was one of jubilance in anticipation of the most important religious observance of the year. Soon hundreds of people would be lining the roads into the city to spend Passover week together. Some were already arriving.

Safely back at Elizabeth's, Sarah bubbled with the wonderful story about the meeting at Simon's house and how Jesus had defended her. And then there was the report about the raising of Lazarus, which brought more rejoicing from Elizabeth and Nahum.

But Elizabeth's news for Sarah was totally unexpected. "Mary Asher will be glad you're back, Sarah," she said, after Nahum left the room. "She wants you to help her with a very important dinner."

"Oh?" Sarah arched her brows. "I'd be glad to help Mary in any way I can. She's such a special friend..."

"Well, if I told you she's serving Passover supper to Jesus and his disciples..."

"Oh, Elizabeth!" Sarah squeezed her hands together under her chin. "I can't believe it. Of all the people she knows, she wants me?"

* * *

Sarah and Mary started very early, working quickly to get everything clean and ready to entertain the important guests. When the lamb was brought to the house after the sacrifice, they carefully prepared it for roasting.

As they worked, Mary Asher told Sarah about how excited she had been to learn her home had been chosen for the dinner. A couple of the Master's men followed her brother home from the well to look at the big room her husband had built on the roof several years before he died. They had agreed it would be the perfect place for their Passover feast.

"I knew I'd need help, and I thought of you," Mary told Sarah, smiling. "In fact, your name hit me so quickly, I knew I was supposed to ask you. I was afraid you wouldn't get back from Bethany in time."

"I'm glad I did, Mary. And I'm so very honored to be asked to help prepare the dinner for Jesus. To serve him in any way would be a joy."

* * *

Toward evening, Jesus and his companions arrived and, after greeting the women briefly, went up to the room where unleavened bread and hasereth sauce awaited them on the table. As soon as they were seated the women brought wine and salt water.

Next came the lamb, with traditional bitter herbs. After replenishing the wine for the remaining ritual, the women went out, leaving the men to themselves to eat and converse privately.

Mary's young son, Mark, happily ran up and down the stairs, bringing empty plates and bowls and reporting on the progress of the meal, while Sarah kept the dishes washed, ready to go again.

When the last wine was delivered, Mary filled a plate for Mark. "You must eat your supper, son, so that you can help us bring everything down when the men leave." She mussed his hair lovingly. "Sarah, I don't know what we'd have done without this boy, since Mona wasn't able to help!"

"Mark is a fine, hard-working young man!" Sarah patted the boy's shoulder. "Some day you'll be sitting around the table with the men."

The boy smiled broadly. "It won't be long!" He stood, stretching as tall as possible. "See how big I am?"

"Yes, we see, son." Mary laughed, putting him back in the chair gently, but firmly. "But unless you stop dawdling and finish your meal, you won't be of much more help. I want you to be through eating by the time they come out of that room."

"But, Mother, I'd give anything to follow them, to listen to Jesus!"

"I know, Mark, but those men don't need a little boy tagging along. They have important matters to discuss and you mustn't bother them. Besides, we don't know where they're going and I'd be worried about you. I want you right here with me!"

"Oh, Mama..." Mark muttered under his breath, sighing.

Minutes later, the men quietly left the upper room and walked off toward a nearby olive grove. Mark brought the things down to the kitchen. Then with a big hug and kiss, Mary sent him off to bed.

"Sarah, you'll stay the night, won't you? We still have quite a bit of work to do and it's already getting very late.

"Gladly! I really don't want to walk home alone," Sarah admitted. "Thanks for letting me stay."

The chores soon behind them, Mary and Sarah sat down for a quiet cup of tea before retiring for the night. As they talked about the exciting day, the front door suddenly burst open and a completely naked Mark ran into his mother's arms, trembling and breathless.

Sarah quickly shut the door, nervously drawing the bolt, as Mary whisked him off to his room. "I thought I told you to go to bed, young man!" she scolded.

When Mary had settled Mark back in bed and was returning to Sarah, a heavy, loud rapping on the door stopped her in her tracks. Before she could decide whether to open it or not, a couple of soldiers kicked it open and stood glaring at the two women.

"Where is he?" one of them demanded. "I saw that boy coming in this direction!" He held a flimsy nightshirt in his hand.

Mary was too frightened to speak, but Sarah stood up and replied in a steady, firm voice. "There's no one here except the two of us and a young sleeping child in the bedroom. His mother put him to bed hours ago, and I certainly hope you haven't disturbed him. A small child needs his sleep.

To Sarah's surprise, the soldiers accepted what she told them and left in a huff, bellowing about the imp who had given them the slip.

Mary clutched her throat, her eyes wide with fright. "Oh, Sarah, that was Mark's shirt," she whispered. "He told me he had slipped out and found the men in the olive garden and he saw soldiers come and take Jesus away!"

Sarah caught her breath. "Oh, no! Where...?"

Mary shook her head. "Mark ran behind, hoping to find out where they were taking him, but one of the soldiers saw him and grabbed him. Mark slipped out of his nightshirt and barely got away." Dropping down on a chair, she shuddered. "My little boy could have been killed out there! And if they had gone back there to the bedroom and recognized him... Oh, I don't know what they would have done to him! But, Sarah, you were so convincing... And you didn't act the least bit scared!"

"Oh, Mary, I was numb with terror." Sarah ran her fingers across her brow. "But Mark's all right now. You must calm down and sit with him until he can get to sleep. He's had a frightful experience."

"I wonder where they took the Master, and what they'll do with him." Mary got up to go to her son.

"I'm afraid they'll find some excuse to kill him, unless he defends himself." Sarah shivered.

"But the way he can heal people—even raise the dead—why wouldn't he take care of himself?" Mary shook her head. "If he wanted to, he could stop those soldiers." She went into the other room.

But Sarah had an uneasy feeling that it wouldn't happen that way. After all, he had been predicting that he would die soon. Was that time here now? Would they kill him before he was even given the opportunity to defend himself?

A pang of fear seized her. At this moment, Jesus could be lying somewhere bleeding to death. Or what if he was already—dead?

CHAPTER 37

Before dawn, the news of the Master's arrest spread quickly through Jerusalem's community of believers. By twos and threes they penetrated the huge crowd of curiosity seekers in the palace area, where they had followed the progression of Jesus' trials. Mary Asher, Sarah and Elizabeth joined the throng, hoping to find out where Jesus was being held.

Talk about the accused rabbi flowed freely, and the women soon learned that Jesus had been questioned in the residences of Annas and Caiaphas before being dragged before Pontias Pilate, the Roman governor, who sent him to Herod Antipas.

Supposedly, now he was back before Pilate in the Fortress Antonia, very near where the women stood. Moments later, soldiers led the Master out of the palace with a ring of thorns on his head. When a woman, held up by three others, stumbled toward him, reaching out her hands, Sarah drew in her breath. They watched in anguish as the soldiers rudely pushed the weeping women away.

"That is surely Jesus' mother. I know the women with her," Sarah whispered to her companions, recognizing Joanna, Rebecca and Mary Hiram.

"I can't bear to see how they have scourged our Lord so unmercifully!" Mary covered her face and wept, as did the others.

It was hardly unusual for a large crowd to gather for a crucifixion, but since it was so near Passover, the mob was too thick to stir. As the soldiers placed the heavy cross-beam on Jesus' bleeding shoulders, the unruly crowd cheered and whistled.

"How can anyone make sport of such cruelty?" Sarah shivered, tears falling on the folds of her mantle.

"But why is he letting them take him?" Mary Asher clenched her fists. "I know he could do something!"

Not once had Sarah thought about her own risk in the Passover crowd until she caught sight of a man she remembered vaguely from Capernaum. A wave of fear swept over her. What if Tamar had sent someone to find her, knowing that she was likely to be here? In fact, she and Elon were almost surely in Jerusalem themselves!

Remembering what Sashi had said about the Sicarii knifing people in the crowd, she shivered. But it was too late to worry about that now. She was here, and she couldn't see any way out!

Recognizing another face from the past, Sarah felt her heart race. Then she realized that just because some of these people were from Galilee didn't mean they were all enemies. Many of them would still consider her a friend.

These thoughts made her wonder if any of her closest friends were in the crowd. Not that they were close any more. In fact, they probably would rather not see her. The old heartache returned at the thought.

But it would be good just to get a glimpse of Deborah and David. And—Lucian! He always came for Passover. Though she doubted that he had started believing in Jesus, she reasoned that if he were observing this cruel treatment of the Master, he would be appalled. At least that's the way he was when she knew him.

Suddenly she discovered that in her preoccupation with the past, she had become separated from the other women. Alone in the hostile crowd, she pulled her head piece more closely around her face.

* * *

Had Sarah been able to see Jesus at that moment, she would also have seen Lucian, for he was very close to the Master. Searching desperately for Sarah's face in the crowd, his eyes had fallen on the man about to be crucified. Blood oozed from the lacerations made by the thorns around his head, and mixed with the beads of perspiration on the rabbi's brow. And the doctor in him wanted to treat the criss-crossed bloody welts all over the man's body.

Suddenly Lucian felt an overwhelming compassion for Jesus. So the man had spoken out against the religious leaders. That was no more than everyone else would have liked to be brave enough to do. It simply was not reason enough to put him to death.

Unexpectedly, a statement he had made to Sarah and Nathan years ago came to his mind. An ache welled up in his chest. *"Maybe someday there'll be someone who will have enough nerve and power to fight it and tell people how to treat each other. And I can tell you this—I'll surely be on his side, whoever he is!"*

Why had his own statement, word for word, come back to haunt him? Was this Jesus the one? Lucian's heart sagged. He had talked mighty big back then. But when the man came along, he had not been on his side.

Jesus was right beside him now and when Lucian saw him suddenly stumble, he automatically reached out, steadying him again. The prisoner smiled at him, only slightly, for he was obviously barely able to stand. In those clear, gentle eyes the doctor clearly saw a reflection of himself, a man who had not believed. No—a man who had refused even to think about whether he could believe or not!

But there was something else in his eyes. Lucian saw the love and compassion of a man feeling pity for him. For him, an unbeliever. Suddenly he became conscious of this person's inner peace. In spite of his suffering, he exuded love. Real love.

Now Lucian knew that Jesus was just what Sarah had said he was. If he had only listened to her—allowed himself to meet the man, like she wanted. Then he'd have known. How could he have been so calloused? He was as guilty as Pilate. Or Herod!

He pushed through the crowd, rushing to catch up with Jesus again. He had to tell him he was sorry! Was it too late? Of course it was. But he must tell him.

Sarah had worked her way through the mass of people just in time to witness the answer to her prayers. She saw Lucian reach out toward Jesus.

"Master, let me help you carry that!" She could barely hear his words. Pushing closer she heard him plainly. "Please forgive me, Jesus, for my unbelief!"

As the soldier knocked Lucian to the ground and pushed Jesus forward, Sarah saw the rabbi look back at him, giving a slight nod, the corner of his mouth turning into a near smile.

Pushing through the few people between her and Lucian, she fell down beside him on the dusty road. "Lucian! Are you hurt?"

"Sarah!" He grabbed her and held her tightly for a moment. "Is it really you, or am I dreaming?"

She took her sash and wiped his face where he had hit the ground. People stumbled over them and someone cursed, ordering them out of the way.

Clutching each other tightly, they got to their feet and moved on with the crowd until they came to the end of the narrow street. There the throng fanned out into an open place, and the two made their way to one side.

As they brushed the dirt from their clothes, Lucian continued to hold Sarah's hand. "You were so right about Jesus, and I was so wrong," he said quietly. "How could I have been that blind?" He looked toward Jesus, who was out of sight behind the surge of people. "He forgave me, even after I had rejected him from the start. I don't deserve his forgiveness." With the back of his hand he brushed away the tears beginning to make muddy tracks down his dusty face.

"Oh but, Lucian, don't you see? If we had to deserve his forgiveness, none of us would ever have it. How could we even begin to earn it? He loves us. It's as simple as that." She gazed sadly toward the crowd enveloping Jesus. "He even loves those who are about to kill him."

"Yes, I know that now." Lucian looked into her eyes. "Sarah, I have so much I want to say. I know this is not the time or place. But I hope when this horrible thing is over... Well, maybe you'll be willing to hear me out."

"We'll go to my house later on." She squeezed his hand. "I want us to have a chance to talk."

"David and Deborah are here, too."

Lucian saw her flinch. Did she still hurt to think about the rift?

"They won't want to see me, though, Lucian." She dropped her head. "And it's probably just as well. I don't look forward to another rejection. It's better to let things stand as they are."

"Maybe so, but I'll have to see them long enough to tell them I'm not going back to Capernaum. At least not yet."

Her head shot up and her eyes met his. They walked slowly toward the knoll where the cross would be raised.

"When this is over, I want to be with you, even if it means staying in Jerusalem."

CHAPTER 38

David and Deborah watched Jesus stumble under the weight of the cross. The strong man took the cross from Jesus, and put it on his own back.

"David, this man going to his death is the one who healed our best friend. The friend we turned our backs on." Deborah's voice broke. As she watched Jesus, she knew in her heart that the decision to turn away from him and his followers had been wrong.

"Deborah, what are we doing here in this crowd? I don't want to see anyone crucified." David looked around uneasily. "It's really not our affair. I'm not against the man, or for him, for that matter." He stopped, pulling Deborah back. "Let's work our way back toward town. They'll soon be nailing him on that beam, and I don't want to see it."

Tightening his grip on her arm, he started turning her around just as Jesus, unable to walk straight, swayed over close, brushing against him. Before David could move out of the way, Jesus glanced at him momentarily, as if to apologize.

When David looked into the man's eyes, he was stunned, unable to tear away from his gaze. The understanding, love, and—yes, even pity. The man looked right through to his soul. David suddenly felt naked. Jesus didn't speak a word to him, yet his eyes told David he knew all about him, how he refused to let himself believe in him for fear of losing his business. How he stood in Deborah's way—wouldn't let her have anything to do with Jesus' friends. David had a terrible yearning in his heart to be forgiven by Jesus. And the rabbi seemed to understand—even to forgive. Yes, he could even feel that—forgiveness! He stood motionless, deep in the alien thoughts. The split second in which his eyes met the Master's had seemed to stand still. But now the soldiers had already pushed Jesus forward, away from David.

Confused by this wordless exchange, Deborah touched her husband's arm, as if to wake him. "David?" She shook him gently. "Are you all right?"

"Deborah, he..." He took her shoulders, looking into her face. "I know who that man is."

"Of course you do. It's Jesus, the one who healed Sarah."

"But I mean I know now who he really is! Sarah was right, wasn't she?" He put his arm around his wife. "And you were, too. You didn't want to turn your back on Sarah or Jesus. I insisted on it." His eyes filled. "What have I done to you—to *us*?"

She stroked his arm gently. "We were both wrong, David."

Holding hands, they moved to one side, out of the way of an especially loud segment of the crowd. They were not far from the place where the cross would be erected.

"David, I'm afraid." Deborah clung to him, trembling.

"I know, but let's just stand quietly, until things settle down enough to get away from here." He kept his arm around her shoulders. "Sympathizers are in a dangerous position in this mob." He fought a wave of nausea.

* * *

On the other side of the mass, closer to the site of crucifixion stood Lucian and Sarah. They had worked their way through the dense crowd around Jesus, hoping to be able to speak to those women with his mother.

Suddenly Sarah stopped, paling. As the soldiers pushed the people away from Jesus, she saw a woman stumble into Jesus. She laid her hand on the Master's arm. Both she and the man at her elbow were gazing intently into his face.

Lucian and Sarah couldn't hear a word they said, but as Tamar and Elon were shoved away by the soldiers, tears had drenched both their faces. They clung to each other.

"Oh, Lucian, do you think they had the same kind of experience you did?" He nodded, gazing at the unbelievable sight.

"But I can't let them see me!" Sarah whispered, trying to pull him out of Tamar's line of sight. But it was too late. Their eyes met only briefly before Tamar suddenly crumpled.

"Why did seeing you give her such a shock?" Lucian shook his head, as the crowd parted for Elon to remove his wife from the scene.

Before Sarah could reply, the Roman soldiers began driving the nails into Jesus' hands and feet, which silenced the crowd momentarily. But when they raised the cross, the revelers cheered and whistled, shouting insults and obscenities at Jesus.

"I want to get you away from this place." Lucian started to turn her around.

"No, Lucian. I'm sure his mother and Mary Hiram will stay as long as there's life in him." Her voice trembled with grief.

"The soldiers won't bother them, as long as they stay back out of the way. With us, it might be a different story," Lucian reminded her.

"But I can't leave. Not just yet," she insisted.

* * *

The hours dragged, imbibers becoming more raucous by the moment. Suddenly, when the sun was almost directly overhead, a heavy cloud covered it. An unusual, eerie darkness descended upon the place of execution. A hush fell over the mob. A soft breeze stirred the few tenacious little pink and red wildflowers peeking from cracks in the dark rock. Sarah clung to Lucian's arm, moving a little farther up the stony hillock toward the cross. Now and then the frail robber on the west cross screamed in agony. A few feet away the small cluster of women waited, weeping quietly. Soldiers squatting on the ground laughed loudly over their game of knucklebones, oblivious to the pain and to the waning festivity of the restless crowd of merrymakers.

Blinded by tears, Sarah pulled her headpiece closer to her face as she lifted her eyes toward the Master. His head was lowered, his chin resting on his chest. A few revelers from the crowd continued to jeer and taunt him. Then his whole body seemed to spasm and he tossed his head from one shoulder to the other. Though she heard no sounds from him, she saw his lips move as he looked heavenward. Sarah prayed, too. Prayed that it would soon be over for him. This caring, wonderful man whom she had first met in Galilee and then again in Bethany had been so full of compassion, loving-kindness.

Time seemed to stop for Sarah and Lucian. "Will it ever be over? Will these people ever leave?" Before she closed her eyes against the sickening scene she saw that Lucian's face was wet with tears.

She heard the man hanging on Jesus' right speak in short, painful bursts, "Jesus, remember me—when you return—in your glory."

Then came the Master's labored reply. "Today you shall be with me in Paradise." And he became limp, his head dropping.

Sarah sobbed quietly. He had been so strong and now he was broken. The Son of God, crucified, dying like a common criminal, he who had never done anything but good! How could the priests ever justify such a thing?

The crowd became silent again. Sarah shivered. It was then she heard his voice, soft and calm. “Father, forgive them; for they know not what they do.”

Sarah choked out a cry. The sudden wrenching insight was overwhelming. She looked at Lucian, tears streaming down her face. “Lucian, that’s what he came for.” She spoke in a whisper.

“What do you mean?”

“This is what he had to do to show us what real love is. What true commitment is. He loves us all. He asked forgiveness for those who are so cruel to him. His life isn’t as important to him as his mission.” She couldn’t watch any longer. Her knees trembled as she turned away from the scene of agony.

“And to think I couldn’t even forgive Tamar. I’ve hated her for so long.” She smiled through tears. “But now I can.”

Lucian pulled her back a few steps and in a little while, they had inconspicuously inched back toward the city until they were near the back of the crowd.

As Lucian moved between Sarah and several drunks who had begun to stare at her, the ground started to tremble. The roar of the crowd was silenced at once as the earth shook violently for a moment. Then the darkness faded. By the time the sun appeared in full, many of the people were running toward home.

The crowd disbursed, small groups talking quietly among themselves. It was easy now for Sarah and Lucian to walk toward her house.

As they stepped along with the flow of people, a voice behind them called, “Lucian!”

Turning, they saw David and Deborah coming toward Sarah with outstretched arms. The reunion was too emotional for words. They simply clung together silently for some time.

"We've looked for you, Lucian, since we lost you early this morning." David wiped his eyes. "We wondered about you, too, Sarah. And to see that you've found each other is too good to be true!" He slapped Lucian on the shoulder.

"Sarah..." Deborah began to sob.

Sarah put her arms around her old friend. "Let's go to my house."

"Yes, we've a lot to talk about and that's the place to do it," Lucian agreed.

In the city the crowd had fanned out into many directions. As Sarah turned her friends onto a street that would take them to the northeast, she found herself gazing directly into a very familiar face. The man looked her straight in the eye for a few seconds, bowed slightly and stepped briskly away in another direction.

She couldn't imagine what Sashi was doing in Jerusalem at this particular time. Sure, there were other Arabs around, but he was a spy. At least she thought he was. And this was a dangerous place for him to be.

"And what was *that* all about?" Lucian's eyes narrowed to a questioning frown.

"Just someone from the not-too-distant past. I'll fill you in later." Sarah urged them hurriedly on. "Come on, now. We've a long walk to my house."

There was so much in her past that they didn't know about. She wondered if the four of them could ever find any common ground again. After two and a half years, was the rift entirely too deep and too wide?

CHAPTER 39

At Sarah's the four Galileans groped awkwardly for a common bond from their past—that certain "something" that could mend the shattered relationship once so dear to each of them.

It was amid an outburst of apologies, forgiveness, and tears that they discovered the "magic potion" that had been there all along. Though a little older and perhaps much wiser, they had never lost that special love for each other.

"Well!" Sarah clasped her hands together as they began to relax in their chairs. "Now that our silly misunderstandings are settled, let me bring in some tea and cakes. I want to hear everything that has happened in Capernaum since I left." She started toward the kitchen.

"That ought to take about two minutes!" David chuckled.

Deborah slapped his knee playfully. "Oh, Sarah, I meant to ask you," she said, getting up to help with the tea, "Isn't Tabitha still with you?"

"Oh, yes!" Lucian looked around. "Where in the world is my good friend, Sarah? I want to see her!"

Deborah brought in the tea tray and set it on a small table. Sarah placed the plate of cakes beside it and dropped down on the nearest chair for the difficult task of telling them about Tabitha's death. They were shocked and saddened.

"She stayed with me through everything. And it cost her life." She was crying now.

Deborah put her arm around her shoulders, her own tears flowing unchecked. "What a dreadful thing to happen to that dear woman!" she said. "But, Sarah, I don't understand why Tamar wanted to harm you and Tabitha. She and Elon forced you to leave, so what reason did she have to bother you after that?"

Sarah thought for a moment. "I'm just beginning to realize how much you don't know about what my life has been like since I saw you last." Sarah sighed. "You never really knew why Tabitha and I left Capernaum so suddenly, without even saying goodbye."

"No, but there was so much I didn't understand..." Deborah shook her head sadly.

"I'll admit I was angry at first, and stunned," Lucian confessed, "But I sent Santimar to Magdala to Tabitha's cousin to find out if you were there. She told him just enough to make us stop searching for you." He looked at Sarah, hesitating before he went on. "She said the stranger seen at your house the day you left had something to do with Tamar's past, and that his being there had put you in grave danger. She made it clear to Santimar that we were not to breathe a word about it to anyone. But she assured him that you and Tabitha were safe." He turned to Deborah. "I hated not telling you and David, but for Sarah's safety—"

"It was better that they didn't know," Sarah broke in. "And your life was also in jeopardy, Lucian, even knowing as little as you did." She told them about the stranger whose brief conversation with her and Tabitha at her house in Capernaum had caused the problem. "The irony was that he didn't tell us anything about Tamar's past, except that her name wasn't really Tamar. And, by the way," She smiled sheepishly. "the man I saw in Jerusalem this afternoon—that was he—Sashi."

Sarah went on to relate the events following their escape, including the attempted rape in the caravan, and the Sicarii's part in things.

"Sarah, Tamar was hunting for you the morning after you left. And..." Lucian shook his head. "We're sure she had been in your house during the night. We found your mattress slashed!"

"But how could Tamar have known where you were, Sarah?" David asked.

She told them about the dressmaking and the customer who unknowingly gave Tamar her whereabouts. "My friends went to work immediately, making arrangements for us to come here to Nahum's. You've no idea what an underground movement these people operate!" She laughed. "I decided then and there, though, that I'd better stop sewing for hire. And since then, I've been a maidservant."

"A servant!" Lucian exclaimed. "Oh, Sarah—"

"Now wait a minute!" She held up her hand, laughing. "I'm officially a servant, but let me tell you what kind of serving I do!" She interrupted. "I mend the linens for Elizabeth, teach her to do fancy needlework, make all her clothes, make new draperies... In other words, I do all the things I love to do! And I have the companionship of a dear, wonderful friend at the same time!" She folded her arms, smiling. "So you see, I'm hardly a slave!"

"But all the danger you've been threatened with!" Lucian was plainly shaken. "It makes me sick to think of what you've gone through, and what could have happened to you." He dropped his head. "That's more painful to me than you can imagine. You must have hated me for the way I abandoned you."

"Don't you know I could never hate you?" Sarah reached both hands toward him, sitting down on the floor in front of him. "You told me the truth about your feelings. I wouldn't have wanted you to pretend something you didn't feel. No good relationship can be based on a lie. No," She shook her head. "it was my own choice. A hard one, I'll admit. But I had to do it that way and Tabitha felt the same. She was with me whole-heartedly in that decision. She died, knowing that we had done the right thing. We had discussed it many times." Her voice broke.

Lucian squeezed her hands. "Girl, you've been through so much."

"But it hasn't been all bad." Sarah smiled, a faraway look in her eyes. "I've made some dear friends through all of it." She shrugged. "Of course, I'll have to admit feeling sorry for myself a lot of the time. I guess I never really stopped until I saw what Jesus went through today. At times I honestly wondered if following him had been worth the price." She shook her head sadly. "But now I know that the peace inside me has always been worth whatever I had to give up. The hardest thing, of course was giving up you three. I really had second thoughts about that!" Tears welled up in her eyes.

"But every time my life was threatened, someone was always there to rescue me, as if an angel were following me around. Like the Sicarii!" She laughed, remembering. "And now my prayers have really been answered. The three dearest people in the world are with me and when we part this time, I'll know you aren't angry or disappointed." She looked down. "If only Tabitha could be sharing this..." Her voice trembled and she paused for a moment. Looking around at the three, she raised a cautioning hand. "There's one thing. Tamar saw me today, and you with me, Lucian, I don't know what to expect from her now."

Just then there was a rap on the door. Everyone froze for a second. Sarah took a deep breath before opening the door to Sashi. He stood smiling at her surprise.

"Madam, if I may..."

"Sashi!" Sarah pulled the hesitant man into the room and closed the door. "Come on in and meet my friends from Capernaum."

"But—I'm sorry I've intruded..."

"Not at all! You can trust them," Sarah assured him. "In fact, I've just been telling them about your part in my escape from Capernaum."

"Did you also tell them that my presence there made you have to escape in the first place?" The Arab dropped his head.

Lucian raised his hand in protest. "From what she told us, it appears to have been a combination of unfortunate circumstances. All of us can share the blame, but you're the one who saved her from imminent danger." Lucian stood and extended his hand. "Thank you, sir, from the bottom of my heart." He shook the man's hand firmly.

Sashi bowed low. "But I came to bring more news to Sarah." He looked toward her, sobering.

"Wh-what is it, Sashi?" Alarmed at his somber expression, Sarah put her hand to her throat.

"Maybe you heard what happened to Elon and Tamar today." He raised his eyebrows.

"Oh, you mean about their encounter with Jesus?" Sarah breathed a relieved sigh, gesturing to him to sit down. "I surely hope it was as it appeared! The way Tamar was sobbing, I think she might have been touched by Jesus, and her heart changed."

"That could be true, but my news is about what happened later." He shifted in his chair. "You see, both of them were stabbed before they reached the inn where they were staying."

Sarah lowered herself weakly into the nearest chair. "I—I just can't believe..."

"Who did it?" David asked. But when Sashi looked at him without answering, he reddened. "Or should I not have asked that?"

Sashi smiled at him. "It was not I."

"Oh, Sashi, what have I *really* been involved in?" Sarah's hand shook as she wiped her forehead.

"It's a long story, Sarah, and I don't know all of it myself. I do know that Tamar was not who everyone thought she was. I mean the social climbing, the desire to be a part of Herod's elite, that was all a sham." He sighed. "You see, Tamar--rather Jeda..."

"You called her that when you saw her at my house in Capernaum that afternoon. Jeda." Sarah nodded.

"That was her real name. I knew her when she was brought as a slave to King Aretas."

A collective gasp coursed through the room.

"Slave?" Lucian shook his head. "It's difficult to picture Tamar..."

"Well, she became more than that, actually. She was a companion to Princess Rafi, the king's young daughter. Those two girls loved each other dearly. Then Aretas did something for which he hates himself to this day. He gave Rafi to Herod to be his wife. Of course, you've all heard about how Herod discarded her for Herodias."

"That's common knowledge." David nodded.

"Well, Tamar's bad experiences started before that," Sashi continued. "Aretas sent her to Peraea to be with Rafi. She was only a child, and terribly lonely. And one night right after Jeda arrived, so the rumor goes, Herod, roaring drunk, went into his bedchamber looking for his wife. Jeda was there, preparing Rafi's bed, and...Well, you can guess the rest."

Sarah shivered. She could hardly believe this was really Tamar he was talking about.

"She ran away," Sashi went on. "Went back to Aretas. And, of course, the old king was furious that she had deserted his daughter, and I guess he got pretty rough with her. She talked another servant into helping her steal some of his jewels and they escaped to Judaea." He cleared his throat and took a sip of tea.

"The two of them went to Jerusalem. Tamar was originally from Idumaea, so she claimed, and probably had been up to Jerusalem many times. So she knew her way around even though she hadn't been there since she was very young. I guess Jeda had a pretty rough life ever since the day she was born."

"I think I get the picture now." Lucian nodded knowingly. "She has been trying to get in with Herod in order to get information for Aretas, right?"

"That's what she claimed," Sashi concurred. "I really think she still cared about Aretas, and intended to help defeat Herod. I happen to know she was approached at Tiberias by one of Aretas' spies and told to work for him. The old king didn't know she was already his ally." He laughed. "Anyway, the spy got caught and had to blow the whistle on her to save his own neck, which is another story I won't go into."

"Then Herod had her and Elon killed?" David asked.

"Not Herod. He never knew about any of this, as far as I know. Herodias intercepted the report on the spy and had them murdered, I'm sure."

"Poor Tamar." Sarah shook her head sadly.

"Before you feel too sorry for the woman, maybe you should know that she was the one who murdered your husband."

"What?" Sarah sat bolt upright, as did the other three.

"You remember I told you that Jeda got another servant to leave Aretas with her—help her steal from him?"

"Not Esli!" Sarah covered her face with her hands.

"His real name was Reuel." He looked sorrowful. "I believe he loved her very much when they were in Jerusalem. Up until she..." He fidgeted in his chair. "She left, taking most of their money."

Everyone in the room was in a state of shock. "I can't believe how little we knew about Tamar." Sarah shook her head.

"I talked to Reuel in Jerusalem after she had left, and several times later. He hated her, but I'm sure he was never really a threat to her. He didn't even know she was in Capernaum until he went there to work in the pottery shop. He had learned to make pottery in Nabataea and was only trying to make a life for himself. He was basically a good man." He sighed. "But Jeda was paranoid. Thought everybody was after her."

"But how did you know about the murders at the pottery shop?" Deborah questioned.

"It was my business to keep up with Jeda, among others."

"Then you work for Aretas," David concluded.

He hesitated. "I hope you're aware of what Herod would do to all of us if he got wind of this conversation." He raised his eyebrows.

"You needn't worry about any of us," Lucian assured him.

Sashi stood up to leave. "And now I must go if I'm to be far away from here by this time tomorrow. Time passes too quickly."

CHAPTER 40

After Sashi left, the four sat in silence. Finally, Sarah got up to pour more tea. "Poor Tamar," she mused, shaking her head. "It's hard to believe she was involved in so many complicated schemes. It's as if she were more than one person."

"Yes, but she was caught in the web of deceit she had spun." Lucian sat back in his chair. "I could almost feel sorry for her, if she hadn't killed Nathan and tried to kill you." He looked lovingly at Sarah. "She was a witch, no matter what caused her to be one!"

"And Elon, poor fool, had to pay, as well," David remarked.

"Yes, he told me once that he put up with the way she acted because he loved her." Sarah sighed wearily. "I guess he just couldn't help it. Poor, weak Elon."

"Well, he wasn't going to put up with her much longer," David told her. "Rumor had it that he was planning to divorce her. He had found out she was having flings with other men, especially in Tiberias. And he might be alive right now, if he hadn't waited so long."

"Sarah, you know this means you can safely go back to Capernaum with us!" Deborah exclaimed excitedly. "You will, won't you?"

"That's my question, too, Sarah." Lucian looked at her hopefully. "You realize, of course, that you have inherited Elon's property."

She looked surprised. "I hadn't thought..."

"You still have your own home there, too." Lucian smiled.

"But didn't Elon sell it?"

"Yes, he did." Lucian grinned at her mischievously. Deborah and David exchanged mysterious glances.

"Lucian, you didn't!" Sarah exclaimed.

"And he paid about three times what Elon could have gotten from anybody else." David chimed in.

"All right, I'll admit to being a sentimental fool, but I would have paid even more than that to keep those two from having that house! So it belongs to me now, Sarah, and if I have my way, you will rightfully own everything *I* own." Lucian's eyes sparkled.

Deborah's mouth dropped open, waiting for Sarah's answer.

Lucian's eyes held Sarah's for a long, tender moment, begging her to say yes.

"Why, Lucian, I do believe you're proposing to me!" She teased, her eyes fixed on his. She reached for his hands. "And I think you already know my answer." She squeezed his fingers tightly. "I want to be your wife more than anything else in the world!"

After a round of joyful congratulations, David and Deborah said their goodbyes for the time being and walked arm in arm outside, where the faint light of dawn was showing in the east.

Before Lucian left, they decided a quiet little ceremony after Passover would be appropriate.

When they stepped outside, Santimar was waiting patiently in his carriage. "How did he know where to find us?" Sarah whispered before she ran to hug the old man.

Santimar was equally happy to see her, and from what he saw in their faces, he was sure she would be riding back to Capernaum with them.

* * *

Mary Asher banged on Sarah's cottage door, calling loudly, "Sarah! I have good news! Come quickly!"

"Mary! What..." Sarah could only step out of the way, as her friend rushed in breathlessly.

"Jesus is alive!" She stopped to catch her breath, both hands clasped at her chest. "He was in my home. I talked to him myself! I just had to come and tell you!"

Sarah looked at her blankly for a moment. "Mary, you haven't met..."

"Oh, I'm sorry, Sarah." Mary put her hands to her face, embarrassed. "I'm sure you're all planning your wedding, and I've just barged in and interrupted..."

"The wedding is all planned, Mary," Elizabeth assured her. "And these are Sarah's friends from Capernaum. Come sit here by me." She patted the cot beside her.

"And take a deep breath," Nahum suggested, chuckling. "Now what's this about Jesus?"

"Like I told you, he's alive!"

"The man who was buried—you're saying..." Lucian arched his eyebrows. "Up walking around?"

"You don't believe me." Mary looked pleadingly at Sarah.

"Oh, now Lucian didn't say that, Mary." Sarah laid her hand on her arm. "Please go on, dear."

Mary sighed. "I left my guests to come and tell you the news. Mary Hiram and Joanna are at my house now." She closed her eyes for a moment, breathing deeply. "You see, the disciples were having a private meeting after they all got back together. They were upstairs, where you and I served the Passover meal to them, Sarah."

Sarah nodded.

"Well, they had locked the doors, afraid the Roman soldiers might still come looking for them, not that locked doors would keep the soldiers out." She shook her head. "Anyway, John said they had bolted the door from the inside. Then suddenly, Jesus was in the room with them. Nobody had unlocked the door, and I didn't see him come to the house. Why, they say Thomas couldn't believe it was really him until Jesus showed him his hands, where the nails had been."

Mary paused briefly, looking at Sarah and Lucian. "It was him, all right. I know, because they had asked me to bring them some tea and cakes later. I knocked on the door, which was still locked, mind you, and James opened it. Well, you can just imagine how startled I was when I took the tray over to the table and there was the Master, sitting right there at the table! Why, I nearly dropped the whole thing, but he reached out and caught the tray." She sighed.

"I was speechless. I bowed to him and he smiled, calling my name! And then I left quickly, for they were in the middle of a very private talk. I heard the lock fastened behind me."

"Amazing!" Lucian was smiling broadly, shaking his head. "Where is he now?"

"We don't know," Mary shrugged. "Off with his disciples, I guess."

"This is all too wonderful for words." Sarah laughed excitedly. "Thank you, Mary!" She hugged her friend.

After Mary, Elizabeth and Nahum had left and things were quiet again, Lucian sat down beside Sarah, taking her hand. "It takes a little time just to absorb news like that, doesn't it?"

"I'll say!" She took a deep breath. "I thought at first Mary was just imagining things. She can be very excitable," she explained, laughing.

Neither David nor Deborah had spoken a word since Mary Asher brought her news. David leaned his elbows on his knees and shook his head. "I'm sorry, but this is too much for me!" He looked up at Lucian. "I saw the man on the cross. I *know* he died! And I have trouble believing he's alive now." He shrugged. "Not that he doesn't deserve to live, but I'm afraid those people are seeing what they want to see. They just can't accept his death."

"I have to admit I don't know what to make of it, myself," Deborah confessed, leaning her head back against the chair.

Sarah didn't say anything. As much trouble as her friends had accepting Jesus at all, how could they be expected to go this far?

Lucian turned to face Sarah. "You haven't made any comments at all, Sarah. Have you begun to doubt his power?"

She was slow to answer, for she knew she must weigh her words carefully. "Lucian, when I first heard Mary telling about it, I have to admit that I was feeling a bit doubtful. Mary is very truthful, but as I said before, I thought she just might be imagining this. But when she told us about Thomas, and how she took the tea and cakes to the men—well, I could see by her eyes that this wasn't hysteria, or imagination. Then I remembered that Lazarus, a friend of mine in Bethany, had been buried four days when Jesus came and brought him out of the tomb. Alive."

She looked around at each of her friends. "Now that may be hard for all of you to accept, but you see, I knew this man and I saw him after he was brought back. He had been so ill the last time I had seen him, and here he was, in perfect health." she smiled.

"I also remember quite well how I was touched by Jesus' power. I knew it was real. I felt it surge through me. So you see, Lucian, I have no choice but to believe this, as well." She looked into his eyes. "But I'd like to know just how you feel about it." She was almost afraid to hear his answer, because if he couldn't believe, it would always be a barrier between them.

Lucian took a deep breath, as if he didn't know how to begin, and Sarah's heart raced. "I know this may come as a complete surprise, but I do, indeed, believe this story." Lucian looked first to Sarah and then David, who dropped his head in obvious disappointment.

"I wish I could give you a scientific reason for my feeling about the man, David," Lucian went on. "It would be nice if I could tell you in logical terms how it has to be true, but all I can say is that what I experienced out there near the cross, I can't ignore."

He raised his hands, palms up. "I touched the man, but more than that, he touched *me*! I saw something in those eyes, David—something that I could never explain in a million years. I saw compassion, love, tenderness, honesty, God. Yes, I saw God himself in those eyes. It was like I could never look away again. He seemed to say 'yes, you can believe in me, for I am God'. And I think I might have had less trouble believing he was alive again than even you, Sarah." He squeezed her hand.

"David, I know I haven't really explained anything. How can anyone describe something so abstract? But I guess I'm trying to because I'd like for the people I care about to know this feeling. I understand how Sarah could believe so easily, and why she was willing to give up everything to follow him. He touched her, more than just physically. I know that now. And that's the secret to believing. Your very *soul* has to be touched with his love." He shook his head. "And to think—I could have been sharing all of this with Sarah, if I had listened then."

Sarah's gaze fixed on Lucian's face. His words were music to her. This was surely too good to be true. There was Lucian, trying to convince David to believe.

David slumped back in his chair, drawing a deep breath and letting it out slowly. "I'm afraid I'm going to have to work on this before I can truthfully say I accept it," he confessed. "I'm not exactly rejecting it. I'm just not sure. Perhaps in time..." He looked at Lucian soberly. "I, too, saw a lot in his eyes, Lucian, and I know he's special. So don't give up on me."

"I promise." Lucian reached to slap his friend on the knee. "But we should come to an understanding right now about what we expect of each other in the future."

"How's that?" David arched one eyebrow.

"Well, we're feeling fairly safe here, talking among ourselves. But we'd better face the fact that we're going to be dealing with other people than just the four of us," he reminded them. "The followers of Jesus will be even less popular with Herod than ever before. He won't trust us, and we could face some real trouble if we're known believers."

Sarah's heart skipped a beat. "What are you saying? That we couldn't admit we're believers?"

"Oh, no! Of course not," he responded quickly. "As far as I'm concerned, I could practice medicine in Alexandria, or one of many other places where doctors are always needed. We could make a good life anywhere. But we must not hold David and Deborah to our convictions."

He looked at David. "Our friendship will always be there, David, even if there comes a time when you don't think it wise to acknowledge it publicly."

"Lucian, I appreciate that." David reached to shake Lucian's hand. "I hope we can be as strong as you two someday. But it's good to know you'll understand." He brushed the back of his hand over his misty eyes.

Sarah was so proud of Lucian. He knew what he believed, and yet was so full of love and understanding for their friends. She knew that Jesus would be pleased with this believer!

* * *

Lucian and Sarah were married quietly in the home of Nahum and Elizabeth. It was only a few hours after the simple but jubilant celebration that the Galileans started out toward Capernaum, the physician's new wife sitting contentedly beside him in the carriage.

Sarah's thoughts went back to her childhood, good times and bad; to her first marriage, the happiness and tragedy; to her illness and healing. When she had touched the tassel on Jesus' robe, all she thought about was being healed. To question the price of that touch never occurred to her that day in Capernaum. And though she questioned it later, she was glad God had always given her the strength to keep her commitment to Jesus.

"God will be with us." Tabitha's words had been repeated time after time, and they had been proved true. If only Tabitha could be with her now. *Maybe she is*, Sarah thought, as a warm feeling enveloped her.

"You're too quiet for a new bride." Lucian looked at her inquiringly.

She snuggled closer to him, locking her arm around his. "I was wishing Tabitha were here to see us together, and how happy we are. Had it not been for her, I might have given up."

"But you didn't, and I'm glad. How very fortunate I am to be married to such a wise woman."

He reached across her lap. "What's that in your hand?"

"A little twig I snatched off the small shrub by Elizabeth's fence. Bittersweet." She twirled the little branch of orange berries in her hand. "It's a little like my life. Bittersweet—and right now, all sweet."

Lucian squeezed her to him. "I'll do my best to keep the rest of your life sweet, my darling."

Just then the sun peeked out, shining on the road ahead of them, and Sarah settled back for the ride that would take her home. To Capernaum.

THE END

CPSIA information can be obtained at www.ICGtesting.com
Printed in the USA
BVOW072306280512

291158BV00002B/1/P

9 781619 969490